DEN OF THE BEAR

VANISHED, BOOK SIX

B. B. GRIFFITH

Publication Information

Den of the Bear (Vanished, #6)

Copyright © 2024 by Griffith Publishing LLC

Ebook ISBN: 979-8-9874270-4-0

Paperback ISBN: 979-8-9874270-5-7

Written by B. B. Griffith

Cover design by Damonza

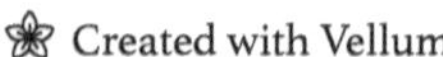 Created with Vellum

"With those gifts from their Father the Sun, the Monster Slayer and the Child of Water set out for home again. And as they made their way back along the Holy Trail they beheld a wonderful vision.

For the gods spread before them the country of the five-fingered Earth Surface People who would someday be known as the Navajo, once all the Monsters were disposed of."

- Diné Bahane'
The Navajo Creation Story

1

THE WALKER

The second my feet hit the desert floor, I know I'm on Chaco Rez. The horizon line seems sharper, like the edge of a knife. And something about the sky when evening comes on makes you feel small, almost like you're bobbing in the open ocean, unable to tell what's looking up at your feet—or down at your head.

I always hate when the soul map calls me to the Rez. That means someone died here. And there aren't enough of us as it is.

I know this stretch of road. I replaced that beat-up old sign in the near distance more than a few times in my day. It says Welcome to the Navajo Nation—or it's supposed to, anyway. Back then, whenever Ninepoint and I swapped it out, we gave it about a week. First, the gangs tagged it up. Then the bored high school kids tagged it up, the real comedians, usually with some spice like "Wanted: Indians" or "Thanks for the Dirt, White Man!" or artfully drawn dicks. Then the tweakers and drunks would take potshots with their deer rifles and bird guns until, pretty soon, it was illegible.

Eventually, someone's auntie raised enough funds for us to swap it out and start the circle all over again.

This particular generation of our welcome sign is late stage. I can see the blood-red sunset through the bullet holes from here. A late wind tussles with the metal, making it groan a bit against the wood.

Someone died here at the welcome sign. That's a bad omen, quite literally a bad sign. And I don't like it one bit.

The veil is already here, sweeping for the soul, swaying like the trunk of an elephant on a slow walk. It knows where it's going, and it will get there at all costs.

"Where is it?" I ask. Unlike this cosmic piece of cloth, I'm physically pulled in a million directions by my job. The veil sorta exists everywhere, just out of sight. It strolls onto the scene. Not me. Every second I'm here, I feel the hundreds of places I'm not. I gotta sprint from spot to spot, across the world.

I guess today is one of those days where the veil pays no attention to me. Sometimes, I swear it's part cat.

"I know you can hear me, you creepy old towel. My head hurts. I'm having phantom back pain. And I don't really want to chase any of my people around today. Let's just get this over with."

The veil takes no pity on me. If anything, I get a mild flutter of acknowledgement of my existence, which I'll take to the bank. What it does do, though, is move down the highway toward the border. And since the veil generally knows what it's doing, I follow.

To the back of me, Rez side, I hear the faint whistle of NNPD cop cars. I would know that whistle anywhere. I swear even over a decade later, I bet I can pick out the car.

The way the siren lilts a little if you open up the gas, that's car six. Danny and I had that car a few times, and it wasn't exactly new then. Seems strange it outlives me, but then again, NNPD wasn't in a place to refresh the fleet a decade ago, and decades bleed to decades real quick.

A truck is stopped way out, maybe a mile over the border on the Rez side. No other sign of humanity. But the veil ain't goin' that way. The veil is moving off the road by the sign, and now the veil is still.

I'm about to say something snide when I hear a voice, very small and muffled, say what I think is "Can't see."

I look left and right, up too. The night is upon us now, and the sky is a mottled bruise.

A choking sound nearby gives me a better bead, and I see him standing stock still past the roadkill ditch on the north side of the road. Here we go. Male, white dude, bald, early fifties, wearing a uniform of some sort. I check the thread and find it's a prison guard uniform, grays and blacks, but well worn.

"Can't see," he says, but his voice sounds like he's got a real bad head cold, and it's getting panicky.

"I'm right here," I say.

He freezes where he stands out there in the desert, which is getting blacker by the minute. Then he turns around, and I see why the head cold.

"Can't see," he says again.

"Here," I say. "Let me help you."

I sense movement from the car on back on Rez land. I'm pretty sure it's his car. And since there's no sign of a wreck, I'm pretty sure whoever he was riding with passed out, likely on account of what I'm seeing right now.

I come up to him and put a hand gently on the back of his skull.

"It feels wrong. Like it should hurt," he says, feeling gently at the edges. "How come it doesn't hurt?"

"Don't worry, brother. Nothing hurts anymore."

That's when he seems to get it. And he's sad. Some people are okay with the Big Exit, and some people are neither here nor there. Escorting these types across is easy enough.

The sad ones hurt.

I pull a brick from his face. A black brick. I look back at the truck on the side of the road. Moonlight winks off little square bits of impact glass on the hood. The brick went right through the front windshield.

He winces, and so do I, but once I pull the brick out, his face sort of fills back in. In death, you present yourself as how old you think your soul is, sorta like a Peter Pan situation.

"What happened?" he asks.

I used to ease into this, but I got a lot of these to get to tonight, and I'm still not super comfortable about the fact this guy got bricked on the front doorstep of the Navajo Nation, so I cut to the chase. "You're dead, man."

"What?" He scratches at his nose, pats at his eyes, pulls his cheeks back.

"Yeah, feels alright now, but it ain't," I say.

"Get the fuck outta here," he says in a white-guy way that would be hilarious under other circumstances. "I just picked up the wife. We're on our way to Manuelito's. It's a Friday-night tradition."

That stings a bit, but only because I love Manuelito's too, and I'll never taste it again either. "Let's take a walk," I say.

He sees the car soon enough, then I'm the one following him.

"Ellen is in there," he says. "Ellen! It's Paul! I'm here! I don't know what happened. I just got lost or something..."

He slows when he sees Ellen. Then he stops when he sees Ellen crying over his own body. The brick was a one-in-a-million shot. His face is pulverized. A six-inch square of black cinder punched right through a life. Ellen is still shaking him. The living brain sometimes tries to power through things like this, refusing to accept it. But in the end, when it comes to brains versus bricks, the brick is gonna win. That's why brains are special. A brick is a brick, but brains can work wonders and then be gone, all in an instant.

It's a tough thing to see, no matter how many times I see it.

Paul gets it well before Ellen. The dead usually do.

"Oh, honey," he says, sadness heavy in his voice. "I'm right here."

He reaches for her, but he knows. And Ellen can't feel him any more than he can touch her. Touch is over now. I know that better than anyone.

Those cop cars finally get to us. I don't recognize anyone on the force now except for Sani Yokana, Chief of Police, and there's no way he should be here at this time of night on the outskirts of Rez country. The fact that he is tells me shit is running lean at NNPD. But he steps out of his beat-up old Bronco like a pro anyway as two cruisers pull in behind him. Two cruisers is a lot in this country.

Paul gets lost in the lights. They cut through him and around him. That happens sometimes with souls. I whistle for the veil—time to get him in and get gone.

The chief and some deputy I'm way too dead to know come up on the car, and the deputy pukes. Chief Yokana does not. He only bows his head and takes his hat off.

Ellen is full-on drenched in blood now. Her head is right below Paul's, and Paul's soul is trying to rest on her shoulders but falling through again and again although Sani can't see that.

"Ma'am, are you hurt?" he asks.

She can't get an answer out.

"Ma'am, can you get out of the car?"

She doesn't answer. Yokana pulls his hair back and bands it for dirty work. He's all silver now. I think that tends to happen when you hang around my crew. Even if he doesn't know the whole story of what's going on here, his hair sure does. He can't take the brick out like I did. That's not what you do at a crime scene. But he can reach in and unbuckle Ellen, at least give her room to breathe.

She won't leave Paul's body, and he doesn't push. My people understand that certain things have to happen before family—before clan—are willing to let go.

So he backs out of the car and checks on the deputy who's puking air at this point. He slaps him on the back and says, "Get the flares. Start popping them, and keep popping them until you're a quarter mile out. Cars come up fast out here."

The kid staggers away, back to his car, and I follow Yokana back to the Bronco, where he puts his hat back on and reaches through to the scuffed-up CB wired onto the middle dash. "Westbound semis, are you on?" he asks then clicks off to wait.

Static.

"Westbound semitrucks, this is Yokana, are you on?"

A rustle in the static. "Ten-four, Yokana."

"I got a bit of a mess at the eastern flats border. Off 64 near mile marker one hundred. Anyone pass by? Over."

Static.

Then a reply: "I saw a stalled vehicle at the welcome sign, Chief. Over."

Yokana looks at his watch. "Any chance you got a time check on that? Over."

The reply is scratchy, distant. "Say twenty back. Strange thing. I followed them out of Santa Fe—"

The feed cuts out. Sani clicks the CB a few times and talks to nothing.

Then it kicks in again with the trucker still talking: "thought they'd just pulled over to let 'em pass, but that red truck coming up on them was some suspect shit, Chief."

Sani looks down the highway like he might see a red truck push itself slowly out of the pitch-black curtain thrown by the flares.

"Red truck?"

"Yeah, ripping up the road, dude hanging a brick out the window—"

The CB takes a total shit—static like nothing can catch. Whatever that good soul saw, he's out of range. And to be honest, I wish I was with him.

Sani keeps looking west down the road. I know that look. That road leads to the Rez. His Rez. My Rez. And some red truck that a long-hauler says was suspect is headed that way. Long-haul truckers know shady shit on the road when they see it.

But first things first—I gotta get Paul where he needs to go.

I turn back to the car. But Paul is gone.

"Did you take him?" I ask the veil.

The fact that it's still here, billowing in some cosmic death wind I can't feel tells me all I need to know. Once the veil nabs a soul, it bounces out of here. So no.

"Well that's just great. Way to drop the pass. Where did he go?"

The veil billows harder, maybe a bit confused like. Or maybe I'm reading into things. But it's not moving, which means it doesn't know.

"What do you mean you don't know?" I ask, turning a circle.

The flares that puking cop set up are throwing everything not on the road into a smoky soup.

"Paul!" I yell. "Paul, let's not make this tough, okay? I got a lot of shit to do today!"

He wants to play hardball? Fine, I'll do it myself. I flutter my fingers and spit into my palms, slap my hands together, and rub them back and forth a few times before reaching out into the air, through the air, and pressing the pause button on his timeline. Sure, the fluttering and spitting and all that isn't strictly necessary, but when your life becomes your job, it's the little things that keep you sane.

Backward we go. Very slowly, I rewind the tape of the living world. The guy couldn't have dipped out more than a couple minutes ago. Only the veil and I operate in this timeline. Everything else reverses while we stay static. Smoke wafts backward, towards the flares. The desert moths flutter away from the flames in reverse, bursting back to life. Chief Yokana's mouth eats his words in reverse. And here comes Paul, walking backward in a trance, toe-heeling his way out of a ratty knot of gutter weeds off the side of the road.

He's walking funny, aside from the backward stuff, that is. His shoulders are low, his neck stooped. His arms are stick straight at his sides.

I hit pause.

"Alright, Paul, enough of this shit." I nod to the veil. "Go on. Do your thing."

The veil hesitates. Right. I forgot it doesn't really like when I mess with time. I can rewind a story, but it has to take the soul in real time.

I walk around to Paul's front and come face-to-face with eyes gone pitch black—front to back, side to side, all black. It's enough to jump me back a few steps, and after ten years on this job, that is saying something.

"What the hell's gotten into you, Paul?" I ask.

Paul doesn't answer, of course, and he won't until I follow him and find out what he's staring at so hard it bled the color from his eyes. I can see where the color went too. It's streaking down his cheeks like... well, kind of like I look when someone really sees me before I take them to the veil.

I have a fever-dream memory of Ana looking that way too in a vision I had of her in a hogan ceremony. All Walkers get it from time to time, the eye bleed. I bet even Black Bear got it.

And just like that, I'm up to the tenth time today I've thought about that bastard Black Bear.

He was banished seven months ago, kicked out of the living world forever. But nobody celebrated because he took Caroline with him, a sacrifice for her daughter. With every action that crosses the lands of living and dead, the balance must be kept. But still, for months, the people of the Arroyo held their breath, looking for any sign she might return.

Then summer waned. No Black Bear. No Caroline.

Then the crows stopped working.

Used to be Joey could've had everyone in the Circle looking for her, but ever since she disappeared, it's like the crow totems are blocked. Without Caroline's to complete the Circle, they shorted out.

Now, fall has come. The Arroyo still rebuilds. The Circle remains committed to their search—no crow left behind—but I can see their strings. I can see what they feel in the dark of the night when they're awake and staring at the ceiling, and I know that in their heart of hearts they are considering, more and more, that this trade Caroline made, this deal she brokered, whatever it was and however it went... that it was final. That Caroline is never coming back. That whatever connection she and Black Bear had to this world is gone, a door slammed shut.

Even Owen and Joey have these thoughts. Even Grant.

But they don't see what I see. They don't see things like Paul, here. Yeah, most of my day-in-day-out is nothing special—find soul, console soul, escort soul. But lately, when it comes to dying on the Rez, souls have seemed... off. Like this eye thing. And the wandering.

"Alright, you weirdo. Let's see where you went," I say. Then I press Play in the cosmic DJ booth and let the world catch up to itself.

Paul starts walking, but not like he's the loving husband of Ellen Richter, who were on their way to Manuelito's for a Friday-night tradition but are now a family completely ruined by a brick. No, he's walking like he's in a trance, licking his lips for something out there in the dark.

I glance back at the veil, which looks about as unsure as a cosmic shower curtain can look. I follow, but it hangs back, the little chicken.

"Don't worry. I got this," I call back, my voice dripping.

Paul walks off the road, through the gnarled ditch

weeds peppered with road trash. I gotta pick my way, but Paul somehow suddenly seems to know this grim stretch of desert like the back of his dead hand.

He steps flat-footed around and through little openings, following snake paths and breaks in the ragged bushes, face-first like a hooked fish.

We come to a clear-cut patch of dirt about a hundred feet off the highway, and Paul sits down right on the ground. It's too dark to see whatever he's sitting in, but I can sure smell it.

Carrion. Animal death.

My reach doesn't go too far with the animals. I can sense when their souls have been cut short, but that's about it. And there are a lot of them here.

Paul isn't moving anymore, so I speed us up to real time. An ambulance has arrived back on the road, along with a state cop from the New Mexico side, and Sani and the poor deputy without any dinner left in him are walking my way with big high-beam battery lights. They step carefully—that slow, smooth way that won't surprise the rattlesnakes known to hang out just off the warm dirt of the roads.

"It's definitely coming from here," Chief says, sniffing.

The young cop has the back of one hand over his nose. "A deer, maybe? Or skunk?"

"Maybe," Chief says, voice low.

I wait until their lights illuminate the scene for me, then we all freeze.

Sani steps back and mutters a countercurse in Navajo and spits on the ground then clears the air with his hand. The kid retches again and tries to hide it, but he sounds like a cat caught on a furball.

There are dead birds. There are also dead mice. And

dead squirrels. And dead coyotes. The mice are the smallest circle, four of them, crushed into little fur pancakes at the four corners. The birds are next, more carefully done, doves interspersed with crows, all of them pierced through the back with stripped branches of wood, wings spread. Every little head turned to the right, each watching the next in death. The sand around their feathers is disturbed. They were alive when they were staked.

The squirrels are the same, but belly up, split open, intestines wrapped around their necks.

The coyotes are the most impressive—or disgusting, depending on your point of view. They've been quartered, their little stumps of bodies propped upright, resting on their heads. Their paws are in their mouths.

All in all, twenty animals desecrated. I've seen a lot, but this is a new one.

And in the center of all of this madness is Paul's soul. He sits on top of a pile of black bricks exactly like the one that caved his face in, but these are surrounded by filthy pennies. He's like a cursed statue at the center of some unholy wishing fountain.

Chief and the young cop can't see Paul, with his black marble eyes and runny face, but they sure as shit can see the bricks. Even the kid can make the connection.

"Is that like some sort of altar?"

"Maybe," Chief says again, his voice even lower.

And Paul says, for my ears only, "It's coming. Black bricks and blood. Bones on the road."

I try to make sense of that while Chief Yokana has made the clearly uncomfortable decision to step into this hellish circle to get a closer look at the bricks, muttering his countercurse the whole time.

"Bones on the road, Walker. Pennies and blood. Boons already won. Souls already lost."

Only one person I know speaks of boons. And I have only one question for that person or any of his lackeys.

I stride my ghost ass right up to Paul and grab him by the back of his dead head. "Where is she?" I growl.

"Boons already won, souls already lost. Bones on the road. Pennies and blood."

He looks at Yokana coming closer to him, unknowing, and he cackles and reaches out for the Chief.

Things are devolving. I whistle for the veil and hear it whooshing toward me.

"Chief, don't move!" I yell to the ether.

Silence on his end. He doesn't even get a hint of an echo. Paul, or whatever Paul has become, reaches for him while his eyes melt in waxy lines down to the corners of his mouth.

He's within an inch of Yokana's knee when the veil sweeps over the whole horror show and gobbles Paul up in a blink.

This time, the Chief does freeze—the young cop too. Rules are rules, and worlds are separate worlds, but when the veil washes over you, you feel it, the dead and the living.

Both of them look like the blood inside them stopped for a second.

"Chief, I don't feel so good," the cop says.

"You and me both," Yokana says quietly. He backsteps out of the circle the way he came, smudging his bootprints as he goes.

Back at my side again, the veil shudders, flutters out something that could possibly be a burp, then pops out of existence. I get another tug.

Another soul calls. Time to leave Chief Yokana and the young deputy and the circle of death they found. I swipe open the soul map and step in. The eastern flats disappear, but my mind can't stop hearing Paul's warnings.

Boons already won, souls already lost.

Pennies and blood.

2

OWEN BENNET

The baby is crying. I blink myself awake in the dark of the bedroom and peel my cheek from a pillow damp with sweat and drool and maybe tears. *Who knows, these days?* In the rare times I'm able to sleep, I sleep so hard that it's like I'm falling through the bed and out of this world. If only I could somehow fall into whatever world Caroline is in. Then maybe we could fashion something of our life back together. Then maybe we could name this child, for God's sake.

Every time I wake up, I feel the oncoming dawn like another stone on my chest. I've spent seven months getting closer to that strange mental space where one must have a reckoning, a space where I have to start thinking more and more about how to prepare this child for life without a mother. And how to prepare myself for a life without Caroline.

I pause, my eyes adjusting to the low light. Moonbeams settle like cold gauze over Caroline's side of the bed. Her nightstand, her night guard to keep her teeth from grinding, her dog-eared copy of some trashy romance from the Rez library—far overdue now although I can't bring myself to return it.

I listen for the child. My brain is trained to be so hypervigilant of her sounds that I've started hearing phantom cries. They often start in my dreams and bleed into that first half-second of liminal space between asleep and awake. Half the times that I check in on her, thinking she needs me, she's asleep. I'm told this is normal by people who have no real idea how abnormal my life actually is.

Nope, this cry is legitimate, a strange-sounding one tonight. Nothing like *I'm hungry* or *I just pooped all the way up my back*. This one stops and starts. It's halting, like she's afraid.

I'm up in a flash and out to the main room, where I find Grant already at her crib. He still sleeps in his little bedroom at the apex of the frame. Usually, Kai's with him although recently, she's been working hard with Joey to rehome the returned Arroyo crew. Grant would probably be at the Arroyo too except he thinks I need help with the girl. And truth be told, I do. He was the one that convinced me to move her crib from my bedroom out to the main so that he could take care of any night-shift needs that might arise and I might be able to get some more sleep. I've had more than a few people tell me I look tired these days.

He reaches in and asks, "What's all this now? What's all this?" with such perfect fatherly pitch that I can't help but feel like a trespasser here.

I'm too old to be a dad, too in my own head to be able to love her like I should, not when I know what she cost, not when I'm staring down the realities of how hamstrung she'll be, growing up in this place without a mother. Caroline and I chose Rez life, for better and for worse, but she doesn't have that choice. I find it hard to believe she won't resent me for that, for the life she fell into—once she can.

I've never told Grant any of this. I know I should, but he's already giving me quite a bit, and I'm not used to asking for help. I'm supposed to be the one who gives help.

Grant is dressed and ready to go, boots on, hat near to hand even though the clock says it's just past four in the morning. A cup of coffee steams on the table in the moonlight. The child still cries, but it's not a scared cry any longer. Grant sways with her until she starts to drift.

I stand there awkwardly in my underwear. "You coming in or going out?" I whisper.

"Headed out," he mutters back, looking down at her.

"You don't have to do these night shifts," I say then backtrack. "I mean, thank you, but I know the elder twins have you set up out there with Joey, and I know they need your help, and I know your heart is there..." I trail off. All that came out sounding like it was rehearsed.

Grant looks up at me for the first time, and I wish I could say the sad smile on his face was a trick of the light. He hands her to me as though he senses my need to appear useful. Thankfully, she doesn't start fussing at the handoff.

"You ain't gotta do this all by yourself, Dad," Grant says.

Yes I do, I think. But I say, "I know. It's just I also know you have a lot on your plate too."

Another thing I hope is a trick of the light is the way the shadows hang heavy on his shoulders, the way the bell looks like it's pressing into his neck, pinching his clavicle like the necklace was wire, not leather. He thinks I'm not being totally honest about how much I'm still reeling from the birth and the loss, but I know for a fact he's keeping secrets too, starting with how heavy that bell has become.

Grant rolls his shoulders and turns his head this way and that. His neck cracks audibly. "I can deal with a full plate," he says.

"I know you can," I say even though I don't. I have no idea how he can rebuild the Arroyo, help me, be there for Kai, and keep that thing around his neck safe. And for a second, I feel like we're both looking at each other, deciding what not to say.

The baby is watching me through lidded eyes, but carefully, in that unabashed way that's somehow both a question and a charge of some sort. She pushes her tiny swaddled feet against my hip and sighs heavily. She sighs a lot. Coos and cries too. More often than not, though, she just has this expectant quiet about her. That's part of the reason that every time she does make a sound, one of us is on it.

"How *are* things at the Arroyo?" I ask since he's still got his hands on his hips and looks like he's about to try to impart some fatherly wisdom on me when it really should be the reverse.

Grant looks out the big front window into the dark flatness of the desert. Chaco is out there somewhere. I can tell when Grant's talking to him. I try to find the bird, but in all that dark, only Grant would know where to look.

"Diggin' out," he says. "Gonna be diggin' out for a long while yet."

He knows that's not what I mean. I know about the digging. Grant doesn't want to lay anything else on me, but I think we all know it's a little late for that.

Tsosi, one of the elder twins and half of the beating heart of the Arroyo people, woke up last week with a midgrade fever that has ticked slowly higher in the days since. Three days ago, he was apparently very agitated and got up too fast from his seat at the fire and suffered a fall. I managed to cobble together childcare from the volunteers at the clinic long enough to pop down to the Arroyo and check on him. Without an X-ray, I can't be sure, but I think he has a hairline fracture, along with a nasty hematoma. Neither of which is likely to fully heal at his age.

Maria, their caretaker, was beside herself. I tried to explain to her that no amount of constant attending could have prepared her for a feverish old man suddenly lurching up from his seat and falling over, but I think the twins could happily pass from this earth at the ripe age of a thousand, and she would still have cause to berate herself that they didn't live to one thousand and one.

"It ain't good," Grant says finally. "Tsosi can't sit anymore, so they have him propped on a lean-to by the fire. He ain't eatin' neither."

"Responsive?" I ask.

"Sometimes. Other times it's... I dunno, it's like he's talkin' in his sleep."

"I'll find a way to get down there today. I'll bring something for the fever and for the pain. Maybe he has some sort of general infection. I'll pack a broad-spectrum antibiotic."

Grant shakes his head. "You can try. But he won't take it. The twins, they're as old-school as they come."

I still have issues distinguishing between *old-school* and *stubborn* when it comes to refusing modern medical care up to the point of no return, but now is neither the time nor the place to get into that, and we both know it.

"We're gettin' together today to try and figure out what to do," Grant says.

"You head out. I can take her from here. I'll never get back to sleep anyway."

He sighs and settles his hat on his head and fishes his keys from his pocket. He looks like he wants to hug me, but the baby is between us, and I've never been much of a hugger. To become one now would be tantamount to admitting things are coming apart, and I've learned not admitting things are coming apart is a key component of them not actually coming apart.

Grant closes the door softly behind himself, and the baby sighs again. *Figure out what to do* could mean so many things these days. About Tsosi and the Arroyo. About Caroline. About this child. About ourselves. But if I'm completely honest with myself, I believe we're at a crossroads here that no amount of figuring can get us through. Something is going to have to break to get our worlds moving again the way they should.

The baby wrings her hands, and something flashes in the dark. I move us to the window to get a better look in the moonlight. Her tiny fingers are gripped vice tight around my old beaded bracelet, the one given to me years ago by a thyroid patient. My first gift on the Rez. I'd know it anywhere, but I'm having a hard time believing it.

The last time I saw that bracelet was when I left it on Caroline's bedside table at the hospital, on a mission to talk Black Bear into taking me and sparing her—a mission she beat me to, in the end.

Once she disappeared and Sani and his team grew frustrated enough with dead ends to let me clean out her hospital room, I looked for it everywhere. I thought it was gone, lost in the swap, taken with her, maybe.

My mind flashes through every conceivable way it might end up here, with the baby. Maybe it fell into the swaddling blanket, got packaged up, tossed about the wash, pulled out with the rest. Maybe it clung to the corner of the car seat, or maybe—

My mind says it before I can snap it shut.

Maybe she's trying to tell you something. The baby. Or Caroline.

Or both.

It's not much. Already, the rational side of my brain is piling dirt over that flicker of hope, trying to kill it with logic. But I gently pry it from her grip until she gives it, and I put it back on my wrist anyway. And it calms my heart just a little.

3

GRANT ROMER

Rollin' into the Arroyo in the dead hours before the dawn, you'd think you were coming up on a tar pit halfway done eatin' a ghost town. The Navajo Nation ponied up for the white canvas pup tents the returned folk sleep in. A string of them are spaced out evenly along the lip of the canyon. A handful of gas generators give light to the whole thing. Extension cords crisscross the mud. Joey, Kai, and I dug trenches between tents with the help of those who could. The whole thing looks like the front lines of a war, which fits.

The pit fire still burns outside the twins' double-wide. Joey is there now with Kai. A few of the returned are there too. All of them are just back of Tsosi, who lies under the open night sky on a buckskin throw, his brother seated at his side.

I park the truck well back, and every step I take their way drags me down at the neck. That, more than anything, is how I know Tsosi's in a bad spot.

Joey sees me and greets me with his "*Ya'at'eeh*, Keeper" as clockwork as ever. Kai and I pass a nod back and forth.

Maria and Tsasa glance my way, but their focus on Tsosi is relentless.

Whatever council was going on here quiets when I arrive. Used to be I thought it was 'cause I'm white, and maybe it still is a bit, but mostly now, I think it's the bell. Even those who don't know what it is know it's best not to have it around the dying.

Hos moves over for me. His attitude these past seven months has been somethin' along the lines of *You saved my life, so I'm gonna pretend you ain't sleeping with my sister.* And believe it or not, that is a huge improvement.

I sit down and hold my hands out to the fire and pretend the bell don't feel like a vice grip slowly twisting itself closed around my neck. Every death we deal with wraps it a turn tighter, and death is all we seem to deal with these days.

Tsosi's covered with blankets but still shivering. Beads of sweat drip down the lines of his brow. Totems are all around him, feathers and woven balls and dreamcatchers spinning. The smoker threw everything he's got at this sickness—crystals and slow-burning sage and even some of his sacred loose cigarettes, so old they're yellow.

Chaco is at his side. I can come and go, helping Dad stay afloat, but Chaco and I figured he should stay. His presence calms the twins, and the Arroyo needs calming, especially now.

"How is he?" Chaco asks mind to mind, meaning Dad.

"Not great," I answer.

Chaco fluffs up and settles down again. A sigh. A lot of those going around.

I try to catch Joey's eye, but he's watching the way people are standing by their tents, looking our way. He sees the looks same as me. He hears the silence, feels the fear.

Tsosi mutters, turning his head back and forth like he's in a bad dream. His eyes flick this way and that under lids as thin as parchment paper.

"They're watching," I tell Chaco. "The returned. They come back to mud and pain and now this."

"They walked the path back themselves," Chaco says. "That was their choice. They could have taken the river. They want to be here."

I ain't sure *want* is the right word, but somethin' about this place keeps us coming back. I set my hat on my knee and try very hard not to run my hands down my face. People watch me now, especially when I'm quiet and they know, or they've heard, I'm probably talking to the bird. So the last thing I need to do is rake my fingers down my face. But I can't help pulling at the bell and rolling my shoulders.

"I know you think we're lean on hope right now, but you don't see things like I do, Grant," Chaco says. "Change is here. Pieces are moving."

"I think a lot of us want off the ride," I say.

Tsosi's mutterings form into words. We all lean in. Joey kneels, holding his long black braid out of the way to listen.

"Of a time long, long ago, it is said—" He looks like he wants to say more, but his breath picks up, and his eyes flicker rapid fire under the lids. He starts to shake under the deerskin. Tsasa pats his hand, slumped low himself.

"He's afraid," Chaco tells me.

"He can't be afraid. The elder twins ain't afraid of anything."

Tsasa leans low, says to his brother something I can't

make out. Tsosi calms, but his eyes still flutter. This time, Tsasa speaks.

"Our people are people of unending flight. In the days of the ancients, we went from place to place, always trying to settle. Many times, we thought ourselves safe. But every time…"

He trails off as Tsosi opens his sticky mouth. "Every time, the *Anaye* came."

His shaking comes back. Tsasa holds his brother's hand, speaking to him in that language only they know. Chaco flutters over to him and settles softly on his chest.

His mouth opens, and he sighs fit to let his spirit go, and maybe it tries runnin'. The bell sure feels heavy enough. Maybe it's Chaco settlin' there that keeps it in.

After a calm span of seconds, Tsosi speaks clear as day, lyin' there on the deerskin.

"The Anaye come. The Eater of Men comes. He Who Kills with Eyes comes. And in their wake they will leave bones and blood."

Chaco flares his wings like he's tryin' to catch the words to keep 'em from hitting the air. Somewhere in the back, a generator stutters and wheezes before catching again. The fire pops, and I hold my hands out to it to catch whatever protection it can throw.

The Anaye are ancient monsters. They walked the world in the beforetimes. They terrorized and consumed, and the names he said—Eater of Men, Kills with Eyes— these things were exactly as they sound.

The tents lining the lip light up here and there like wish lanterns. Dawn's still a ways out, but the people are stirring. Everyone's heard by now that Tsosi ain't doin' too good.

Joey looks toward the flats opposite the canyon, where

the hogans stand. He takes his deerskin lanyard, the one with the pouch that holds his crow, and he gently pushes it back and around his neck so it's out of his way. I know what he's thinking. Used to be he could get help from the Circle. But Joey said when one crow totem goes missing this long, it blows a fuse, and they all go dark.

"I think it's time we take grandfather to the hogan," he says.

For what, I ain't sure. But I got an idea. We gotta shore up. Prepare as best we can. Because somethin's coming, and it ain't good.

4

CAROLINE ADAMS

I'm having a hard time figuring out the time.

It feels like only hours ago, Owen was saying to me about how my baby wasn't breathing. Which wasn't right because I specifically made a deal to keep her breathing, a swap. Me for her. Then Owen took her for emergency CPR and wall oxygen, and everyone scrambled, and I was left alone in the hospital bed for just a moment or two. And my bill came due.

When you're on forced bedrest, it doesn't take too long to really hate your bed. My sweat-and-blood-soaked hospital bed, the thing I'd been confined to for what felt like weeks, finally won. It took me down. The sheets, the mattress, all of it just turned to sand, and I sank, and I sank. Too weak to fight, I could only watch as everything dimmed and I thought, *Well, here we go. Time to meet Ben.* And the thought brought this wave of peace and sadness upon me at the same time. And regret. And pretty much every other emotion. Longing. Anger. Heartburn.

The darkness covered me like a weighted blanket, and with it came this growing pressure squeezing me all over.

Just when I was sure I was gonna be one of those corpses that wee themselves, *pop*, the lights turned on.

My vision wavered back together like one of those old TVs on the fritz does after a few good whacks, and I could see again.

I remember Owen describing what being dead was like. He talked about a river and a bunch of souls like bobbing tea lights and the sound of water and a gently glowing beach. I mean, aside from the whole being-dead part, it didn't sound all that bad.

This place I'm looking at right now is not that.

All I see is desert. Desert forever. A few hills and mounds here and there. A handful of rocks that look just as lost and awkward as I feel. Certainly no beach. For there to be a beach, there needs to be water, but I don't see water. I don't hear it either. No sounds at all, really, unless you count the roar of silence.

I've been sitting here for a while now, trying to figure out if I'm dead or not. Both sides of the argument have their points. Honestly, I'm leaning toward dead and all the baggage that comes with *that*, but next I see a shack out on the horizon.

Or I think I do, anyway. I blink, and it's gone. But *something* was there. I putter around on the sand a little bit, like a few feet here or there might give me a better line of sight across all this hot nothing. When it doesn't, I sit. I sit, and I think about whether seeing a disappearing shack in this endless landscape is a point for the Dead column or for the Alive column, and just when I conclude that "weird hallucinations" are probably a point for the Dead column —considering I have firsthand nursing experience of how such things can happen to a brain starved of oxygen at the last moments—I see it again, closer this time.

On the Rez, the shepherds and cattle drivers keep up a series of cabins strewn all across the canyons so they have a place to go if a really ugly storm rolls in. Owen and I visited a few of them on wellness checks. They're basically four walls, a firepit, and a stovepipe. The shepherds call them safehouses. This shack I'm looking at is basically the same, but it doesn't exactly scream *safe* to me.

I'm not the type of girl to walk into horror-movie shacks. I'm what you call an empathic personality, super vibe-sensitive, and yes, that description makes me cringe too. But really, I am. I can literally see feelings like smoke wafting here and there, and even though this shack doesn't smoke, it's got trouble written all over it.

But if my choices are the shack or endless sand...

I suck at my teeth. Owen wrapped my totem pouch around my fingers when I was giving birth—something to squeeze, I guess, to give his own fingers a break, and I haven't stopped squeezing it since. I fish the crow out again, skin to stone. Nothing. Same as the last dozen times. I hold it up to the sky anyway like maybe it's just got bad cell service. Flick it a few times. Nothing. Might as well be a paperweight.

I have a creeping suspicion I've been puttering around this little patch of sand for a lot longer than I think. It's easy enough to say, *Don't go in there, idiot!* when you're munching popcorn on the couch, watching some poor bimbo waltz right into trouble—harder when the choice is your own. I can't really explain why except to say I think maybe part of the reason people go into the haunted house is because it's *there*.

I take one step toward the shack, and the old wooden door opens with a whisper. A man, wearing the peeling body of another man, walks out, pulling bits of his old skin off like lint as he approaches.

I know who he is even before he calls out, "Welcome home!" in that same halting, half-mad lilt he had back on the Rez, like he's trying out the words for the first time.

Black Bear—the other side of my wager.

I turn and walk away. You can do that, you know. Just turn around. I do it all the time when things get to be too much. Bail on dinner plans. Bail on parties. Leave jobs. Leave cities. It usually works. Until it doesn't.

I take a step that doesn't land quite right and trip for no reason. Then I freeze—literally freeze, mid fall.

Black Bear speaks up behind me. "I am sorry to say, Caroline, but your steps are no longer your own."

Stepping forward won't work. Stepping backward won't work. Nothing works.

A hand grabs me around the waist in far too familiar of a fashion, and Black Bear slowly turns me around like a piece of candy in a Jell-O mold.

He still wears the peeling face of the Gambler, but *peeling* might not be the best word anymore because that's what happens after a bad burn at the beach. This is way worse. *Sloughing* might be better, like a snake trying to scrape off the last of its skin. The whole thing is so repulsive that I'm fully expecting to find a monster beneath, something with tentacles that spits and snarls and wins first prize at the ugly awards.

What I see instead is a young man—native, definitely, with eyes of glittering brown set deep atop high, angled cheeks and a sharp, broad nose. He looks almost Navajo, certainly related but cut from older stone.

After he pulls the last of his mask away and drops it to the ground, he rubs down the length of one arm and degloves a strip of skin that falls to the sand, watching me all the while. He wears nothing but buckskin pants fastened at the hips with woven horsehair, the leather so worn that it shines with an oily patina. He's not tall—maybe he has an inch on me—nor is he particularly big. But he has a twitchy sort of strength. Coiled and loaded.

His skin is witchy white now, and where his veins touch the surface, they're poison black. The skin of a one-time Walker who never quite stopped walking. Owen said Ben's looked the same when they met on the far side of the veil.

I wish he looked more like a monster and less like a man. It's throwing me off. Making me think maybe he came out here to help me.

"You have crossed the threshold of my house," he says, blowing right past my personal space bubble until his face is inches from mine. "But I will allow it because it is now *our* house," he adds, looking at me with a gross fondness. He lifts his arms to show me the shack—as if I'd miss it—and his armpits smell like a damp basement. "I had hoped to have something larger by now," he says, "but that will have to wait."

He takes my hand in his, his touch like old newspaper, and before I realize what he's doing, he plucks my totem from my grasp.

"You no longer need this," he says.

I try to scream, but my mouth won't move. He sees the scream in my eyes, though, and he likes it.

He places my crow in a pouch on one hip and pulls a glittering black bear from a pouch on the other. "A different totem rules here."

He tucks the black bear into the space in my hand where my crow was, and just like that, I'm able to move.

His totem burns, too, but not in the slow, piercing cold way of the crow. His is like hot oil covering my palm.

"I don't want your filthy totem," I say and toss it back at him.

The second it leaves my hands, I'm frozen again.

Black Bear gives me a *tsk tsk* and bends down to pick it up. He places it in my grip again, and I'm able to move. I pull my shaking hand up and look at the totem in horror.

"I am sure you will try to run again. But you will find you cannot move without my totem, and my totem only works here."

I hold on to the oily burn and take in deep breaths.

"Do you understand now?" he asks, peering at me with wide, unblinking eyes.

I make no moves, but I'm huffing fast, trying not to panic. If I drop this hideous thing or he takes it away from me again, each breath I take could be my last.

"Good," Black Bear says. "Now. Come inside."

5

KAI BODREY

Riding in a cop car sure ain't a first for my brother, Hos, but I'd be lying if this ain't a first for me. That's pretty hard to believe, considering all the shady shit he had me do. And of course, of the two of us, he's the one with the window down, taking in the breeze. Not a care.

Sure, you could say Sani Yokana's Bronco ain't a true lit-up cop car, but I know he has a light when he needs it. And Yokana ain't just any cop, neither. He's the Chief of the Navajo Police. He's King Cop.

Hos sees me all tense and slaps me on the stomach with the back of his hand. "Relax. If they're here to arrest you, they arrest you. And they sure as shit don't let the windows roll down."

He pokes his head out like a dog. Might be something about jail that does that to a person. I'm not lookin' to find out.

"Chief, where are we goin?" I ask again because my boots are still covered in Arroyo mud and I'm pretty sure the Arroyo needs paths from tent to tent more than whatever bullshit the NNPD wants.

The only reason I got in his car when he asked us to ride along is because he asked Hos, and if Hos is in some shit, I need to know about it. Plus, when I was lost during the flood, Yokana showed up out of the storm with a flare to guide me right, then he let me go where I needed to go without asking questions. But the longer this ride gets, the less sure I am that I made the right decision.

"Not long now," Yokana says, eyeing the mile markers. We're out eastern flats way. Driving IH9 for at least twenty miles. Just when I start to think maybe we're going off Rez, Yokana slows.

Out here, there ain't signs indicating turnoffs. Just desert that looks a bit more driveable. Like maybe a few cars ran it over before you, so your car's got a shot. Yokana takes one now.

"This is the battery road," Hos says, sitting up.

Yokana grunts something that may be a yes.

"The hell is a battery road?" I ask.

"We used to swap booze for batteries," he says. And when I keep staring at him, he says, "You know how fuckin' expensive batteries are? And how many you need when your sorry ass don't live along one of those?" he asks, pointing at the looping electrical lines that follow the main roads but definitely do not go as deep as we lived —not even close.

"Two jars for ten double D's," Hos says, almost to himself. "We'd swap it at Baba's, this old breakfast spot way out."

"There's a restaurant way out here?" I ask.

"Not a restaurant. Just Baba's, this little cabin painted sky blue. She's a mean old bag, but she makes a hell of a breakfast and never kicked my ass out for being too drunk." He leans forward. "Hey, Chief, is Baba's still out this way? I fuckin' loved that place. We'd pop a few jars and eat eggs cooked in backfat grease and a shit ton of cheese."

Yokana doesn't answer.

Hos and I know that kind of quiet. It's the kind of quiet that says you'll see. And then you'll probably wish you hadn't.

It's high noon on one of those really nice fall days, but once we leave the BIA road, the sun gets cut at the knees by the rocky foothills, and the temp drops like a rock.

The smell of charred wood wafts into the car, and somethin' else too, heavy and sweet and a little off. Hos rolls up the window and gives me a grim look.

Baba's is still smoking when it we round the bend to see. It may have been a bright little blue house once. Now, it's a black smudge.

Another cop car is already there, roping off a wide square perimeter. A woman is walking around, taking pictures with a big barrel-lens camera. We park, and Yokana just sits for a sec. All we can hear is the tick of his engine cooling down and every now and then the click of the camera shutter.

"Like I said at the Arroyo, Kai, this is more something for your brother to see, not you," he says.

"And like I said, if Hos is in some shit, I need to know."

Hos cuts in. "Look, Chief, if anything I did got Baba and hers in trouble, I'll own up to it. I been doin' a lot of apologizing and could stand to do a lot more."

"It's not like that," Yokana says. "I'm more hoping you might have some thoughts on the crime scene. From your days upstate."

"Is that what Baba said?" Hos asks, looking at the shack cockeyed.

"Baba's dead. Same with Jules, her husband, and their two daughters."

The silence stretches. That sweet smoke turns my stomach. I breathe through my mouth, but somehow, that makes it worse.

"Chief, you gotta know I would never—"

"I know it wasn't you. You were a bootlegger and a petty thief. I got a long list of who it wasn't. What I need to know is who it was."

He pushes his car door open with a squeak and heaves himself out, looking the full weight of his years. He walks toward the tape, leaving it up to us to follow. We share a glance, then we both get out.

Baba's is completely gone, nothing but four crumbled walls and a door that looks propped up by rocks. The crime scene tape is wrapped around four metal fenceposts staked into the ground fifty or so feet from what's left. Yokana stops at the line and speaks with the photographer.

"Any others?" he asks.

She shakes her head. I recognize her from the cultural center. This must be a side hustle. Judging by how green she looks, it's one she's regretting right now.

"Take a breather," he tells her. "It'll be here when you come back."

She nods, glances at me and Hos, then turns to walk back into a patch of sun where she rolls her neck and pulls out a packet of cigs and stares down the road, back the way we came.

Yokana ducks under the tape, and we follow. He stops us well short of the wreckage and points at the ground where a little red tent with a number one sits in the dirt. At first, I can't see anything, but then Hos squats down, and I see what he's looking at. It's a penny, a dirty penny that almost blends into the desert.

There's more too. A whole line of pennies and little numbered tents, spaced evenly one after the other. Hos follows them, and I follow Hos. Yokana lets us take the lead.

The pennies lead us down a worn footpath. Hos turns back to me more than once as we walk alongside, like he wants to check I'm still there. I catch him doin' that a lot these days.

The trail comes to an end at a pile of black rocks stacked like one of those cairns you can come across in the backcountry—Hos says they're markers the migrants leave each other. Strangers saying hello.

Safe to say this one five feet from the burn zone feels more like the opposite of hello.

The top of the rock pile is covered with junk—more dirty pennies but also cigarettes and even some bullets, each placed carefully on and between the rocks, in a rough circle. At the center is a charred human hand holding a blistered, half-eaten apple—most of a hand, anyway. The fingers are nibbled to bone up to about the first knuckle.

I'm freaking out and breathing fast, so I try to cover it up by asking "Coyotes?" and pretending I gotta burp. I know damn well no coyote or buzzard or night animal of any sort leaves a severed hand dead center on a pile of rocks, holding an apple.

Hos doesn't freak out. Hos squats down and brushes at a black rock with his finger. A bit of the black flakes away like burnt barbecue. He grunts and stands, wiping his hand on his jeans. "It's blood. Charred blood."

"All that black is blood?"

The whole cairn is black—twenty, maybe thirty stones worth.

Hos nods and looks back at Yokana, who watches him with a flat and unbroken gaze.

"You weren't kidding, old timer," he says quietly. "This is some shit."

"I'm not much of a kidder," Yokana replies flatly.

Hos walks to the front of the wreckage, where most of the door still stands. I follow, trying to keep that burp from becoming something worse. Hos pushes at it, but the door doesn't move. The rocks are piled too high.

The walls to either side are charred rubble, though—no door needed. A step to the right gives me a clear line of sight on four charred bodies in the dead center of the cabin. They're as black as the wooden walls, skin bubbled off bone.

That burp comes back with a vengeance, and I take in a big breath to keep it down.

"They were trapped," Hos says. "Locked in and burned alive."

That's enough for me. I walk back to the light, where the photographer offers me a cigarette, but I don't get a chance to say no, thank you before I puke on the dirt. The smell and the nibbled hand and the bubbly bone—I puke again and spit and stand, tryin' to pass it off like I didn't, like I can take it. I have no idea how Hos can—or anyone, for that matter.

"You do this for a living?" I ask the photographer, wiping my mouth.

"I ain't ever seen nothin' like this," she says, looking tired.

Hos does a full circle of the place and comes back around from the other side. He stops at the pile of bullets and all that shit and spits, muttering a countercurse. But if you ask me, there ain't enough sage on the Rez to clear this air.

He comes up to me, and for a quick second, I think he's gonna call me out a pussy, and I flinch, but he sets his hand softly on my shoulder instead, a kind hand. And I remember again that the brother who made me flinch all the time is gone.

"You okay?" he asks.

"Hell no, I ain't okay. What is all this? Aside from somethin' out of a nightmare I ain't had yet."

Hos looks over at Yokana, who watches us quietly, his old black hat in his hands.

"Come on," Hos says. "Let's get back to the Arroyo."

I DON'T QUITE BREATHE RIGHT until we come down the hill back to the BIA road and that hellhole winks out behind us. I can't get enough of the open windows. Now, I'm the dog hanging out.

"What do you know, Hos?" Yokana asks.

My shithead brother, whom I love, has been very quiet since he sat down in the back of the Bronco.

Yokana glances at him in the rearview mirror. "Anything helps," he says.

Hos looks out the window, one finger hooked on the bar up top. "We used to do a few booze runs out on the southern flats, where the Rez bleeds into the Zuni land.

Did some drug mule shit out there, too. Shit I ain't proud of." He looks over at me and looks away, ashamed.

"It was for good money," he says, on reflex, but ain't nobody in this car about to call him out. Not anymore.

"Sometimes, we'd find little rock piles like that with animal bones. Witch shit. It got to the point we had to give Dunk and his squad a burn stick to make the run. Some of these piles even had cigarettes. One had bullets and lollipops."

"Like fucked-up totem piles?" I ask.

Hos softly pops my shoulder with his fist. "Exactly. More and more of them. Except back then, I was hopped up on all sorts of chemicals and really didn't give a shit what me or anyone in our crew saw in the open desert. I cared about the money. Then I got arrested for that shit we pulled in Santa Fe and got sent up."

Hos shares a glance with Yokana in the mirror then shrugs. "Not sayin' I didn't deserve it, Chief."

"Keep talking," Yokana says in that same flat voice he says everything.

"So I'm in juvie, right. 'Just juvie,' they call it. But these kids are nuts. And the lockup's out near Roswell, with all the aliens and shit? The whole place was bad medicine. Meth vibe amped. None of these boys I was in with was going anywhere after this stint but down Turquoise Road to the Pen."

Hos shivers and rolls the windows up.

"The local boys rolled deep there, if you know what I'm sayin'. We Indians held our own for sure. But the one group we never fucked with was the Mexicans that rolled in hot off the border with the lady-skeleton tattoos. I learned that quick when one of the meth head ABQ white boys did, and then he ended up choking to death on his tongue that night."

"Lady Skeleton?" I ask.

Hos rubs at his neck. "The Mexicans call her Santa Muerte. Saint Death. She's the patron saint of the dealers and the cartel boys. Killers pray to her for luck. I saw it with my own eyes in the yard. Boys who came in, caught off the border without a word of English or a cent to their names, out in the yard burning cigarettes on a little shitty altar they made out of loose rocks. I saw one kid pull out his own dog teeth with a pinched set of pliers and offer them in prayer, rubbing blood from his mouth into the brick."

Yokana clears his throat and cuts in. "We know about Santa Muerte. The cartels always try to cut through Navajo land. Too many of them—not enough of us. But there's no drug money or cartel glory in torching Baba's. All she wanted to do was cook breakfast and take an occasional drink."

Hos glances behind us, where the sunset chases. If I didn't know better, I'd say he looks scared. As it is, I think he's just being careful. Bodreys are tight-lipped. This ain't coming natural to him.

"That ain't it, Chief," he says. "These Santa Muerte people... Pulling their own teeth is a start. The real nuts ones don't give a shit about money or drugs. All they care about is death. All they want to do is meet her."

He glances at me. "Or him," he adds.

Yokana turns back onto the BIA road, and I can't think of any other time I've been so happy to see streetlights.

"So you're telling me they're here looking for death?" Yokana asks, broad brow furrowed, working things out in that big King Cop head of his.

Hos cracks his window again and takes a deep breath of good old desert night air. "I seen pictures of the statues in the border towns down Mexico side. Death holds a scythe in one hand, which ain't nothin' new, but the other hand holds the world. And I gotta say, it looks a lot like that hand back there holding that apple."

"And the gnawed-on fingers?" Yokana asks.

Hos watches the razor-thin horizon reflected off the rearview mirror. "That, I got no idea about. That's new."

Yokana grumbles again. I work my jaw back and forth —Hos talking about kids pulling their own teeth making me feel phantom pain. Hos checks again if I'm still here, and I nod yeah. He spits out the window, and it gets whipped back behind the car. Clearing the air of the witch shit.

Because we wouldn't be here, seeing all this and talking all that if Yokana thought whoever torched Baba's went on their merry way afterward. Nah. My guess is Yokana thinks whoever lit that fire is still on the Rez.

My guess is he's worried this is just the start.

6

OWEN BENNET

My twelve-thirty appointment is uncomfortable. And by that, I mean my patient is visibly uncomfortable. Not that talking about syphilis with your doctor is particularly comfortable. But let me tell you, the alternative is worse. *Not* talking about syphilis—just living with it until it progresses into neurosyphilis then delirium then dementia is bound to be a lot more uncomfortable. Plus, your hair falls out.

The patient, a young rig worker from Shiprock named Tonteel, swears he came by his affliction honestly, but I know all about the camps that pop up around rigs in this part of the country. No doubt they come by the money honestly, but the way they spend it is another matter.

He's sitting on the crinkly paper, wringing his hands. He looks at the floor then back up at me and clears his throat. I resist the urge to rub my face. I'm going on five hours of sleep in the past forty-eight.

"It's nothing to be embarrassed about. And no, your penis won't fall off. But I'm going to need you to be honest with me about where and when so I know what to prescribe."

He still seems hesitant. Going to the CHC can be tough for the younger men here. Or, come to think of it, maybe it's the baby I have strapped to my chest like a beer belly. She's facing outward, arms and legs starfished, watching him in silence.

He glances at her and looks away. Yes, it's definitely the baby.

"Don't worry, she doesn't know what a penis is," I say before I realize how absurd that is. "I don't think it's a HIPAA violation if she isn't developing memories..." I add weakly before trailing off. I clear my throat. "You know what? You just sit tight. I'll find someone to take her. It's... uh... single parenting and all that. Real treat."

I smile wanly and head out. In the hallway, I shake my head. I don't know what the hell I'm thinking. Or not thinking. I wear this carrier so often, and my schedule gets backed up, and well, I guess I just forgot she was there. When she's not crying fit to wake the Rez, she can be a remarkably quiet child.

Thankfully, Dee is here, eyeing me from behind the desk, cracking her gum. "I was wondering how all that was gonna work out in that visit," she says, pointing me up and down with the bedazzled nail of her forefinger.

I waddle up to her. No sudden movements, to keep the baby quiet. "Dee, can you do me a favor?"

She stares at me with a droll look. Then, God bless her, she motions for the child. "Of course," she says as I ease the girl out and pass her over. "Come here, sweetheart," she says, switching tack completely to cute baby voice. "You hang with Auntie Dee for a while, mmkay? No need for you to hear your father talk about dirty dongs."

"Dee," I say, flatly.

Dee brushes the child's cheek, still talking baby. "Oh, *now* we gotta protect your precious ears."

"Thank you, Dee," I say. And I mean it.

And she knows even though she waves me off.

THREE BACK-TO-BACK APPOINTMENTS LATER, I'm wandering around the break room in a fifteen-minute cancellation slot, sipping motor oil coffee. I look out the window at the falling dark and realize my shift is almost over. I pluck my phone from my hip.

"Does anyone have my child, by chance?" I ask over the two-way.

Dee chimes in, "I did, but then a buzzard came in and asked real polite, so I gave her up."

"Dee."

"Sort of like a reverse stork."

"Dee."

Nascha, our chief medical assistant, cuts in. "I have her, Dr. Bennet. We've just been walking the halls."

I find them on the first floor, walking *that* wing. By *that* room, the one that haunts my dreams in the rare moments I have them. Nascha walks this hall for a reason. It's the only one the baby can cry in without disturbing many patients, because it's part of an ongoing investigation into my missing life partner, an investigation the NNPD will never solve.

The staff here have been a lifeline for me. The only reason I'm able to come in to work at all is because we all pass her off throughout the day. When Nascha says she's *walking the halls* with her it's usually code for *she's crying her face off.*

And she is. It's no fault of Nascha's, of course. She has two grown children and two grandchildren. She's a savant at this. Sometimes, babies just cry.

"It's okay, girl," she says, cooing, unpanicked. She speaks some Spanish to her then some Navajo. I meet them at the stairway before *the hall* and hold my hands out to take her.

"Sorry, sorry. I got caught up in back-to-backs."

She looks me up and down and says, "You finish your coffee. Let's take a walk."

Nascha has this way of saying things that makes them happen. So I sip my coffee and follow while my daughter stops and starts her fussy crying in Nascha's arms, like she's not sure precisely how bad she wants to feel.

Caroline's room is up ahead. It's not quarantined any longer—no police tape. But Dee doesn't like to put anyone in there. The MAs and RNs don't like to go in. The janitorial staff won't go in. Even Dasan, our seventy-five-year-old handyman, won't go in. And he faced down a den of rattlesnakes.

Not that I blame any of them. I don't want to go in either. I walk by this whole wing a little faster than usual every day. Something about the loss and the shame of not being able to do anything about it turns my stomach. I don't like looking at it, and I don't like turning my back on it.

But Nascha doesn't care, which is why we love Nascha.

"Real talk, Dr. Bennet," she says, walking and bouncing her.

"You can call me Owen. You helped deliver her, for crying out loud."

She shifts the girl to the other side, facing forward. It occurs to me that my daughter should probably be crawling by now. Six to twelve months is that window. But I'm not about to let her loose on a hospital floor. I make a mental note to push her to crawl more at home. I don't know how one does that. *A carrot?*

"You don't want to be here, Dr. Bennet," Nascha says.

That stops me, then I have to fast step to keep up as she walks closer to *that room.* "Well now, that's not fair—"

"I'm not talking about fair. I'm talking about what I see. You've put your heart into this job for ten years. I know what that looks like. And I know what I'm looking at now."

The baby wails. I've found the really loud wails come in sets, like waves, and I fear we're in the middle of a swell. I'm having a hard time coming up with a retort. Or a justification or a refute. Or anything, really. Because Nascha, as always, is right.

And then we're at *the room,* and I don't think Nascha even thinks about it, but I sure do. That's when my child goes completely silent and stares at the door, to the point that both of us stop cold.

Nascha looks at me, unflinching. "I think she wants to go in," she says.

Of course she does. Somehow my seven-month-old child, who can't tell day from night, wants to visit the scene of her mother's disappearance. Seems logical.

I fuss at my tie. It's tied way too short, and the tail keeps creeping out to the side. I wouldn't have allowed such a shoddy presentation a year ago.

"Fine," I say. "If it keeps her quiet. No harm."

This time, Nascha does hand her to me, gently. I settle

her in the crook of my arm, and all the while, she stares at the door.

"I got rounds," she says. "So I'm gonna let you do this. But think about what I said, Dr. Bennet."

"Thank you for watching her, Nascha. Really."

She kisses my child on the top of her head. That's something I don't know if I've done. Although I must have. Every sane father kisses his child on the head. I just can't quite remember the last time. And by the time I work that out, Nascha is gone, and I'm alone.

I mean, together with my child. But together and alone.

"What do you want in there?" I ask her. "It's empty. Has been for a long time."

She stares.

"Fine," I say. I push the door, and it glides silently open.

The room is lit. We didn't keep it as some broken place of memories. It's still a hospital room. And I try to walk in like it's just a hospital room. But my body isn't having it. My free hand starts to tremble. I see places here —spots of air now—where I was pumping my child's lungs to keep her alive. And the biggest spot of air is there on the bed, where the *nothing* I see punches a hole in my chest.

I swallow a big pine cone of pain that comes out of nowhere and settles right at the pit of my throat. "See?" I say, hoarse. "Nothing."

But my child smiles.

She's looking at the bed, and she's reaching for the bed, and she's smiling. And immediately I think, *Could be gas*, which is a thing I've realized new parents attribute a lot to, and not without warrant, but this smile is something real, something true. It falters and drops and comes back. She's working at it.

Whatever pity party I'm having in here, my child is having none of it. Without quite knowing why, I set her on the hospital bed on which she was born. And I find that I'm standing, watching her, in the same spot where I had her over my knees, pumping her tiny heart, willing her to breathe. And for just a moment, I allow myself to smile too.

She rolls over onto her stomach and pushes up on all fours, holding her head up. That shock of white hair above her forehead hasn't gone away, and at this point, I doubt it ever will. The rest of her hair started blonde but has been darkening over the months to something like brown with flashes of red when the light hits it right. She has Caroline's facial features: button nose, pinched little lips. But her eyes are my eyes, clear blue.

"What are you looking at?" I ask.

But that's not quite the right question. She's looking at me, at the thin blue sheets of the bed, at the light overhead. I know what she's looking at. What I don't know is…

"What do you see?" I ask.

Until I had a child, I counted it an obvious medical fact that the reason we don't have memories of ourselves as babies—the reason core memories only really start to form around two or three at the earliest—is because, at that age, we don't have the neurological development to support them. The medical term for it is "infantile amnesia."

These days, I'm not so sure.

She's looking out the window now. At first, all I see is the light of the fading day. Then a shifting disc of black in the bottom corner catches my attention.

"Hey, Chaco," I say.

I've seen him circle the CHC a few times before. Probably, Grant is checking up on us. Or maybe he sits here, looking into this room a lot, mourning in his own way. He glances at me, bobs a nod, but then he's back to watching the baby.

She can see what happened here, somehow. I believe she understands that her mother disappeared from this place. She looks back at me, too, as if she also understands that part of me disappeared with her.

"I'm sorry," I whisper, and the words claw their way over the lump in my throat. She was basically down one parent out of the gate, but ever since Caroline left, I've felt like half a man, half a father. No heart for my work—no heart for anything. She's had half a dad too.

"I don't know where she went," I say, helpless.

As I clear my throat, she looks back at me and gives me that flicker of a smile again. Chaco shifts around, and his wings scrape the window like a strumming tree branch. I try to loosen my tie against the goosebumps that run along my neck.

I don't know where Caroline went, but something tells me my daughter does.

Maybe I've been looking at this notion of infantile amnesia all wrong. Young children understand a lot more than we think, especially about the nature of what happens outside of life. They're the closest to it, after all. If we adults were to remember these things, they might well break our minds, things like where we come from and where we go.

Here's what *I* think. I think infants have full cosmic understanding but no way to speak of it. Then we grow up and find the words but lose the understanding. Maybe because the understanding can't be expressed with the words.

I pick her up and walk her to the window. She reaches for the glass. Chaco taps back a hello.

"You know where she is, don't you, baby girl?"

She speaks no words, of course. But she's saying something nonetheless.

The trick is learning how to listen.

7

GRANT ROMER

Joey and I walk single file along a dug-out trench to the open desert beyond the Arroyo, where the hogans sit. Kai tells me there were six of them back in the day, but in my time here, I've only ever seen three get any sort of use, and that was before the flood. The elder twins have the last on the line.

Joey says a prayer as we pass each of the dark hogans. Some of them lean hard toward the ground now, like the flood kidney-punched 'em. I try not to look too hard into the gaps in the mud walls or the sagging square doors, facing east. Always east, toward a dawn they may never have use for any longer. I don't look because, for one, it makes me sad for things lost. And for another, my mind plays tricks, telling me things are in there. I ain't a fan of derelict places. I like light, life, moving air.

Chaco is incoming. I can see him on the horizon and feel him coming back to me, settling in that place in my mind that is his alone. The rest of the Rez crows aren't here yet, but something tells me they're coming. I can hear them out there, flocking. Cawing here and there. Comin' to a quorum. They do that when big change comes.

"How's Dad?" I ask Chaco as he swoops low.

I tip my head and hat left so he can find his spot on my shoulder. He lands with enough force to buck me forward a bit. Every time he does this, it reminds me how big he's gotten. He's come into his own again.

Chaco flares his tailfeathers and sets himself right, blinking away the road dust. "Struggling," he says. "But he has help. How is Tsosi?"

"Same."

"Hogans?" he asks, a question and a statement.

"Joey says we need a sweat. He says we don't have much time."

Chaco looks back down the trench to where the double-wide still glistens in the night and the fire still adds its sparks to the stars in the sky. He doesn't reply, but he settles as close as he can against me without tipping my hat off, which is saying enough.

THE TWINS' hogan wasn't spared by the flood either. The waters washed all sorts of junk inside, and the mud that followed dried uneven. The ground is cracked and crusty and a bit lopsided. As it is now, a sweat won't work.

That's why we're here.

Chaco takes off from my shoulder and lands on the dome top and starts pecking at the chimney hole, clearing it out. Time to get to work.

Joey tells me the goal is to do a big sweat, a healing sweat, something fit to heal body and blood. Maria will bring the twins' sacred items. Tsasa will chant and paint with sand as long as he has it in him. Both twins come from a long line of Singers. If anyone can call out so that the gods will hear and favor us, it's him.

But first, we gotta purify the place. No holy spirit worth a salt is making a house call at this hogan the way it is now—doesn't matter how much we sweat.

I move to duck in, but Joey holds me back with a steady hand on my shoulder. He looks at the hogans down the line, and something in that look tells me he saw somethin' in their darkness too. If holy places get forgotten, things that ain't supposed to be there tend to move in. I've seen it happen.

Joey pulls a big stick of herbs from the cross-body pouch at his side. I can smell the sage, but other stuff is there too. Cedar. Maybe sweetgrass. A home blend. High-octane shit he got from the Smoker. He takes out a Bic lighter and fires it up, letting it burn in the gathering dark until the smoke jets out like white lightning, then he tosses it through the east entrance, smoke bomb style.

Chaco backs off the chimney up top. I don't even flinch when I see the shadows move inside. Me and the shadows are old acquaintances. I bet if I could hear across worlds, I'd be hearin' some shit right now. Soon, all you can see through the east door is white, but nothing comes out the top.

Chaco hops back up the roof. "They blocked the chimney," he says. He dips his head in and looks. "Chindi. Spirits we don't need anywhere near here. They think they found a new home. And they're pissed off."

The smoke builds and spins, and things circle with it, black chunks in a slow blender of white.

"Chaco says they're stubborn," I tell Joey.

I won't say the name aloud. That gives them power. Joey knows what they are anyway.

"It's a big smudge stick and a small hogan," he says. "We wait."

I can tell Chaco ain't sittin' well with this. He's walking around the top of the dome, chancing little bird-looks down and in.

"Don't mess around up there," I tell him. "Joey says wait."

Chaco ticks his head. "The smoke won't chase them out unless they can get out. That's the point of the smoke. The evil rides out on the smoke."

"Yeah, I know about—"

"I'm gonna get some speed going and knock the chimney free," he says, matter of fact. "But I'm probably gonna fall in."

He looks my way from up top, framed in the dying light like a statue on a castle. I was about to say hell no, but he ain't a fledgling anymore, far from it. And he can make his own decisions.

I pluck his feather from the brim of my hat, the one that helped bring my baby sister back from the dead, and I run my finger along it like a luck charm.

"Alright then," I say, trying to sound casual. "Hit it hard."

Chaco flares his wings, showing that streak of red I remember from the old days as he flaps his way straight up, six feet or more in the span of three wingbeats. He takes one last look at me, and I somehow manage a nod. I know he knows I'm scared shitless. When I was small, he seemed huge, a crow damn near half the size of a grown man, and I never worried about him like this. Then he burned, and I thought he was lost forever.

Now I'm big, and even though he is too, all I really can remember is how he came back to me small.

He hits the chimney with the sound of an axe to wood, but he still has to push, scrabble, and push more before he can drop down.

Joey has his hand on my shoulder. I hold Chaco's feather, spinning it slowly.

I can't see what he sees in there, but I can feel it. Trapped fear. Echoes of pain. I feel his shock as the Chindi rush at him. I know his thoughts. These spirits are not riled out of anger. They're riled out of desperation.

But to my mind, desperate things are more dangerous than angry things.

"Get out of there, Chaco," I say. "Get out. Now."

"They're trapped!" he chirps back.

"They're crazy! They'll drag you down like drownin' men. Get the hell out!"

Joey grips me harder, both of us watching the hogan.

I feel a flash of pain from Chaco, a cold moment where he makes a decision to strike. I feel his heart beating. Racing, now, he pumps his way up, aiming for something. I can almost see it, dirty black in the white. He homes in and drives upward. He pierces something and snatches it like a tattered black flag in his mouth, and with one, two, three bursts of his wings, he shoots out of the chimney like a mortar shell, and the smoke follows. A dirty white stream pours screaming into the night, and the coyotes howl after it.

Joey plucks his fingers from my shoulder. We all take a breather as Chaco flaps down and drops whatever was blocking the chimney at our feet. He shakes his beak, rubs it on the dirt, and squawks a few times like he's spittin' the evil clean. The smudge stick is burning well and true now, and it gives us just enough light to see what my bird brought.

It's a hand, picked clean to the bone. The fingers are all curled up except for the pointer, which hooks right at us. Joey blows the air clear and says a ward. He takes a road-worn bandanna from his back pocket and lays it on top.

The first big burst of smoke is gone. Now, the hogan seems to be breathin' normal. Already, it looks better, but I wait for Joey's lead.

He pulls a pollen pouch from his satchel. "Walk the circle with me," he says.

We take a slow lap around the hogan, Joey, me, then Chaco hopping his way along at the rear. Joey finds the horizon and lines himself up with the north side of the hogan, where he stops and turns to the pine boughs that make up the exposed wall. He takes a fistful of cornmeal from his pouch and tosses it high on the mud-thatch roof, singing quietly to himself as he watches it skitter down the sides. He thumbs a yellow smudge down the center of the top pine bough, then walks on, doin' the same at the west side and the south side.

At the east side, he takes a pinch of pollen and spreads it carefully along the cracked wooden mantel of the door. He nods at my hat, which I remove, before he sprinkles a fair amount over my head and on each shoulder. Chaco leans into a puff he tosses the bird's way.

"Now we go in," he says.

Joey ducks in first, no questions asked. I hold my breath and duck in next with Chaco at my feet. I expect to see signs of the fight, but the hogan is clear.

The smudge stick has settled to a low simmer that casts a soft glow on the curved walls. Mud's all piled at the edges like snowdrifts, and there's shit all over the floor: rocks, dried brush, caked leaves. Spiderwebs leap the cracks in the walls, wavering silently in the heat from the smoke. But sure as shit no ghosts—no traces of anything bigger than a bug. Not even a single animal track or drop of bird shit. Animals are smart enough to stay away from the dark side of the spirit world.

Odd thing, though: there is a penny.

A single penny, dead center.

Joey's pondering the cracks, running his fingers lightly down where we'll need to do some quick-n-dirty patch-work. I tap him on the shoulder and point at it.

"Find a penny, pick it up?" I ask.

Joey sees it and narrows his eyes. "Better to check with your bird," he says.

Chaco gives it a good, long look. He flares his wings once as he soft steps his way closer then walks a slow circle around it, switching from one side-eye to the other.

"I don't like it," Chaco says.

"Maybe it came in with the mud flow of the flood."

"Maybe," Chaco says, in a tone that says he believes no such thing. Before I can get another thought out, he snaps it in his beak quick as a mousetrap.

I hold my breath.

Nothing happens.

Chaco waddles to the east door with it in his beak.

"Where you goin'?" I ask.

"I'm putting it under the kerchief."

"Why?"

"Because I don't like it."

I scratch at my head, and pollen sifts down into my eye. I blink it carefully away. "You like it more or less than the skeleton hand cloggin' up the top?"

"Both are messages," Chaco says.

"Sayin' what?"

"Not sure. Nothing good."

I turn to Joey to translate. "Chaco's gonna put the penny with the hand. He thinks both are bad shit."

Joey grunts agreement and turns back to the walls, checking cracks, seeing where the mud is sagging away from the frame.

"You sweep out the floor," he says. "I'll patch the sides. High time we got this place in order again."

Joey and I work wordlessly, side by side, reclaiming the hogan that was lost. Chaco rebuilds the top of the chimney twig by twig, always with one eye to the dark horizon.

8

CAROLINE ADAMS

I'm a frozen doll on a shelf. Literally.

Once Black Bear got me into his creepy little shack, he plucked that hideous totem from my hand and froze me where I stood. Then he picked me up like a middle-aged mannequin and put me on a raised platform in the back, next to a kiva fire burning on a bed of ashes so thick the smoke looks like grease. And that's where I stand, unable to speak, unable to move. I can't even technically breathe although that clearly doesn't seem to matter much here.

The only consolation is that I feel like he froze me with a pretty serious resting bitch face for him to see every time he walks into the room. So I do have that going for me, but not much else.

The sun doesn't set here. Doesn't rise, either. I don't feel hungry or sleepy. And once the initial sleep-paralysis terror of being frozen screamed itself hoarse in my mind, I was just left with... me. My own thoughts. My line of sight.

So I think a lot. And I watch.

Black Bear is an odd duck. I mean, he's definitely a monster. Nobody kidnaps women—kidnaps whole tribes, for crying out loud—without being a monster. But he's an odd duck too. This is what happens when you're trapped in a monster's living room. You see his domestic life.

For one, he talks to himself a lot. I thought I did a lot of one-sided conversing with myself, but this guy takes it to the next level. Sometimes he rants. Sometimes he rambles. Whatever two parts of his brain are talking, they don't seem happy with each other.

Other times, he sits at this old, stained card table in front of me, and he stares at his greasy kiva fire for so long that I think his eyes are gonna crisp over.

The worst is when he just stares at me. After a while, I think he stops seeing me. But he doesn't stop looking at me.

I get the feeling this shack is bigger than it looks. Half the time, he's here, but half the time, he's gone. Off collecting.

This place is chock full of all sorts of junk. Some stuff looks super expensive, like a set of cups made out of gold, the metal all saggy because it's been beside the kiva fire for who knows how long. A rug woven with beads that glitter like diamonds in the firelight is heaped like a bath towel in one corner.

Other things look worthless but have spaces of honor. A ratty white feather hangs from twine right in the center of the room. A strip of dirt lies perfectly unmussed on a cheap plastic crate by the door. A woven hat band, cracked by salt and sun, hangs from an iron hook on the far wall next to where my crow totem is perched on two rusty nails. And these are just the ones I found today. The floor is barely walkable. Black Bear steps across piles of plastic trash, over buckets full of rocks and coins, and around mounds of musty clothes.

Sometimes, he'll take one or another of these things and hold them for a while and rub them on his face and over his lips. Sometimes, he'll lick his finger and put it in the dark dirt between the floorboards and then take what sticks and rub it over his teeth like a coke fiend. I've seen him take the ratty hanging feather and mouth it like a popsicle, which was gagworthy.

But it's the black stones that worry me most, the ones he fashions into his boons. He keeps them piled by the card table along with a little rock hammer and a coarse brush, all of it covered in black dust like pollen. When Black Bear gets close to me, I see the black dust on his face. It rings his nostrils. It hangs heavy on his eyelashes and darkens his cheeks. It gunks up his tear ducts.

Other rooms are here, other doors. When he leaves, I hear them open and close. The walls are thin enough that his voice carries. His tone is all over the place, from demanding to fond to distant. Sure, he's nuts, so that might be all in a day's work, but I swear I can sometimes hear other voices, small and soft, calm, placating, but in that practiced way I remember from nursing when I had to sit bedside with the real hot messes.

A million questions bounce around my head. Like if my child is alive. If Owen has her in his hands. If she's taking food. If she's crying. What it sounds like. What she smells like. If she has hair. I wonder about the color of her eyes. My mind starts to flush itself into a mental downward spiral until I shut it down by focusing on what's around me.

What I hear. What I see. What he's saying, but mostly who he's talking to.

Because maybe it means I'm not quite as alone as I think I am.

9

KAI BODREY

We carry Tsosi to the hogan on a slab of sheet metal from a busted camper that Joey cross ties with stripped pine for handles. It ain't much, but at least it's draped in deerskin so that he doesn't have to feel the cold.

We walk the trench the boys dug out, and a lot of people follow us. Maybe twenty, each with a little flashlight or lantern, all slow stepping toward the hogans in complete silence.

The night is one of those early fall nights when the air is full of waiting. Trees waiting to sleep. Earth waiting to cool. The animals waiting to go to ground. A darkness is out there just past the horizon that I can't quite name, but it feels good to walk as a line of light. Feels like a bit of a fuck you, which was what the Arroyo used to be all about. But nowadays, I feel like all we do is play defense.

Tsasa leads the way, with Maria at his elbow, so the goin' is slow. But that's okay by me. Hogan work is tough work, so if it takes a few more steps to get there, it's all good. I carry the black lacquered pot that Zahara left with us. Four white-hot embers are inside, but the outside is as cool as river water.

Up on his stretcher, Tsosi mumbles, but I can't make sense of it. Tsasa seems to understand a few words here and there, judging by the way he nods. Sometimes, he'll even look back at his brother until Maria has to steady him and keep him walking.

I look for crows. Aside from Chaco, who sits as still as a stone gargoyle by the glowing chimney top in the distance, I don't see them. And I don't know how I feel about that.

While we walk, Tsasa talks. "Of a time long, long ago, these things are said..." And just like always, whenever he starts like that, the night feels a little closer.

"When our people found this world, it was not a place fit to live. Everywhere we went, we tried to make a home. We settled. Planted. Hoped to harvest. And every time, we were driven away."

I hear grumbles of *Ahe'hee*, which basically means *preach it* because nobody walking this line is quite sure what era of our people Tsasa is talkin' about yet, but the fact that statement stands true regardless is a bit of a point in and of itself.

"Monsters have always chased us," Tsasa says, softly. He pauses and looks back at his brother, and I can see in his eyes the strength he gets from all of us coming up behind.

"C'mon, Grandfather," Maria says. "Let's get out of the night."

Tsasa looks from our line of light to the deep night beyond. The darkness looks so empty that it's like the night sky forgot to load. He nods to Maria. "Quickly," he adds.

Joey is still putting some finishing touches on the walls as we arrive, his body glistening in the still night. I can't think of a time since Knifepoint that he's been around so much. I know it pains him not to have the use of his crow —it's tucked away in his totem pouch, hanging from a braided strip of horsehair around his neck—but it's nice to know he's gonna be here. He bumps my fist in welcome, and I duck down and in. The hogan is clean swept and sage blasted. Grant is carefully digging out the fire pit, placing dirt in a bucket at his side.

He sees me and gives a tired smile. "How's it look?"

I crawl over and touch my forehead to his in response. He smells like clean sweat and campfire smoke.

Hos and the other stretcher bearers carefully set Tsosi down outside, and together they gently push, and we gently pull, and his makeshift gurney slides inside. When he's settled, Grant pulls at the bell around his neck like it's burning him. He swallows hard.

I want to tell him to take it off. I want to say, *Hold it in your pocket or your hand or anywhere else.* But that's not how the bell works. You put it on, and you don't take it off. So instead, I tell him to take some air while I get the fire up.

He nods, grateful, and ducks his way out, quickly, almost like he's gonna be sick. He won't say it, 'cause Grant's about as forthcoming about being in pain as a block of wood, but I know he's hurting bad.

I sit Indian style and set the lacquered pot in the spot between my knees. It's just Tsosi, Hos, and me in here. The others ring the hogan, waiting. Talking in low murmurs. Hos watches Tsosi with a lost look that tells me he's trying to prepare for the old man dying in here.

"Hey," I say, snapping him out of it so that he blinks and finds me. "Gimmie the trowel," I say.

He passes it over. I take one coal from the pot and put it deep in the tinder. It kicks up a little fire instantly. Whatever Joey and Grant and Chaco did in here worked.

Hos adds snapped branches, and I add the rest of the coals. We do it without talking. Bodreys have fucked up a lot, but there are a few things we do pretty good. One is booze running, and the other is building fires. When you live on the back side of nowhere and your life depends on fire, you understand it on a different level.

I keep glancing out where Grant went. That pull at his neck when Tsosi came in wasn't good. It was heavier than his usual pulls.

"Just go check on him," Hos says, not unkindly.

I glance at my brother, and he's got a little smile on him, which is crazy because before he came back from the other side, seeing Hos smile was basically a never-in-a-lifetime experience.

He shrugs. "Like I said, for a *bilagáana*, he's aight."

"Hosteen Bodrey, I never thought I'd live to see the day—"

"Alright, alright. Just making sure, though, you are *not* kissing him, right? Because if you're *kissing* him, that's a whole other deal—"

I roll my eyes and duck out while he's midsentence.

Joey is talking to Tsasa outside the entrance. Maria is at his side, one arm locked in his, taking no chances. He speaks in low Navajo and points at a lumpy handkerchief on the ground. I find Grant and grab his hand, and he leans into me harder than usual.

"The bones and the penny," Joey's saying. "That's all

we could find, Grandfather. Could be they were washed up here in the flood. Or dropped by the birds."

Tsasa leans against Maria and sighs in thought. "No matter how they were brought here, by water, by bird, or by spirit, they are evil omens calling out to the Anaye. The sage burn broke them, but the Anaye will return. They chase us still. As it was in the long ago, so it is again."

He sags against Maria and looks toward the hogan, where his brother lies in the glow of the fire. His hands tremble.

The Anaye are the monsters of legend, real bad bitches that chased us from world to world. The Slayer Twins had to face them down one by one so that we could carve out a home that wouldn't keep getting destroyed, so that we could make families that wouldn't get slaughtered.

That's the story, anyway. And I used to think these stories were just that—stories. Then the Gambler walked across that water toward me. Now, nothing's off the table. And the look on Tsasa's face says he and his brother can't protect us all like they used to. He's afraid. And frustrated. A powerful man grown old.

A strip of wind passes by us on its way out into the dark desert. Back when we would do booze handoffs at night, truck to truck, out in the naked desert, we'd some-times get a strip of wind like that. Just one gust. And I always wondered where the hell it came from and where it was off to all alone.

There are things going on in the Dinetah—the Navajo country—that we got no idea of. Some stretches of our land ain't seen humans in a long time, not whites and not Diné either. People say the last true wild part of the world is the oceans, but my guess is they ain't ever been on the Rez.

Tsasa asks for Maria's help into the hogan, his eyes on his brother.

"Night is coming to the Arroyo," he says. "It is time to prepare."

Joey leans down close so he can hear. "The sacred herbs are here, Grandfather. Fetishes too. With your voice, we can heal him."

Tsasa shakes his head. "Grandson, my brother and I have met enough of the holy people to know that this is not a time to pray for healing."

He turns to Maria. "You know my prayer sticks? The ones in the back of the camper?"

She nods, her eyes shimmering in the moonlight.

"And the shell. The big one. Not the little one. You know the big one?"

"I know the big one, grandfather," she says.

"And the bundle of crow feathers. And the pollen. The old bag of pollen. Not the new bag, the old bag. The one way in the back."

"I know the old bag of pollen, grandfather," she says.

He squeezes her arm and rests his head on her shoulder for a second, and I get one of those quick flashes of how old he really is. He looks like a child there in her arms.

She clicks her tongue to Joey, who comes over and takes him while she starts walking the trench back to the double-wide, and I have a strange, heavy feeling that the twins might never get back there again, that this walk we took was a dead man's walk for them. I try to shove the thought out of my mind, but it's hard in the going.

Tsasa hardly has to duck to get inside. Joey guides him to the center of the hogan, where a place has been made for him next to the head of his brother.

Tsosi's eyes are closed, and his face looks skeletal in the shadows cast by the fire, but he's breathing, and it's steady. That's about as much as anyone can hope for.

Tsasa sits and, with a soft nod, takes the blanket Hos drapes over his shoulders. He places his hand in his brother's hand, and Tsosi squeezes back.

"Our people are at war again," he says. "Night is coming to the Arroyo. True night. And when true night falls, we sweat to prepare warriors."

I sit here, in this hogan, feeling the gathering heat, and I'm tired. I look around and see the same weight in every eye. Hard to see where the hell these warriors are supposed to be.

Joey watches Tsosi with concern that borders on sickness. He touches Tsasa's shoulder. "Grandfather, if we don't do a big heal for him... we may not get another chance."

"Night is falling on our home," Tsasa says, matter of fact. "If we do not send out our warriors to meet it, there will be nothing left to heal."

Tsasa chooses another log from the stack at his side, and Joey helps him settle it on the fire. He smooths the dirt around his brother's head with careful sweeps of his knobby hand and positions the fetishes and bowls and other objects of power he called for. No shaking this time —he's going to work.

It takes me a lot longer than it should to realize that these warriors he's talking about aren't people he hopes to summon up in the swirling white smoke of the sweat. They ain't gonna spring up out of the ground at the clacking of his sticks or come riding down the horizon on pale horses as visions once the heat and the smoke take hold.

They're us. *We're* the warriors everyone's waiting for. Me, Grant, Joey, Hos, and Chaco. Five of us against whatever Anaye are comin' our way.

Grant and Joey look how I feel: lost, tired, half buried in mud. Every step we take feels like it cakes more of it to our feet until even just walking forward means pushing through the weight.

Tsasa wraps his forehead with a strip of simple cloth to wick away the sweat and begins humming. He's drawing with a single finger in the fine top sand, figures and symbols I can't see anymore though the smoke. His design moves sunwise, east to west, around back to east again. He hums a low tune I feel like I know even though I can't quite make it out. Quiet for now. But I get the sense he's just warming up.

10

THE WALKER

The calls of frayed souls seem to come in big batches. I'll have a quiet span of time, then everybody dies at once, all over the place. At first, I thought these waves were just chaos, but the longer I've been at this job, the more I see patterns.

Patterns are everywhere. Some are easy to see, like how the nutjobs who torture animals around an altar can be the same nutjobs that bar doors and burn houses. Some are harder, like how all of this is tied to Black Bear. Or Caroline.

I try not to read too closely into these patterns because I'm not exactly the most mentally stable of creatures, and I feel like madness lies there. But sometimes I catch myself looking anyway—staring hard at the lights of the soul map, the great rope I walk on, which looks a bit like Vegas at night, on steroids, from up high—staring so hard that the lights start to waver.

And that's when I have to remind myself that I just work here. This map isn't mine. Forces govern it that would easily break my mind.

So I'll just stick to sweeping up the threads and whatever sanity I have left. I've seen what happens when you stare too hard at the patterns. When you try to force yourself to figure them out. To fight against them. His name is Black Bear.

Just when I think this bad batch has passed and I might get a chance to comb the rope for signs of Caroline again, I get a tug that takes me right back to the Rez.

The soul map swirls open to Main Street, and it's a bloodbath.

Main runs from the cultural center roughly up to Wapati casino, but this stretch looks like a bomb went off. Someone ran a truck headfirst through the front window of Manuelito's—my favorite fucking enchilada place—and I don't exactly need to pull plates on the thing to know it's the same house-paint-red piece-of-shit truck that wrecked lives out by the welcome sign. The same truck that cut a trench in the dirt pulling out of Baba's with hell in the rearview.

And here it is again, windshield shattered, hazards blinking. It's hung up on the concrete wall it blew through, dripping fluids down the busted sidewalk.

The cops aren't here yet, so the wreck is fresh. A crowd pools at the edges of all the glass, but what they see inside must not look too good because that's as far as anyone goes.

I step over a stream of water from a popped fire hydrant, and I realize I'm not gonna have to spin the tape back on this one. This time, the boys are still here.

I high step my way through the shattered window and steel myself.

Bodies are stuck to the yellowed diner tables with rusty knives. Four of them, pinned at the hands and spitted through the neck. Blood is nickel thick on the tables already.

Splayed hands. Speared heads. Same MO as with the animals. But weirdly enough, the worst part for me is the missing front teeth.

I call out to the souls, "Whatever they did to you, the pain is over now. You're with me, and I'm here to take you home."

The quiet is awful. Blood streams syrup-thick off the table in one long, soft hiss. A body can hold a lot of blood. It'll mark that spot forever, even after it's all cleaned up in the living world.

"C'mon now," I prod again. "Your time here is over."

I hear a shudder from behind the bar, where in my day, the lifer waitress Jo would sling hot Mexican food, cold pie and coffee. But Jo is long gone, and it looks like whoever has her shift now booked it out of the back along with everyone else who could run.

The shudder sounds like someone trying to breathe when they don't have to anymore. I step my way through the blood and the glass and around the counter, and I find all four souls huddled in a corner by the sink. They hold each other, young and old. New friends in death.

"Hey," I say. "It's okay. It's over. Whatever happened is over."

The girl whose head is pinned to the table twenty feet behind me is the first to get it. Her eyes go wide on me, but then they flit to the far end of the dining room.

She shakes her head. *No,* she's saying. *No, it is not over.*

I hear a popcorn crunch. She winces and tries to push herself deeper into the corner. All four of them squirm against each other to get away from the sound.

Another crunch.

The boys are at the far end of the bar, waiting for me.

One of them is huge, bigger than Danny Ninepoint. He's the one making the crunch sound, and the crunch sound is the teeth. He runs another over his blood-black lips and pops it into his mouth. I don't even wince at the crunch this time because that's what he wants, and I'm not gonna give it to him.

The other is smaller, but he's on point like a hunting dog. A huge dollop of black blood drips in an even line across his eyes. Shaved heads, black T-shirts, tattoos up and down to the point they all blend. They can't see me. But they sense I'm here.

The one eating teeth pauses and takes a cigarette from behind his ear. He lights it with an entire matchbook that he leaves burning on the counter. After a big, bloody drag, he sets it still burning next to a spare tooth.

"Santa Muerte!" he calls. "This is for you!"

"If only I had eyes to see her," says the short one, blinking through blood that clots his lashes.

"Get fucked," I say. But apparently, they don't have ears to hear either.

"She's here, somewhere," says the big boy.

She? "Listen, assholes. My sister hasn't punched the clock in this gig for years. And fuck you for even uttering—

"Santa Muerte, you come for blood, and we offer blood."

A lot more cussing dies on my lips. *Santa Muerte.* I've run into their kind before. It's a cartel death cult, and they snuff out a lot more than their fair share of lives. Cartels do run through the Rez, but the death cults usually stick close to Juarez.

Another crunch. And another. The big boy thinks

about eating the tooth he just offered to me, but he pulls his hand back. "I am hungry still," he says in raspy Spanish.

The short one has his elbows on the table now, rubbing blood deeper into his eyes with the palms of his hands. "Then eat," he says.

The big one looks over at the bodies, grunts, and gets up. "Which was the youngest?"

"None were young." He sniffs towards the carnage." That male was youngest."

The big one lumbers over to the booth and sits down next to the body of a guy that looks maybe twenty. I'd still call him a kid.

"You're sure Santa Muerte is here?" he asks.

Blood Eyes pushes himself off his stool and joins him at the booth. He pulls a black bear totem from his back pocket and uses it to wick together a little pool of blood that he gobs on his fingers and jams into his eyes. "*Something* is here," he says. "I'm... so... close to seeing."

A soul stirs from behind the counter. "Don't look him in the eye," says an old man huddled with the others. "That's how he got me."

Patterns. Black bear totems. It's all connected. I hear another crunch from the big boy across the table. And this time, he ain't eating teeth.

"So hungry," he says, chewing, his face to the table like a dog, a dead guy's finger in his mouth.

And something about these two hits a chord way back. When you deal with death, you see monstrous things, but believe it or not, you rarely see *actual* monsters. These two are different. And they're here, on my Rez. Blood on the eyes. Blood on the mouth. One an eater of men, the other one you can't look in the eye.

"I know you," I say.

The big boy scents me. That's his thing. He can sniff my people out but can't really see for shit. His partner is the eyes. And to look at them means death.

"You're Anaye. The terror of our people in the time before." I shake my head, trying to add it up. "But you were destroyed by the Slayer Twins."

The big one slurps a forefinger. Blood Eyes feeds his sight with another palmful of blood cooled to jelly. Neither of these assholes can hear me. From somewhere outside this nightmare, I hear cop sirens, and the relief they bring washes over me like water. Please let it be the chief. Please let Sani Yokana come in here, guns blazing. Please put these things in the dirt.

But the Anaye don't seem concerned. The Eater has moved to the thumb. Blood Eyes is wandering the room with a cigarette out like a dowsing rod, looking for me. He's pretty close, too.

"An offering, Santa Muerte," Blood Eyes says. "A smoke, from Black Bear."

The Eater wipes his mouth with his own boon. "Santa Muerte *is* here," he says, picking his teeth. "The more I eat, the closer I get."

"My eyes are almost opened," Blood Eyes says.

"But I need more," says the Eater, rubbing his stomach and leaving it streaked with bits of skin. "Only, I need younger."

The four dead under the counter hold fast to each other, scrabbling their feet on dirty linoleum kitchen tiles they can't really feel. Their need to leave is so strong that I can feel the pressure behind my eyes. I look around for the veil. This scene is a complete clusterfuck, but I got a duty to the souls first. I kneel down and reach out a hand to them, but they're like caged cats.

"I know the young one you need," Blood Eyes says. "And I know where she is. I need her too. Her blood will make me see."

That gets me standing again.

"Hold on a sec. Who the fuck are you talking about?" I ask, getting really close to the thing. Its cigarette dowsing rod closes in on me, but I don't even care. "You are *not* eating that little girl, you shithead."

His cigarette twitches, and he sniffs.

He sniffs, and he smiles.

"Santa Muerte is here, alright," he says. "We cannot see you yet, but we will, and when we do, we will fall down on our knees."

The Eater snaps the hand off the kid and tucks it into a back pocket of his bloody jeans. Tendons hang down to his ass. "Adios, Santa Muerte," he says, working at his huge teeth with a tongue like a garden hose.

Blood Eyes pulls fistfuls of dirty pennies from his pockets at the door and scatters them behind him. "For their eyes and the eyes of those to come," he says, his voice more breath than words.

And just like that, they're gone. I go after them at first, but the pull won't let me.

The dead. Shit. My one job.

I walk back around to them.

"They're gone?" asks the boy, the one whose hand is now in the Eater's back pocket.

"Yeah, they're gone."

He starts to stand, but I sit him back down again. Nothing good is gonna come from looking over that counter.

"How about all of us just sit here for another minute, okay?"

When the veil finally comes, it squares up to me like I'm the one late. I think it's looking for me to talk to it, but I have no words. Thankfully, I don't have to convince these four to get the fuck outta Dodge. They jump into the veil like it's a waterslide, and I would too if I went through what they went through. In my favorite fucking enchilada place, too.

The second the veil pops out of the picture, I'm out the door. I swipe right to open the soul map and step through.

Owen has to know what's coming for his little girl.

11

OWEN BENNETT

I'm dead asleep when she wakes me this time. My body has that sunken feeling like it hasn't moved since I closed my eyes. My left arm is in an awkward position over my face, and it's half asleep to the point that it startles me. It feels like it's someone else's.

I sit up and flutter it back to life and listen for her. Just when I think her voice was likely another dream, I hear her again. She's not crying at all—she's talking. Babbling, really. Long strings of unintelligible words. I flatter myself that I hear *Dada* in there somewhere.

Then I actually do hear *Mama* in there, which chills me.

She's moved on, but the end of that last baby soliloquy was definitely *Mama.*

I've never heard her talk like this before, rolling sound after sound off her clumsy little tongue. It's not happy babble. It's more urgent than anything.

I walk to my door and find her standing in her crib, leaning against the bar, waiting for me.

She sees me instantly, and the babble picks up a pitch.

"Mamamama." She squeezes the bars with her chubby fingers. "Mamamama."

"What is it?" I ask because she can't possibly be saying *Mama*. Everything I've read says babies don't actually speak with intention until about a year. They don't even really have the ability to command sound until ten months or so. This is nothing but an exercise in understanding her own mouth. It can't possibly be anything else.

I hear the telltale crushed-gravel rattle of a car on approach. A quick check of the clock puts us at three in the morning. Grant is still burning the candle at both ends on my account.

Headlights swing across the window as he makes the turnoff, but they don't shine like Grant's headlights. Grant has crystal-clear LEDs, bright enough to spot a coyote at a hundred yards. These are dirty yellow.

The baby stops speaking midbabble and turns toward the window. She plops down on her rear and scoots back, away, up to the headboard.

There's that chill again. I'd call it a blast of AC if we had it.

I walk carefully to the window and peer out through the slats as the car slows, not Grant's truck at all. Far from it, this thing looks like it got hotwired off the side of a road. The rust streaks suck in moonlight like mold.

Her babble starts up again, but quiet. "Mamama... nonono..."

I turn back around and find her standing against the far wall of the crib, holding a long black feather that glints a touch red in the moonlight. Chaco's feather.

"How'd you get that?"

"Nononono—"

Outside, a car door opens like a rusty gate then slams shut with a hollow rattle. That's when I realize I have to get us out of here immediately.

Fire drill. Caroline had us prep for this.

I fell asleep in yesterday's clothes, so at least I'm already dressed. I grab my crow totem on principle even though it's basically bricked. Wallet. Keys to Caroline's truck where the car seat is.

The doorknob clicks softly. *Please tell me I locked it. Please tell me I locked it.*

I locked it.

The knob rattles violently, and something very big leans against the door. The hinges squeak.

"Time to go," I whisper, picking her up with her blanket and feather and all and bundling everything under one arm while I grab the emergency stroller bag on the way out the back.

"I need you to be quiet, okay?" I whisper to her, but one glance tells me she knows this. She knows it with an intensity that scares the hell out of me. She buries her face against my shoulder, her gummy mouth open, the feather tucked tight in her fat fist.

I shut the back door as softly as I can. It's as dark as a pit out here. Clouds have eaten the moon, but I think that's in our favor. My daughter picks her head up to watch behind me as I creep like some weird baby thief, arms full of various baby spoils, stealing off into the desert. She coos, and it's loud enough that I press my hand over her mouth and drop into a terribly painful crouch ten feet from Caroline's truck.

I glance back. The house is lit up like a lantern, so I see him clearly. I'm six foot three, and he is every bit of that and at least a foot more. He's wide, too. He fills out a tarp-sized black T-shirt easily. Streaks of inky black mottle the scruff of his chin and cheeks and run up and over his bald head. It's either motor oil or blood. And I don't believe it's motor oil.

I know I should run in absolute blind terror, but I can't stop watching him, especially as he walks his way to her crib. It's horribly invasive, having this thing in my home, where I putter about in my robe and eat standing up over the sink. My daughter is supposed to be asleep on the thin slab of mattress he's picking up now.

And smelling.

And licking.

His tongue leaves blood streaks where she laid her head, new red blood.

A bit of stomach acid eases its way up my throat as I turn around and find the bumper of the truck with my free hand, easing my way to the back right, where her car seat is. I gently ease open the door and slide her in, refusing to look back in case I get struck stupid again by the horrendous nature of the thing smelling and licking its way around where we live.

The clicks of her harness sound like rifle shots to my ears. There are so many. Never have I begrudged the three-point harness like I do now. One buckle for the chest, two at her sopping diaper. *Did I bring more diapers?* Maybe they're in the fire drill bag. Maybe not. No going back now, either way. Time to fill the world with your urine, young child. Walking back into that house for diapers would mean Daddy's death. And then yours.

I slide along the car to the driver's side and almost need a diaper of my own when I hear a light clicking on the roof of the truck: a crow, walking. Not Chaco, either. Chaco is throwing all his ethereal weight behind holding the Arroyo together. This is just a regular old carrion-eating crow.

I hear a large thump from the A-frame. I believe he's lifting up our bed—my bed, the bed Caroline and I shared —as if he might find me hiding under it.

I slip behind the wheel and fire up the truck before I can think of how shatteringly loud it will be. And it is loud. Grant souped it up.

But the roar from the thing inside is louder.

I throw the truck into drive as he shoulders through the back door like it's a shower curtain. Dust kicks into the back floodlight as he lopes after the truck, skidding to a stop where we were parked moments after I'm out and down the dirt road. He roars again, and it sounds primeval.

I gun it down the driveway and hit the main road, working on instinct and memory, missing the big rock here, pinning the brakes at the hard left before the washout there.

And just like that, we're away. For now.

A mile out, I finally look back at her. She's droopy, almost asleep. But she holds that feather tightly.

Caroline would know what to do. We've all dealt with monsters before, of one kind or another, but she's the only one that seems to have taken any points of improvement from all those encounters. When I think back on those battles, the things we endured feel like they happened to another man. She was the one who came out stronger. I came out older. But somehow, here I am, and here she isn't.

Be kind to yourself.

It's her voice in my head. I often pretend she's speaking to me. Sometimes, I even manage to halfway convince myself her voice is real. I'll be the first to admit that the past seven months have had a decidedly dissociative effect on me.

"No time for kind," I fire back. "Not if we want to live. That thing was licking our child's bed. I have one job. Keep her alive. And I'm barely doing that."

There will always be monsters, she tells me. *You are not one of them.*

The girl drifts to sleep as I watch, her face catching the dim green light of the dash. I try my hardest to see her for who she is: my child, a girl born of myself and Caroline, a member of my family. But all I feel is the rattle of the dirt under our tires. I'm tearing down dark desert roads with a child in tow that I cannot seem to connect with, cannot understand, can't even properly name.

Don't be your own worst enemy.

I clear my throat to quiet her voice. It would be best now to just talk to myself for a bit. I don't want Caroline to see me like this, even the Caroline that is almost certainly nothing but a figment of my imagination.

I spray down the windshield to wipe it of the desert grit and turn on the high beams. Real high beams. Grant Romer high beams.

The only place I can think of to go is the Arroyo. So that's where we're going.

12

GRANT ROMER

I blink away unsettling dreams. Most of them these days are of this bell choking me one way or another. Hanging. Pulling. Dragging. My brain keeps comin' up with ways.

I'm on a blanket in the mud trenches outside the hogan. The night is still and deep. The moon hides behind clouds. The only light is the glow of the fire within. I rub my eyes and feel the grit of dried sweat. Kai lies next to me, still asleep. We took a break from the sweat, but I can hear Tsasa still singing softly. He hasn't stopped for hours.

I clear my throat of desert dust. It's been a while since I slept on the full-blown earth. Can't say I recommend it. I look up at Chaco on top of the hogan, still as a weathervane.

"How we doin'?" I ask my bird.

Chaco stretches his wings. "Quiet before the storm."

Yeah, I feel that. So does the bell.

A voice comes from the hogan, weak and wavering, but I know in an instant it's Tsosi. I crawl inside, hoping to see him recovered, the two of them swapping out lines tellin' stories like in the old days. And for a second, I can see it in my head, the way it was.

Tsosi is still lying down, wasting thin. But even as his body seems to be disappearing around him, his voice still remains. Eyes closed, he tells of the story of the monsters that came. And all the while, Tsasa nods and paints symbols in the dirt around himself. The heat in the hogan is deep and dry, and when the night breeze dies down, the smoke can make it hard to breathe, but Tsasa doesn't seem to care. Every time his hands get sweaty, he grabs ash from the edges of the fire like a gymnast with chalk. His fingers are black, and his cheeks and nose where he wipes the sweat are the same. One hand draws in the dirt. The other clasps his brother's hand as Tsosi speaks.

"The Anaye have found us again," he says, barely fluttering the words out. "The monsters of old. The ones that chase our people from world to world."

Tsasa nods and retraces the delicate grooves in the sand around his brother's head. I try to catch Joey's eye, but he's downcast, lookin' grim. I don't think he's slept since he first floated the idea of a sweat. He holds the pouch that carries his totem like a kid cradling a broken toy.

Tsosi licks his lips, and Maria puts a cold sponge there and expertly dribbles a stream of water for him to drink. "We must name them, Tsasa."

Tsasa sucks at his teeth. "Names give power."

"True. If we were seeking to avoid their summoning. But they are here. Black Bear has conjured them with boons we thought long dead. Nothing can stop that now."

Tsasa traces a rainbow over his brother's shoulder, and the soft rustling his finger makes reminds me of a field mouse nesting. His hand trembles, and he pauses then takes a deep breath and wipes away sweat with ash. "Then name them, brother."

"Of the Anaye, there were many. But two brought us great pain."

Tsasa starts to hum softly, lifting his brother's voice to strength I know he wouldn't find on his own. He finishes the rainbow and moves back to the lightning.

"Binaye Ahani. He whose eyes mean death." Tsasa frowns at the name. Tsosi rumbles on, low. "And Yé'iitsoh. The big giant. Eater of our young."

Tsasa throws more herbs on the coals and pulls in fists of smoke to clear the air. The elder twins seem to have more than a passing history with these things, and it hits me again that they're a hell of a lot older than even I think.

"All Anaye eat, but these two eat and eat. Binaye Ahani with his eyes, Yé'iitsoh with his nose and mouth—"

Chaco flaps his wings a handful of times up top, and the sound stills all of us. He glances over the rim of the chimney and takes in the whole of the place, all the pieces of the story, in an instant before backing clear of the smoke.

"It's the Walker," Chaco says, "He's here, and he ain't happy."

13

THE WALKER

I see Chaco before Chaco sees me. That's what happens when you drop out of a soul map. I crash the party everywhere I go. And I come in hot, speaking to Chaco before I even set my feet on the dried mud.

"Where's Owen?"

"Nice to see you too," Chaco calls down. "We're doing just fine here, thanks. I mean aside from all the mud and the impending loss of about a thousand years of oral history if Tsosi kicks the bucket. Please tell me you're not here for him."

I check the soul map for Tsosi's thread. It ain't lookin' too good, but it's still here. I set the thought aside. One horror at a time.

"No, not yet," I say, before I realize how that must come out. "I followed Owen's string. He's supposed to be here. Or near here." Walking the rope isn't an exact science. I still throw some wide darts every now and then.

Grant steps out and looks up at the bird. "Ben's here? Where?"

Chaco nods my direction, but Grant was already basically facing me. I think enough time with the bell does that.

"They're talkin' Anaye stories in the hogan. I think it's important."

"They ain't stories no more. The Anaye have been crushing souls for miles. And now, your dad's caught up in it."

It's been far too long since I took a good look at Grant Romer. He and Chaco both look like they've been through the ringer. The bell used to sit on his chest, but now it burrows like a lime tick. Grant is a strong man, but the world of the dead eats strong men same as the weak. And he's held the key to that world for way too long.

I share a look with Chaco that's not good. The bird knows too. And usually, he's a mouthy bastard, but this is a kind of worry even he can't put words to. He's trying to figure out how much of what I just said—what he sees in my look—is what he should translate. Because he knows my fears better than anyone.

The bell is killing Grant.

"How did we let it get this bad?" I ask Chaco.

"One thing at a time, Walker. We find Owen first."

Right. Owen. I look back at the swinging gates as though he might be rolling up, but he's sure as shit not. "Something happened," I say. "He was coming here."

I look toward the hogan and find the soul string of the twins. Tsosi is talking about the old monsters, the big baddies that the Slayer Twins picked off one by one. Tsasa is absently painting a masterpiece in dirt that speaks a lot more to *war* than to *healing,* so I know the twins likely already know what I know.

I look up at Chaco. "There are two of them. One ate blood with his eyes."

Chaco clicks his throat. "Binaye Ahani."

I nod. "And the other..." I remember the way the big man ate the fingers of that dead boy in the booth like they were chicken wings, the disgusting intimacy of it. "The other is something else. Something worse."

Inside the hogan, Tsosi coughs hard. Chaco ducks his head at the sound. That kind of cough is rough to hear. It's the sound of a man working his last breaths out.

I kneel down at the east door, not wanting to get too close, not wanting to give the wrong idea. This isn't a work call yet.

Tsasa holds his brother's hand and pats his cracked lips with water. Tsosi's eyes flick to the door even under their lids, in that way the sunset folks get a sixth sense, but he doesn't break his story. He mumbles around the sponge. These two take death in stride—always have.

"The Big Giant rained misery upon us all," Tsosi says, his voice laced with disgust and thick with phlegm.

Tsasa picks up while his brother tries to slow his breathing enough to clear his lungs.

"He wasn't just an eater of men," Tsasa says. "He wanted *children*. He wanted to kill the *future* of our people."

I look at Chaco hard because I really want to make this stick. The bird seems as pulled apart these days as I am. "Chaco. Look at me. They are here. Blood Eyes and the Eater both." I gesture out at the Arroyo. "They want all of this. But they want the child most. Black Bear sent them for the girl."

Chaco shakes his head in a whir and stands. He tests

the night air as if to taste the truth of what I say. But he knows I'm right.

"These Anaye want to eat her and pour as much blood as they can out on this land in some sick sacrifice to worship me. I don't know how Black Bear got to them, if he brainwashed them or created them, or what. All I know is he's a greedy bastard, and he won't stop until he proves his point."

Chaco stills and looks into the darkness. "And what point is that?"

"That he can grab you by the throat no matter where you are," I say.

Grant walks through me on his way to look Chaco in the eye up top of the hogan. "These things eat children?" he asks. He caught half the conversation, but it's the most important part. "Naw," Grant says, shivering. "You can't mean—"

"They're here for your sister, Grant," Chaco says. "To finish the job for Black Bear. And they almost got her, but Owen got both of them out. He's coming this way."

Grant shuffles through his stuff beside the hogan, looking for his cell phone. He finds it and holds it up, useless as always out here. He tosses it back onto the pile and puts on his shirt. "I gotta find 'em. Meet 'em halfway."

"I'll go," Chaco says, pinning his head back like a notched arrowhead. "I'm faster."

"No," I say quickly. "I'll go. Tell Grant I'll find him."

Chaco points his beak at me. "You? What are *you* gonna do? You can't even talk to him."

"This fight is bleeding more and more into my world. Those freaks are killing people in my name. I'll find him and get the point across. Plus, I'm faster than either of you. I spin time, bird."

Chaco concedes the point and relays it to Grant, who nods but keeps dressing.

"Fine, but I'm still coming," Grant says.

"The Arroyo needs you here, Grant," I say, looking to Chaco to translate, and when he does, Grant's face darkens.

"You mean the Arroyo needs the bell here," he says.

I don't want to come right out and say it, but yeah. We gotta control the controllables here. Chief Yokana always said that. The bell is an X factor, and we need it here behind whatever protection we have left.

Grant looks back at the glowing hogan, and for a second, we all listen like kids at the stairs, hoping to hear the comfort of voices below. Tsosi has gone quiet, but Tsasa still hums, which is something.

"The bell ain't safe here, neither," Grant says. "It ain't safe nowhere."

Chaco fluffs his wings and pins them back again. "It's a lot safer here than you running *toward* these maniacs."

Grant drops his shirt back to the dirt. He has the peculiar pain of being caught between two families, both of them in deep shit, and him just being one man. I can see the pain in his eyes, how he would rip himself in two if he could. But he's always been a practical kid, and he knows where he needs to be.

Tsasa's song rises softly. The Smoker comes back from his foraging, his face grim as he ducks inside with a new bundle of sage, milk jugs full of cold water and tea, and a few fetishes of his own. He pauses when he sees Grant and Chaco and susses out that I'm nearby too. He follows Chaco's line of sight and manages to nod my direction. He keeps thinking I'm coming for him on account of his throat, and his throat ain't in great shape, but it's not his time yet. He has things to do here still.

All these folks do.

I can feel strength building here, like a signal fire blazing out into the night. The question is whether it'll be enough when the darkness arrives.

"Take care of them, bird," I say. "And yourself."

Chaco stretches to his full height. He's big now, the size he was when I first saw him staring at me outside Sancho's. We've come around again. He looks west, where night takes the day. That's where these things will come from. It has often been that way with our people.

I swirl open the soul map and look for a particular shade of blue, the bright soul thread of a good man trying to save what's left of his family. He's here somewhere, close, but he's on the move.

I step through and leave the Arroyo behind.

14

CAROLINE ADAMS

I'm sitting down at the crusty yellow card table by the kiva fire, and I'm telling Black Bear the story he wants. Again.

This is what he does. He comes into my room—and yeah, I know it's really disgusting that I'm starting to think of this smoke-stained crack den as my room—and he walks around, mumbling to himself, holding this and that, smelling here and there, until he comes up to my spot on the shelf and jams that awful totem in my hand, and I can move again. Then he points me toward the ratty table and says, "Tell me again."

So I roll my neck, take in a deep breath of whatever passes for air here, and go to the table.

"You want the same—"

"The same," he says, low, cutting me off, then holds up a finger. "But different." He looks up at me with bright brown eyes like I might challenge him again. Like he kinda wants me to. But the last time I did that, he took the totem away from me for a long time, longer than normal, long enough that I forgot how to breathe for a while before he finally jammed it back into my hand.

He places his long, thin fingers flat on the yellowed card table and stares into the fire. "Go," he says.

I clear my throat.

"Well," I say, "It usually goes like this—"

"Usually?" he asks, his fingers inching toward the oily totem in my hands.

He likes to ask a lot of questions.

"Usually, yeah. I mean, you get into a routine."

This settles him, and he sits back. His hands inch away from my lifeline. "Tell me."

"I worked—I *work* at a clinic. A health clinic. It's mostly like a big doctor's office crossed with a small, really old, kinda busted hospital."

He narrows his eyes, and I can tell he's trying to put it all together. "You... work? A job?"

I cross my arms and lean back. "Yes, a job. Is that hard to believe or something?"

He looks above my head, lost in his own thoughts. When he gets like this, I just let him reboot. Eventually, he nods. "And he... *Owen*... works there too."

I hate the way Owen's name sounds coming out of this guy's mouth. I never should have told him Owen's name, but it sort of slipped out on the first telling of what to me is nothing more than an average Tuesday doing house and family stuff but seems weirdly sexual to Black Bear.

"Yes," I say, trying to move on.

"And that is how you met. That is how you came to love each other."

Another creeper question. His eyes are brown like sap bleeding from a rotting tree, his smoke the color of coffee-stained teeth, and it simmers on him. I've come to understand that when it gets close to boiling, that means the madness is taking over. Heck, for all I know, the smoke *is* the madness. Maybe that's what happens when you die but don't leave. The smoke that's supposed to leave you—call it your soul, call it your aura or whatever, the smoke that *is* your life—maybe it starts turning, like milk. And this guy is all curdled.

"Yeah, you could say that," I reply, watching him warily but trying not to look like I'm watching him warily.

"And after your day of work, you come home together?" he asks.

"If the schedule works out and one or the other of us isn't on night shift."

He brushes the air of that. Evidently the concept of *night shift* at a health clinic is too much for him. "And what do you do at home together."

"We eat dinner, sit on the couch, watch TV, talk... I dunno, normal boring things middle-aged people do."

And this is where he starts to nitpick. *What dinner? Which couch? Tell me what it looks like. What do you talk about?* I tried to lie at first, to say we eat a nice sit-down meal, which we never do, or that we watch the sunset together, which I don't think we've ever done either, but he sniffed that out and took the totem away. Now, I have to dig for details of what we actually do, which is a lot of pretty routine, boring stuff. Routine, boring stuff I miss more than breathing.

What I do is I change into my comfies. I wash my feet because I sweat a lot at work, and I have a thing for clean feet. Owen does not sweat at work, nor does he change into comfies because I'm pretty sure slim-cut slacks and an oxford *are* his comfies. But he does take the tie off and roll his sleeves. Then we eat takeout or leftovers or the healthiest of the quick-cook meals we can get, and we sit on the couch. We talk for five or so minutes about how the day went. Then we talk about the baby. How she moved in my tummy. What she might look like. Who she might be. How she might sound. If we're ready for her.

This is what Black Bear wants. These details in the routine are what sets him boiling. They turn him on. But he took my child away from me, so he can go to hell. I'm not giving him my memories of her too. Sure, I know they're not memories of *her,* her, like of the actual girl. I only have a hazy half memory of that, of her near my face. And sometimes, I wonder if it's a memory at all or if it was actually a dream. So these prememories are the only ones I have, the only ones I trust. And they're mine.

But Black Bear is still hungry.

"The couch has a stain on it from when I spilled a cup of chicken posole on it," I say, which is true.

His eyes light up. "When?"

I shake my head, trying to remember, "A year ago, maybe?"

"Where?"

"The right arm. That's my spot. Where I always sit."

He nods as if he knew all along, as if I was in therapy and that was some huge breakthrough. He wets his lips with a chalky tongue and looks around the little room.

"A couch..." he says. "A couch."

He's starting to bubble. I think he's actually scoping the layout for where a couch could go. He shoves back from the table and looks at the white trash lawn chairs like he's only now seeing how gross they are. He seems to have forgotten me entirely.

He looks out the window into that unchanging jaundice-yellow light of a sunset that never comes. "A couch..." he says again and leaves.

He leaves just like that. With the door wide open and me with the black bear totem in my hand.

So.

This may be my first time as part of a weirdo's doll collection, but it ain't my first rodeo when it comes to making snap decisions that might save my life. And here's what I've learned in that department. If you're trapped and you see a door, run.

So that's what I do. I know he says there's some sort of boundary to his world. But he says a lot of things. I'd rather check for myself.

I'm at the door in a blink, and that's when I see the other smoke.

I catch it out of the corner of my eye, like when you stand up too fast and those fireworks pop off at the edge of your eyeballs. But these are soft red. They're coming from just down the hall.

I stutter step near the front door.

You don't know how much time you have, Caroline. That's Owen, cheering me on, holding my racing heart in his hands. And he's not wrong.

But that smoke says I need to move that way.

Decisions are what matters. Right or wrong. Nothing worse than being caught in the doorway.

I follow the red mist to another door.

Just make the decision, he says in that kind way.

I push it open.

Inside, I find a room the size of mine. Kiva fire. Table and chairs. But the décor is all different. The crap in mine is a mishmash of roadside trash. Old beer cans from the seventies stacked on the walls, plastic TV dinner trays, and bent silverware. Gas station signs and busted-up old appliances. The kind of stuff you'd expect to get dredged out of a lake. Here, the stuff is all older, warped wood and rusted steel. Turn-of-the-century stuff like rubber band guns and carved horses. Toy soldiers and jagged jacks. A first-generation TV the size of a milk crate, broken screen and all, sits in the far corner. The kind of things our grandparents lived with.

And there, by the fire, is a woman.

She's the one dripping the soft red dust that called me. Or warned me. She's the one I heard through the walls. She's frozen, seated cross-legged on the ground. I can see in her smoke how much she wants to talk to me. But the only way she talks to me is if I hand her my totem.

And if I hand her my totem, I become the frozen one.

There's a world in which I hand this woman I don't know—this literal red flag—the totem, and she runs. A world where she leaves me a statue.

But something tells me she's been on the shelf a lot longer than me. Something tells me that maybe I need to take a chance here, that she has something important to say.

Information first, Owen tells me. *Run later, and get farther.*

I put the totem in her hand and feel the passage of the dark power. I shudder as my body freezes and hers wakes up. I can see how her eyes find me, like they've been looking for me forever. Maybe this is when she runs. You would think I would know better than to trust strangers at the end of the world, at my age.

She stretches her neck and picks up her knees one after the other. But she stays.

She looks me right in the eye, inches from my face, and says, "I need to you listen to me while we have time."

So I listen, frozen mid baton-pass as she speaks low and close, sometimes whispering, other times crying, other times holding me, my ratty hospital gown balled in her fists.

I listen. I listen hard.

I listen like I can't do anything else.

15

OWEN BENNET

The road to the Arroyo is dark, and the flood wiped out a lot of the landmarks we used to rely on to navigate at night. A hundred years of tire ruts washed away. It'll take a hell of a lot longer than seven months to get everything straight again.

The truck's high beams light up the far desert, and the fog lights keep me on the road. I drive slowly now. The girl is asleep, somehow, clutching the feather in her fat fist. Children are amazing like that. One second, they're in mortal danger, the next they're conked out in the baby seat. I could sure use a bit more of whatever chemical clears the table in her brain like that.

Instead, my fingers still thrum with so much adrenaline that I'm having a hard time feeling the steering wheel. I swear my heartbeat echoes against the roof. Maybe that's what she fell asleep to. It's one long snare drum.

Three times now, I've tapped the brakes, thinking I somehow missed that the thing trying to eat my daughter snuck under the tarp in the cab. Three times, I've caught crows in the rearview. I've never seen crows fly at night. It's very unsettling. Unnatural. The silence of it makes it worse. I've been around enough crows now to know they're a chatty bunch. They'll caw all day long, especially if Chaco's nearby. So when these don't, it means they're being quiet for a reason.

I think they don't want to blow our cover. Which means that creature that licked my daughter's bed like a dog is near enough that a crow's call might alert it.

Old Owen—the me that jumped in front of a literal bullet—would lure this thing away from the Arroyo to keep my friends and family safe.

New me—dad me—cannot get to the Arroyo fast enough because I feel absolutely incapable of dealing with this alone. And yes, I realize that leading a monster to the masses is likely a form of cowardice in all but the most generous interpretations.

You are your own worst enemy, Owen. Friends are there to carry the load. That's what friends do.

That's Caroline's voice again, in my head.

"Not so sure about that one, honey," I mutter, tapping the brakes again at a flash of darkness, another crow, before wiping my hands on my slacks and pressing on. "I think maybe my current worst enemy is the one that wants to eat our child. But point taken. I love you too."

A crow floats on some unseen draft up to my left, squarely framed in the driver's side window, wings wide and head pinned. I yelp and nearly run us off the road, but it adjusts when I overcompensate, tail feathers shifting this way and that like some softer sliver of the night come loose.

Another joins it. Then another outside the passenger's window to my right.

Two crows drop in and down the updraft from the windshield and float right in front of the truck.

I slow more. "Listen, fellas, I appreciate that we're in this together, but I don't really have time for this—"

The fog lights pick up a black bed of feathers ahead where a hundred crows stand, dead silent, in the middle of the road. If I was going any faster than ten miles an hour, I would've plowed through them like black snow. Instead, my tires hiss to a stop feet from where they're gathering, and they turn to eye me as one, like a single creature.

The two that dropped down ahead of the windshield settle with uncanny accuracy on the hood and waddle over to either edge. They settle their feathers, lean over, and peck at the headlights.

"Hey!" I say and almost lay on the horn before the girl stirs in her sleep, and I hold off, trembling. *Smart idea, Dr. Bennet. Why don't we just honk that thing a runway right to us?*

Still, those are Grant's lights, and they saved my ass in this deep desert, and he won't be happy if they get pecked to pieces. I roll down the window. My voice is a harsh whisper. "Hey! Birds! Get off the hood! Hey!"

Tap tap tap... tap tap tap.

I'd get out of the car and shoo them away if I wasn't both consciously and subconsciously terrified that I'd get killed out there and my daughter would be left to rot in her car seat. I love crows as much as the next guy—a lot more, to be honest—but I'm under no delusions about non-Chaco crows. If I wasn't here, the harsh reality is that they would be pecking on her not too long after they finished pecking on me.

Shut the lights off, Owen.

I swear it's like I can hear Caroline talking to me—her tone, the way she would be sitting to my right, one leg tucked up under the other.

Of course she would be the one to tell me that this murder of crows is actually trying to get a message across. That's a concept I have a hard time convincing myself to believe without her.

Quickly now.

I kill the engine, plunging us into darkness. You really haven't lived in darkness until you live in Rez darkness. The fabric of it is woven from something thicker out here.

"I can't believe I'm doing this," I mutter, turning back to check on her. She's asleep again. The feather rises and falls with her breaths. I count them out of habit. A pediatric cardiologist colleague at ABQ General told me that a healthy, sleeping seven-month-old should take between thirty and forty breaths a minute. I asked him because I had to perform some fairly bruising CPR on her little heart, and even though all signs point to her being fully recovered, I was and still am terrified I did some sort of long-term damage and she'll have to compensate by over-respirating, even after he assured me that hearts don't work that way. You don't mush them all up when you perform CPR, not even infant hearts. They're muscles, not balls of Play-Doh. But I still count.

Thirty-three. Right in line. Nothing to worry about until the next time I count.

Movement to my front snaps my head around. Muddy headlights coming from the desert side paint the road jaundice yellow and throw shadows a long way down the road.

A car is on its way from the deep desert toward a crossroads. Once it gets there, all the driver has to do is look left, and there we'll be. And something about the slow roll of this car, the way it groans its way down the road, tells me we don't want whoever is driving to look left.

A crow caws once, setting my teeth on edge. I brace for the cacophony, but it doesn't come—just the one and done. I think they know what I know: nobody good is driving these roads at this hour.

Another crow settles on our hood with a scraping *plop*. Then another. And another on the hood. Two more on the roof. Then the air rushes with the sound of wings. All of them land on the truck until we're practically painted in crows. A line forms on the wipers that blocks half the windshield. The skylight is completely obscured.

The car reaches the T, and moonlight cuts right through the cab as it comes to a rolling stop with a soft squeal. I find I'm holding my breath. The crows are still. Behind me, the baby lets out a huge settling sigh in her sleep, which brings beads of sweat to my brow. But she sleeps on.

The driver is a man, bald. He looks left to right, slowly, and what I took for shadows over his face are in fact tattoos. Ink all over, just like the one in my house. But this guy isn't the one from my house. He's shorter, more compact.

"Great," I mumble. "Now there are two of them."

He noses about like a blind dog. Either that's paint smeared across his eyes or he's wearing some sort of Zorro-looking mask—

It's blood. Her voice again.

I know it's blood. I just didn't want to admit it to myself. Even in the dark, I can tell. And bloody eyes or no, he's going to see the truck. I could be standing where his car is, not even squinting, and I'd say, *Hmm. Looks like a truck with a hundred crows on it. That's going to be a rough car wash.*

But the car squeaks into a roll again.

Something about the crows was enough to hide us.

Once the rhythmic squeal of his shocks fades, it's as if all of us—me, my daughter, and a hundred crows—take a single collective breath. One great sigh.

It worked. They hid us.

I look back at her, still asleep. "I think maybe these birds are on our side," I whisper. I think maybe—"

In an instant, the whole flock explodes into flight. The wingbeats sound like a single-note blast of a tornado, and when I unflatten myself from the console, they're gone. My daughter is blinking herself awake. She looks at me then at the feather in her hand. And she starts crying.

And I'm not surprised. I'd be scared too. Hell, I *am* scared. And she's a baby. Not a seer, not an oracle. She's a baby who's hungry and likely dropped a load in her pants in her sleep and then was awoken by a crownado.

I hop out of the front seat, trying to ignore how exposed I feel even touching the ground that car rolled on, and open the back cab. I hope the fire drill bag has enough diapers. I also hope it has a changing pad although I think Grant wouldn't begrudge us a little poop on the back seat. We're on the run, after all.

And we're not going to the Arroyo, either. Not anymore. A lot about this night makes no sense to me, but that decision is crystal clear. First of all, I will not be taking my daughter near that thing that just slow rolled its way past us. But beyond that, I can't just go back to waiting for her, for Caroline. It's killing me, and what kills me kills my daughter.

Grant would understand.

Those pus-colored headlights are headed Grant's way. I reach for my cellphone midchange. Maybe I can warn him. She looks up at me as I fumble around with my three clean fingers and drop the phone and curse in a way that makes me happy this child will not remember tonight. If we're lucky, that is.

One thing at a time, Owen. Caroline's voice is like a soft hand on my shoulder.

Right. First, clean her up. Then get her fed. Then buckle her in. Then figure out my life.

I strap on a fresh diaper and dig in the bowels of the changing bag on a whim and a prayer for food. I grasp not one but five pouches of pureed stuff. Sure, I probably tossed them in there because they're all green and she's going through an I-hate-green phase, but I think we're about to the point where even green gets the job done. I find a few packs of the high-calorie formula too, from when I had to force feed her for months to try to get her to gain weight. Grant packed reinforcements in the truck bed too, like any good desert dweller: more food, pureed and solid; protein drinks; energy bars; a big jug of water. I don't even care that it's probably been rolling around in his side hatch for a month. I'll take it all.

"How about some green?" I ask her. She sucks at her fist with some serious vigor. When I hand it to her, she takes it and pops the cap right in her mouth.

I brush a forefinger gently down her fat cheek as she eats. "Desperate times, I guess."

And now to call Grant. He has to know what's coming for him. I fumble around under the truck and pick up my phone and dial again.

No ringing. Straight to voice mail.

I try again, holding it up to that phantom god of cellular service.

No luck. And I know from experience once you've been snubbed by the cell-service god out here, it stays that way unless you head towards humanity. So I leave a message. It'll get delivered on delay, but it'll get delivered.

"Grant, it's Dad." And here I struggle. "I had to take your sister."

Great. Great start there.

"But I did it because something is trying to eat her. And I don't expect you to understand that, which is why I won't blame you if you don't believe me when I tell you a man with bloody eyes is coming to the Arroyo, and I think he means to wipe it out."

I clear my throat, pressing the phone to my chest. I look at my daughter.

"Grant, I have to go find your mom," I say, switching tracks entirely and not quite knowing why. "I can't live like this anymore: half in, half out. Hating when I wake up from dreams where the two of us are together, only to find I'm alone. I can't do it anymore."

My daughter looks at me carefully, sucking away.

"And before you ask, no, I do not know where I'm going. But I have a good week's worth of food and water here, thanks to you and your mother and..."

My little girl coos, looking at me trying to explain myself to a recording.

"And I think your sister knows things," I say. "It occurs to me that I may need to have..." The words I feel forming are foreign to my lips. "I may need to have faith."

She misses her mouth with the tube of green, and I guide it back to true.

"So have faith in us, Son. We will see you again. All of us."

I end the call and toss the phone in the bag. I check her straps, close the cab doors, and settle back into the driver's seat. Now, the only question is where the hell to go.

"What do you think, tiny seven-month-old child sucking pureed spinach out of a tube?"

She coos. I can't help but smile.

I fire up the truck. The high beams and low beams and all the other beams kick in and blast the desert white. "I think we're going to go find your mom," I say, not even really believing I'm saying it. "How does that sound?"

She seems nonplussed, at least in the rearview. Maybe this was what she was going after all along, and she's glad I finally came around to her point of view. She's also absolutely crushing the spinach.

"So, where to?" I ask her. I ask the night sky. I ask nobody and everybody.

Look for the shadows, Owen.

I look out and around, and sure enough, I see what she's talking about. They're shadows, yes, but they're also crows. I thought they'd left. But I don't think that leaving is in the agenda for this group. They know I'm watching them too. The closest of them shift around in a way that makes their feathers look liquid black. Chaco can do that too, walking about in the darkest hour of night in a way that owns it.

This squad dribbles out to the T then shuffles to the right, away from the Arroyo. Toward the desert. One by one, they take silent flight. Their passing silhouettes punch holes in the moonlight. I swear a handful of them even look at us as they take off.

An echo from my past fires in the recesses of my brain. Not Caroline this time, this voice is from medical school, an attending that I hated—a brilliant man who held the keys to a posting at some or other prestigious bullshit—drilling into us his "mantra": *Hope doesn't save lives. Science does.*

I do get that sentiment, but looking at these things take flight, the way they all career one after the other on the same line, even I'm not cynic enough to turn a blind eye.

Even I know that when the crows look at you like that, you follow the crows.

16

GRANT ROMER

There's a funny thing about Diné country that people might not know if they ain't been around here a while. Sometimes, you'll be driving down a dirt road on a random Tuesday, mindin' your own business, and your phone'll buzz in your pocket, and you'll pluck it out and see it's a voice mail from way back, just now come across the wires. If it's for me, it'll usually be Kai, asking if I can pick this or that up on the way home, or Dad asking if I'm stayin' at the A-frame tonight.

Used to be Mom too. Before.

Kai and me, we call it ghostmail. And it happens all the time. But none hurt like this one from Dad.

So have faith in us, Son. We will see you again. All of us.

I feel like I saw this comin'. That child is a heavy child. And I don't mean how many pounds she's got on her. I mean her soul weight. I've seen the way she looks at the crows. I gave her the feather because she kept reaching for it, the first real thing she ever reached for like she knew what she was doin'. And Chaco said sure, so... I mean, hell, I'm pretty sure that feather is sort of part of her anyway. It popped up from the Arroyo when she came back to us. It blew our way on the same dark wind that took Black Bear out. It's part of the balance.

I listen to the message again, my body still dripping sweat and pollen from the heat of the hogan. Dad is on some sort of spirit journey. I'd say the sleep deprivation finally cracked him except that he's heavy these days too. Ever since Mom left, it's like his soul has been takin' on water. It was only a matter of time before he tipped over inside.

I just hope Ben finds them before somethin' worse does and that somehow they stay ahead of this nightmare long enough to find out what happened to Mom.

"One thing at a time," Chaco says, easing my burden with just his voice. "Owen knows what he's doing."

"You sure?" I ask, tossing my worthless phone back on the clothes pile outside the hogan. When I'm about to duck back in, I hear the telltale rumble of an early-model SUV engine rattle across the mudflat. Not just any SUV, either—a classic Bronco, the kind when you tap the gas, it sounds like hippo runnin' through water. Sani Yokana's car.

He comes fast around the gate and skids up short of the tents and campers to talk to Maria. She points our way then goes back to tryin' to keep our squad fed and watered.

Yokana looks our way, and I raise a hand. He parks the Bronco and sets off down the trench our way at a trot, then a run. I don't think I've ever seen Yokana run before. It looks painful, like his knees thought they were well past that shit.

He comes up on us, breathin' hard. "They are heading this way," he says. "All signs point to here. The east border, then Baba's, then Manuelito's. It's a line, and it points right here."

"One of them is, at least," I reply, handing him some water. "Owen tried to call, left a warning. The other might be on his tail."

Yokana looks at me strangely mid-drink. He glances up at Chaco, who stares back with absolute stillness. "Why am I not surprised to find you not surprised, Grant Romer?"

"You said Manuelito's? What the hell they want with Manuelito's?"

Yokana shakes his head and takes another drink before he says, "Food, by the looks of it." He lets that one sit before spitting and waving the air of the words.

So not the enchiladas Christmas style, then.

Yokana wipes his hands on his jeans. "My guess is they're coming this way because they want more."

"That's why we're here," I say, nodding toward the hogan.

"I thought this was for Tsosi. A Blessingway."

"It was, then those two things showed up. Now, it's to get right for what's comin'."

Yokana takes off his hat and smooths his silver hair. "I have seen dark things in my day, young man. But these two take all the light. I feel like we've been living in a world at midnight ever since they crossed into our land. If you're getting right with the holy people, I will get right with you."

He pops the snap buttons of his faded denim shirt and shrugs it off. He's lumpy and scarred underneath, sagging here and there, but if I look half as built in my seventies as he does, somebody buy me a beer.

He tosses his shirt on the pile and sets his hat carefully

on top by the crown. He starts to unclip his gun and badge but pauses and snaps them back on before grabbing a handful of pollen from the buckskin sack hanging from a nail aside the door. He speaks a blessing only he can hear before wiping a streak of the yellow across his sweaty brow and brushing the rest through his hair. He dusts his gun lightly then ducks in.

I look up at Chaco and find him watching the creeping blue of early morning. Soon enough, the sun'll crack over the far end of the canyon. I bet it's gonna be a bluebird high-desert day. But I doubt even full sun can stop this shivering. It's part adrenaline, part lack of sleep, and part the weird pulsing of the bell. I'm keyed up like a dog in the chute.

I make to duck in after Sani, but the bell throbs and damn near drags me to the ground. I gotta steady myself on the mud wall outside.

"You alright?" Chaco asks, worried.

I shake my head, trying to pull the leather loop off my neck. A rapid thumping echoes across the canyon, strange and panicked in the quiet of the early morning. Someone is running along the lip of the canyon. At first, I think it's Blood Eyes, but he's not running our way. And the running looks more like fleeing. A flash of a silver chain tells me it's Hashke Lee, one of the young guys who returned with Dark Sky's lost people. He was in Hos's class at Chaco High School, and he always rolled around with these ridiculous chains.

Chaco gets it before I do. He lets out three piercing *caws* into the dead morning air and it's enough to snap Hashke out of whatever crazy fever dream he's in. For a minute, at least.

He finds us, and he sees us, and he screams, "Run!"

clear as a bell across the canyon before he turns his back to us and tears off into the open desert with no shoes on.

"Hashke!" I yell after him, picking my way over the trenches to run toward him, but ain't no way I'm catching him. He's running full tilt toward the sunrise, and he don't look like he's ever stoppin'.

I look up at Chaco. "What the hell was that all about?"

Chaco clicks his throat a few times. "Hashke was manning the gate."

Usually, the Smoker mans the gate, but the Smoker is tied up in workin' the sweat. He asked Hashke to sit his spell at the front.

"Is he high?" I ask, trying to piece together what I saw.

"He was manning the gate, Grant."

"Runnin' like that into the open desert? He ain't even got shoes on."

Chaco looks at me hard.

"Somethin's at the gate," I say.

Chaco nods in his bobbing way. "Something bad."

I see that something, now. A figure is walking slowly our way. One minute, I'm lookin' at shades of black morning, the next, a thing pieces itself together. Could be a trick of the horizon. Or maybe it ain't.

"He's here," Chaco says, his voice a low rasp.

The bell knows it too. Sure as shit, it knows. The presence of this thing hits me hard enough that I gotta take a knee to get inside the hogan. But someone's gotta tell 'em it's time.

I trip over some shit or other, and the bell wants to take me six feet under the mud, but then Kai is there. All she does is put one hand on my shoulder and the back of the other on my cheek, and it's like she's sucking venom from snakebit skin.

I look up at her. "He's here," I say.

Inside the hogan, Tsosi is still quietly dying while Tsasa paints his story in the dirt around him. The Smoker still works at the fetishes, figuring out what to burn next and how. Hos has his eyes closed, sitting and breathing deep into the chant, so close to the fire that I can see it reflected in the sweat of his chest. Chief Yokana rubs ash from the spent logs between a thumb and forefinger while beads of sweat drip from his nose.

Joey is the first to get what I say. He thumbs the crow totem, quiet in its pouch around his neck. Usually, Joey is our *we need more time* guy. Usually, he takes that crow out, phases wherever he wants, knocks a few heads, and phases back.

But that's because usually the crow totems work.

First time for everythin', I guess.

Joey moves to his knees then stands. Crow or no crow, he knows what he has to do. What *we* have to do because I sure as shit ain't lettin' my friend face that thing out there alone, no matter how heavy this bell gets.

Yokana pulls big fists of smoke his way and breathes deep before he claps his hands free of the ash. His knees pop like crackling wood as he stands. "I'm coming too. This is police business."

Tsasa looks half blind with sweat and grief, but he still tugs on Joey's arm as he stands. He mumbles something that comes together at the end when he says, "His stare means death, but his eyes lie."

Joey narrows his own eyes then steps past me and out of the hogan first. Yokana follows, stooped and old one minute, then strong the second he steps out and stands tall.

I can tell Kai wants to go. But she also knows how

important the fire is. She and Hos are our last line of defense.

"I'll be back," I whisper.

She presses her cheek against mine. Her breath is a different kind of warm from the smoke. It still prickles the skin of my neck after all these years. "Remember what matters, Grant Romer," she says. "You. Me. Our people."

I've been in enough situations like this to know you take those words, and you shove them deep in that pocket of your brain you go to when the world catches fire around you. So that's what I do. I nod. My scruffy cheek brushes a soft rasp against her, then I duck out.

17

CAROLINE ADAMS

I'm frozen, listening to the stories of a woman who lived a hundred years before I was born. I can't tell how much time has passed. I know I should be on the lookout for Black Bear to return, but I can't tear myself away from her words.

Also, I literally can't move. In order for her to speak, she had to take the totem I gave her. And now, my face is frozen in a pinched half grimace, the face of a woman going with her gut, on a wing and a prayer. Or at least, that's what I'd like to think. Probably, to her, I look constipated.

But my gut was right.

Her name is Sara. But that's her white man's name, the one the missionaries gave her when they showed up in her area of the Navajo territory. She says she doesn't know quite when they came and she's forgotten more since, but she thinks it was sometime around the turn of the last century, which makes a sick sort of sense when you look at how Black Bear did up her room. The more I see, the more it clicks. Tattered Old West dresses rot in the corners, her furniture is made from chipped and faded schoolhouse crap. *Little House on the Prairie* from hell.

She's been here for well over a hundred years. In this room. On this shelf. She tells me she's spent most of that time remembering her real name, remembering her clan, trying to keep where she came from front and center.

She won't tell me her real name, and I get that. She says the missionaries tried to beat it out of her, then the government tried to starve it out of her. And none of them got it, so she isn't about to let it go now.

She was one of the boarding school kids. They were forbidden to speak their own language, forbidden to speak at all most of the time. That meant she couldn't tell anyone she couldn't breathe right. When she wheezed and coughed, nobody wanted to get close to her. The nurse in me knows it was likely pneumonia. You can kick it now with simple oral antibiotics, but back then, it was different. She was alone in her bed when her own lungs drowned her.

She remembers the cold, how thin the blankets were, how the freezing metal of the cot stung her.

That's when he came. Black Bear. When he took her, she was only fifteen and terrified to die, and he said he knew a place where she could live, a place where she wouldn't wheeze at every breath, where she wouldn't feel the cold.

He took her here. What he didn't tell her was that she wouldn't wheeze because she wouldn't breathe. She wouldn't feel the cold because she wouldn't feel much of anything.

"I sensed him coming," she says, her face close to mine, her voice a whisper. "When I was sick, he was at the edges. Watching me. Waiting."

Her eyes are dark brown, her face smooth. Not a single wrinkle.

Fifteen forever, I think. *That's a curse of its own.*

"He chose me, just like he chose you. Like he chose Tábaahá."

Tábaahá? So there's more of us.

My face betrays none of my questions, but Sara knows I must have them. "She's in the third room," she says.

We're getting into serial-killer-level collecting here. I can just see the creep stalking the halls of the school where Sara died, a dark presence in the freezing shadows. I bet he walked it like he walked the halls of my clinic, waiting to make a deal. The question is why. *Why us? What about the two of us...the three of us, is so important to him?*

"Tábaahá has been here a long, long time. She's..." Sara's face is pained. I bet her eyes would well up if they could. She looks over my shoulder, through the walls, deeper into this mess, and I know she's looking for her.

"She's from the early times, close to the years of Black Bear himself. A true daughter of the plains. Her memories are almost gone. And once they are, he'll have no use for her."

She tenses, senses something behind me. Her eyes widen. "He's coming," she whispers. She speaks quickly now. "Your memories are your money here. Remember that. And there's one he wants more than anything. We all have it."

Memories as money. It doesn't make any sense. Half of my memories are cringe, and the other half are terrifying. *Why would he want anything I have?*

"You'll find it, and when you do, keep it buried. Never speak it. Not even to me. Now, quickly, back to your room.

You should know by now you cannot run away from this house. I'm sure you tried. I did too, we all do, but that isn't the way."

What is the way? I scream in my mind. But there isn't time.

She puts the totem back in my hand and curls my fingers over it. "Be strong," she says. Then she passes it off.

I blink, stretch, turn to the door, then turn back. I have so many more questions, so many things I could say. But I can hear the heavy shuffle of sand under his feet, coming from just outside.

"I'll be back," I whisper. It's the first thing that comes to my thawed lips. I say it for her, and I say it for me. When I was a floor nurse back in ABQ, deep in a long shift full of codes and blood and fear sweat and bad coffee, I got real close to the squad going through it with me. When you're in the trenches, the people nearby are all you've got. And now I've got one here.

"Thank you," I say. Then I dash.

I quick step out her door and almost stop when I see the third door off to the left. The wood is sun bleached and salt stained and shut tight.

One thing at a time.

The shadow of Black Bear darkens the window, and I duck low, back to the wooden wall, knees popping as I soft step as fast as I can back into my own room. I hear him grunt, shift something heavy, and paw at the door. Panic scatters my thoughts the second they form. *Where the hell was I when he left?* The table. Telling him stories at the table.

Feeding him memories at the table.

I shove that thought aside and stumble back to the card table, glancing my hip off the corner. It doesn't hurt

—nothing here hurts like that—but I have to slap my hand over my mouth not to yelp at the clatter it makes. *How was I sitting? Think. Think!*

Black Bear shoves inside with a ratty old couch that would look at home outside the scuzziest frat house at ASU. He has it slung easily over one shoulder, balanced like it weighs nothing more than a boombox.

He looks around until he finds a corner, and his eyes light up. He flips the couch off his shoulder, and I can feel the way it pushes the wind, and my teeth rattle as he slams it down onto the wood floor. It's stained and cracked, and something snaps inside the frame, but he doesn't care. He pushes it flush to the wall, and the cheap fake leather splits right down the middle. Again, not a care.

He steps back and puts his hands on his hips. "Couch," he says.

Then he turns around and sees me seeing him, and his face darkens in an instant. His watery gaze drops to my hands, flat on the table once more, and when he sees the totem there, his smoke bubbles, and that spark of fury glows again. "Where did you get that?" he asks, his voice deadly soft.

"You gave it to me before you left. It's been here—I've been here the whole time," I say quickly.

His eyes flicker back and forth as he checks this against memories I'm pretty sure flit out of his head not long after they come in. Maybe that's why he needs ours.

He scans the room as he walks back to the table, as though anybody would want to mess with any of his time capsule trash. When I think he's about to take a seat, he shoves his chair aside and leans down into my face. "You stayed right here?"

"I stayed right here," I say, refusing to look away from him because I know that's exactly what he wants me to do.

He sees it in me, though, sees that I know more now than when he left. I don't know how, but he does, and he picks me up by the limp collar of my hospital gown.

I have a terrible urge to tell him more, to tell him an important memory. Maybe it'll calm him down. It's like a kneejerk reaction, and I hate it, and I'm proud when I keep my mouth shut even though I know it makes him angry.

He throws me back against the ratty cushions of the disgusting addition and plucks the totem from my hand at the same time. I land, frozen, half standing, half sitting, like a poorly positioned doll. I fall over, my face on the stained seat, my mouth open, and inside, I scream. Inside, I gag. Inside, I blubber and snot and plead and curse and spit and moan.

But outside, I'm frozen.

"Enjoy your couch," he says.

And he leaves me like this.

18

GRANT ROMER

He's not a tall man, this thing that walks out from between the sleeping tents and darkened campers of the far side of the Arroyo. Not built, either. He don't look much like a monster. From this distance, I can almost convince myself all that black running down his face is just ink.

He wears black boots and black slacks, a black T-shirt too. Grant said Ben wears the same, save the boots. I don't think it's a coincidence this thing dresses like Ben. From what Chaco says, these guys are fanatics.

I feel when he finds us. The early sun plays weird tricks with his ink and the blood as he walks our way, making them look like they're swirling on his skin.

"We can't let him get near the hogan," Joey says, his voice a growl.

"We're about to escort him straight into a cell," Yokana says, shrugging on his old denim shirt and resting his hand on his gun.

I lean my head one way so that Chaco has a place to land on my shoulder.

"That's not gonna work," Chaco says. "Tell Sani this thing isn't here to get arrested."

"Chief," I say, "It ain't gonna be that easy."

Sani settles his hat on his head. "No, I suspect it won't, young man. But this fellow is wanted, and I am still what passes for the law around here." He plucks his badge from his waist and holds it up in the sunlight. "Stop where you are! Hands behind your head."

The Chief's voice ain't lost a step—that's for sure. And the man does stop. He stands where the Arroyo flat turns into the trenches that come our way. The mud cracks around his boots.

The Chief starts forward, but neither Joey nor I am about to let him walk out there alone. The bell throbs with every step I take. Chaco is as tense as a block of wood on my shoulder. When we're about fifty feet out, it's clear that this thing's got his eyes closed. Maybe had them closed the whole time.

"This is a bad idea," I manage to say.

I get a nod from Joey and a *No shit* from Chaco, but that's about it. And we keep walkin' anyway.

Yokana clicks his badge back into his belt and pulls his gun, steadying it with a gnarled but sure grip. "I said hands on your head! You are wanted in connection with multiple homicides within the borders of the Navajo Nation—"

The man cocks his head clockwise, like a dog just catching our sound, and the sun takes that moment to rise above the canyon and pour into the Arroyo. In the new light, it's easy to see where the name Blood Eyes comes from.

His hands flutter slowly like a spider testing strands of its web.

I try to clear my throat, but it still comes out raspy when I say, "Chief—"

Yokana cuts me off. "If you move, I will shoot," he says.

The man moves. He opens his eyes, and Yokana fires. Three shots. Practiced. No crazy unloading, which I would have done.

I square up again through the gunsmoke, and the first thing I see is Yokana's eyes opening up like a camera lens going wide.

He drops his gun.

"Chief?" I get this crazy thought that maybe Blood Eyes shot back or somethin'. The sun is behind him and I'm having a hard time focusing, and just when I can see him clearly, Chaco drills me in the temple with his beak hard as hell.

"Don't look at him! Do *not* look at him, Grant!"

I get it now. All it takes is a bird to the brain. I reach for Joey. "Keep your eyes on the ground!"

But when I grab him, Joey's as stunned as Yokana. Worse, even. It's like he's a cow in the kill chute, getting pulled forward with slow, staggering steps.

"Pull their eyes off him!" Chaco yells, his voice pounding in my head.

"How?" I ask, staring at the ground. It's crazy hard not to look at a thing when all you wanna do is look at a thing.

"How do you think? Hit 'em in the face! I'm going after Blood Eyes," Chaco says then launches before I can even utter a word.

Their collision is strangely quiet, barely more than a baseball hittin' a mitt. Chaco's wings flutter, and I hear the knife slice of his raking claws while I find Joey's feet and trace up to his face. "Sorry buddy," I say, then I deck him, fist to chin. If it takes knocking him out, I will.

He crumples, but at least his eyes close. I turn to the Chief next and hesitate only a second, thinking how it'll look down at the station if I break his jaw. But then I think what'll happen if there ain't no Chief, and I swing at him too—sideways, not up. I pop his temple, and he staggers then drops, groaning. Tough old goat.

Chaco screeches in pain, and that's when I make my mistake. I can feel it happening as I do it. I know I'm gonna look, but that's my buddy, and he's hurt and—

I look just as Blood Eyes slaps my bird off his face. Chaco hits the ground hard, one wing out of place. He does a sad little flop and tries to take off again but doesn't get far. Chaco got a few good cuts in, but it doesn't look like it did much to deter him. He takes two steps after Chaco, like he aims to crush my bird with his filthy black boots, and that's all it takes to make me run at him.

I get about two steps before he looks at me full-on. He has no real eyes I can see, only weeping pits that go on and on and on, and the urge to find out where they bottom out is like a desert pool to a man dying of thirst. I just want to throw myself into it.

Then I'm caught like a fish on the line. I can't do nothin' but bite, and when I do, he sets the hook in my soul. His eyes get bigger, darker. They drip blood then drop blood then drool blood. They become everything, and I can't look away.

My own vision wavers, and in its place, I see a child at a graveyard.

Not just any child and not just any graveyard. I know this place. It's been a few decades, but before I found the bell, I spent a fair bit of time here.

The kid is me, and my parents are buried here. I sit in

my usual spot, this time against Mom's stone. Tomorrow, it'll be Dad's. I alternate so that neither one gets lonely.

"I miss you, Mom," I say. That's what I always say. But this time, she talks back.

"You'll see us soon," she replies. She sounds for all the world like she's right there on the other side of the stone. Us back to back.

Mom isn't supposed to talk back. That's not how it works.

My mouth is clammy with fear. 'No. I can't. I have things to do."

She slams against the tombstone, and I grip the dead grass with both hands.

"Do you even remember my face?" she asks, her voice a hiss. "Or when you think of *mother*, do you think of *her*?"

Caroline. And she's right. More and more, I do think of Caroline as Mom. And it's true, I'm having a hard time really remembering the face of the woman who's supposed to be under this earth.

"It's not like that, Mom. She's family too. Just like you."

"You killed her. Just like you killed me. Just like you killed your father."

That ain't right. A freak accident killed them, a car wreck so bad nobody was at fault and everybody lost. I know this. But what I know ain't holdin' water right now.

A dirty finger curls its way over the top of the gravestone. Then another. Black fingernails. A filthy wedding ring.

I scramble away. "Mom, please—"

"You hold death inches from your heart," she says. "You have for your entire life. Even when you didn't carry the bell."

Two more fingers then all five grip and push. I see

Mom's dark red hair rising over the other side, but it's clumped and matted with grave dirt.

All I can do is watch.

"With you in this family," she hisses, "there can be no ending but death."

Her eyes crest the chipped stone, and they're those same weeping pits, and the bell yanks me down. Onto the ground. Under the ground. The grave dirt squelches between my fingers and pushes into my mouth. I feel bits of things, parts of people. Soon, I'm pushed through the ground and back to the cracked mud of the Arroyo, somehow still staring at this creature. I'm caught well and true, and Blood Eyes is smiling, licking his lips. He's eating this up.

The bell pulls tighter.

"Take it!" I scream. "Please! Take it! I can't carry it anymore."

Blood Eyes comes closer, and I hold it out, tears in my eyes. The air has the bittersweet taste of a forbidden dream, the kind where you make dumb decisions and wake up terrified at what your brain showed you.

Blood Eyes grabs the bell. That much is real. And when he does, the words of Tsasa ring deep inside.

His eyes lie.

I need the truth. And what's true is that my bird is limping his way back up to this monster, clawing himself up while Blood Eyes is lost in the bell. A lion drunk on the feed doesn't give a shit when a bird walks up its back, right up until that bird jams a beak full of dirt in its eye.

Blood Eyes screams and reels, digging at his eye with his fingers, and the spell snaps in an instant. I grab the bell from his other hand, terrified that the darkest part of me finally won out, that I really gave it up. I feel relief and a strange type of sadness I ain't ready to deal with as the bell tucks itself away near my heart in the same place it's been for twenty years. Mine still, for better and for worse.

"Get to the hogan!" Chaco says, but that's all he gets out before Blood Eyes backhands him with a sound like a dropped watermelon. Chaco flies backward and lands crumpled in the dirt.

Blood Eyes wipes his hand on his shirt, disgusted. "Filthy creatures, crows. I'll never understand why my brother eats them."

His eyes are draining blood again, but I ain't about to look any longer. I've learned the hard way that when Chaco says run, you'd better run.

The horrors of being trapped in that stare flit from me like a bad dream as I pound the mud back toward the hogan. I feel like I was lost for hours in the depths of those pits, but I bet it was nothing more than a few seconds. Terror is strong stuff like that. And this guy looks like he's dealing the pure shit.

I hate to leave Chaco, but he's got a lot of history in that bird brain, so as long as this thing leaves him alone, I think he might be okay. That's what I tell myself anyway, trying to forget how broken he looked, hobbling up that monster's clothes with a beak full of dirt. Trying to forget that split-watermelon sound.

I try to run to the hogan, but the bell has other ideas. It *likes* death, and this thing behind me leaves death everywhere it goes.

The bell drags me to the ground like an anchor. My knees cut out, and I stumble right into the dirt trench I helped dig out, and there I stay, exhausted, pinned like a butterfly on cork.

All I can do is listen to the crunch of those filthy boots comin' my way.

19

KAI BODREY

I'm holding the chant the best I can with Tsasa, Hos, and the Smoker. It's hot in here and white with smoke, and all things outside are muted. That's the point of a sweat. But then again, I ain't never had a sweat where shit is really going down outside.

I can't hear the fight, but I can feel when Grant stumbles. His fall hits me like a phantom pain right where I pull in breath. Chaco's muffled cry from somewhere out in the desert seals it.

Grant wouldn't have gone down if Joey wasn't down. And if Joey's down, that means Yokana's down 'cause he would've gone out in front, all coplike. That means everyone's in trouble. I drop the chant, open my eyes, and wipe the sweat from my face and brow up into my hair with shaking hands. Maybe I can at least drag Grant and Chaco back here. If I beat the Gambler at his game, I can beat this thing too. I look at Hos and find his eyes already on me, open for the first time in a long time.

Hos drops the chant and makes his way over to me. The Smoker falters but picks up the thread. He watches

Hos with concern, but that's nothin' new. He's been lookin' after my brother for decades.

Hos wicks the sweat from his arms with his hands and rubs the smoke and heat into his hair. He's dripping but somehow smells cleaner than ever, like every pore has been washed and this is the real him.

"They're hurt out there," I say, quiet and low. "That thing took them down."

"I know," Hos says.

"We gotta go help—"

"When you were a little girl, one time you took a punch for me," he says, cutting me off. "You remember that?"

Swallowing is painful. I look for the water jug. "What? Hos, I can't let that thing take Grant—"

Hos hands me the jug from next to him and talks right over me. "Dad was beatin' my ass over nothin'. Maybe three jars deep, whalin' on me, and you just... stepped in. Took one right in the face. You were maybe six."

I don't like this story, not because I can't remember it but because I don't like that he's sayin' it right here and right now.

"Hos, what the hell are you gettin' at—"

"I ain't ever faced somethin' that can kill with a look. But I been stared down by killers plenty. The scary ones ain't the ones tryin' to cock off and show how tough *they* are. The scary ones trick you into seeing *yourself* as weak."

He reaches forward and takes a handful of ash from deep in the fire. I can smell his skin singe, but if he feels it, he ain't showin'. He looks at the ash like it's an old friend and rubs it all over his hands and arms like soap.

"Little sister," Hos says, "it's time to stop taking punches for me."

The ash mixes with sweat to form a paint that he smears across his own eyes, ear to ear, and when he's done, a change comes over him. He paints two long, thick brushstrokes down from his eyes. Tsasa sings stronger and more clearly than he has since this chant began.

Hos looks at the fire like a long-lost friend. "When I was upstate in ABQ on those concrete yards and those concrete floors, concrete beds, concrete chairs, all I ever wanted was this earth," he says.

Hos grabs another fistful and turns to me. "Watch me," he says, smiling that old, wicked smile, the one I loved and hated. But this time, it's different. This time it's dangerous in a good way. "Witness my coup, little sister."

He unfolds himself and crawls from the hogan, and I scamper out behind. He stands outside, steaming, and cracks his neck right and left. He's my brother still but something else, too, now. Something different. It's like the violence came back the right way.

"Blood Eyes!" he screams, so loud that it ripples the tents across the half-moon flat. The dark creature is crouched over Grant, eyes dripping, but he snaps his attention up.

"Look at me!" Hos screams.

Blood Eyes looks, and I have a sick, wavering moment when I almost look back—he almost catches me—but then I find my brother again. Whatever sickness this monster gives, whatever it is that laid Grant, Joey, and Yokana low, it hits Hos full on.

He staggers back like a boxer who expected the hit, who wanted to taste it and see what he's workin' with.

"That was good," Hos says, wiping his face, smudging the ash, keeping the eye lock. And I can't even think what kind of horrible shit this thing is throwing at him. He's been the "ultimate disappointment," the absolute poster-child cautionary tale of an Indian. You name the crime, he's either done it, been in on it, or covered it up.

"That was good," he says again, nodding. "But I seen it before." Tears are cutting the ash, but his voice is strong. "I seen it all."

Hos walks forward. I catch the monster's stutter step back. I get the feeling this thing has no idea what to do with someone that takes his full gaze right to the face and then keeps walking *toward* it.

Hos clears his throat and spits. "The thing about hitting rock bottom is that there ain't nothin' you can show me that I ain't already beat myself senseless with, no poison of mine I ain't sat in for years."

Hos takes careful steps. "Show me," he whispers to the thing, deadly quiet. "Show me all of it."

I don't know what he's seeing, my brother, but I know he keeps walking. Slow boots making slow crunching sounds. At some point, he starts laughing. Or maybe he's crying. His steps come to a stop, and I see him dig his heels into the Arroyo dirt and hear his low growl. His back is tense, his arms all corded up. He bends down and grips the earth in both fists like it's the only thing keeping him standing.

His voice is as sharp as a razor when he says, "I told you to look at me."

Hos runs at this thing like one of those big freight trains that blares through the desert night. I follow his fists as he pops Blood Eyes once in the face with a boxer's jab, and when the thing recovers, he comes at him with the other fist, right to his throat.

Blood Eyes coughs and wheezes, and for a second, I think maybe he did it. But I should know by now when it comes to people my brother wants down, coughing and wheezing ain't enough.

Hos squares up and tackles him low, hits all the air out of his chest. His black boots scrape, footing lost. He falls, and Hos presses with arms in a cross bar and I think, *We've got this*, then it rolls. It rolls back and throws Hos off and staggers to standing, and all of a sudden, they're out deep in the flats, and it's like we're back where we started.

I follow, walking past Yokana, walking past Joey, looking for signs of life and maybe seein' them.

The sun cuts sharp over the canyon now. If I shade my eyes, I can see the pitch-black silhouettes of the two of them out deep in the mud flats now, near the lip.

They circle each other. Blood Eyes stands straight and follows Hos with small ticks of his head. My brother circles low, arms wide.

"Look at me!" Hos screams again, running, hitting it low, getting thrown and coming right back. Getting thrown again and coming back. Getting beaten about the face and coming back. My brother drips black from his face, and it ain't all sweat and ash.

Chaco fires off a series of caws that rips a line through the air between us. He's limping toward Grant, and he's scared. I pick him up without thinking and sprint there faster.

Grant is belly down, his face pressed to the dirt. He's breathing. I think he's just lost in whatever this thing showed him. Looping, maybe. I've been there. Chaco tucks in at his neck. I don't know what to do. I never know what to do.

The sound of my brother slamming into the meat of this monster pulls my attention back to the flats. The sun stretches their shadows long, well past me. The two of them are wavy now in the early-morning heat. Blood Eyes grabs him and presses his face right up to him. Eye to eye with my brother. How dare this fucking thing.

They stare into each other. Both of them. Grapplers at a standstill, they hold each other and stare. And somewhere in the back of my mind, an alarm is blaring that says they are almost at the lip of the canyon.

Hos breaks the stare first. I don't blame him. I won't blame him anymore. I'd have been burned inside and out by this thing. But then he looks right at me, and I know he broke the gaze on his own terms.

I know he sees me because of how his face softens, blood and ash and all.

"Look at me," he says, again, strong and clear, but with love behind it this time—words just for me.

He bear-hugs Blood Eyes and rips out a war cry as he hucks himself off the lip of the cliff.

The two of them go full sail into the empty air, and there's a moment when the sun burns their outlines against the red canyon beyond before they drop like stones.

20

OWEN BENNET

As it turns out, when you decide to follow crows, you end up in the deep desert. And I mean considerably far out. We're on a swath of land that the BIA map colors a weak lime green, where no designated towns exist for ten or so miles in any direction, with no named roads to speak of. We're following a two-rut path that I would likely have lost five miles back if not for the crows.

These blessed corvids are the one constant here. Over a hundred of them are alighting in batches alongside us like a moving blanket in the air. The BIA map is in the back seat, next to my sleeping daughter. I'm traveling by crow now.

My daughter is quite the trooper when it comes to the rattle of desert driving. My back is about slaughtered, but she's sleeping like a rock, her little hands curled around that feather.

I can't help but think of names. Names are a nice dose of reality in all this, a sign that we'll go on. Or some of us will, at least. Maybe we name her Feather. *Feather Bennet? Will that work in high school?*

I know it's ridiculous, but the girl has to have a name. She can't be "Baby" her whole life. It doesn't show well on a resume.

This isn't to say she has to be a Bennet. She could easily be an Adams. Caroline and I aren't legally married. Neither has taken the other's name. Maybe she'll hyphenate all of it, and she can be Feather Bennet-Adams.

Yikes. I've got to find Caroline. There cannot be a world in which I even consider naming this child Feather Bennet-Adams. That's the kind of thing that happens when men are left alone for too long.

I'm thinking of how best to not hamstring my child with a terrible name when I realize I've outrun the crows. I've gotten so used to them flitting ahead, little black feathers falling down in the distance like tumbleweeds, that I somehow missed when they dropped off.

I punch the brakes. The spreading light serves only to show how empty the desert is, how cold and bruised with shadows. Without the crows, I'm lost.

I throw my hand over the passenger's seat and look back and let out a breath. There they are, all of them, like a black puddle in the road. They shift and hop, mercurial in their direction. Some move toward the flats. Others sluice toward the bushes and brush.

I grab my totem on instinct. One touch tells me it's still broken, disconnected, bricked. *And why was I trying to grab it anyway? To run?* I can't go anywhere she can't go, and she can only go places in her car seat. Even if the totems came to life again, I wouldn't dare carry her across the thin space. I can barely carry my physician's bag. Hell, if I'm being honest, I can barely carry myself.

I throw the truck into park and step out.

The crows have reached a quorum and moved decidedly toward a painfully thick patch of mesquite bushes on the shoulder of the road.

"Shit," I say. A quick look shows the baby is awake. I find my child seems to be awake most of the time I cuss. I'm not quite sure how that works.

I let out an enormous breath that's mostly a sigh and partly the kind of exhale you let out when you're about to lift something heavy. Either physically or mentally or spiritually.

Leaving Grant's truck is so counterintuitive to my sense of self-preservation that it's physically painful. I get twitchy fingers over the keys and a pinch of the nerve between my shoulder and neck. I'm very close to just firing up the engine again and finding another way, any other way. I almost do, but then my child starts crying.

Probably, she's hungry. I've lost track of time. *It's morning, but of what day? What year? What lifetime?* I rummage in the fire drill bag for another puree pouch. I'm pretty sure there's a strawberry one in here. You have to space out the spinach if you can. I'm not trying to create a Popeye child.

A crow call thrashes against the silence of the morning, three times, and something thunks against the roof of the truck. I would say it was an acorn, but we're under endless sky.

Whatever hit us rolls down the windshield and rests against the wiper.

She's really crying now. She's tired, needs a change, needs food, needs to be held, needs a mom, needs all these things. But I can't help but also think it's because the crows want us to do some bushwhacking and we're still hanging out here in the truck.

"Fine," I say. "Perfectly good truck. Loads of gas. Jugs of water in the back. Could probably get us all the way to the Colorado border if it had to. But let's go ahead and leave it here in the middle of nowhere, shall we?"

I flick the key and shut off the engine before I can think otherwise. The silence of the desert expanse hits me like vertigo, and I have to steady myself against the door for a second before I can reach in the back for the baby carrier. She's still crying as I clip it around myself, but at least she's appraising me while she's crying.

"What?" I ask. "You think I'm lugging that car seat around? No way, sister. You're about to get strapped to Dad for the long haul here. Great primate style. Are you prepared for this?"

I pick her up and flip her face-forward and strap her in the baby carrier on my front. She carries that feather the whole time in one hand and has as tight a grip on her mush pouch with the other. "You're my second set of eyes now, okay? My tummy eyes."

She seems to take this quite seriously because the crying stops. Either that or it's because she's become a completely immobilized starfish.

She slams the pouch to her face and starts eating again and eyes the crow-spotted overgrowth in front of us like it's dripping with chocolate or lit up with balloons or whatever little brains like hers like. Black wingbeats flutter beyond with the sound of falling paper.

I grab the fire drill bag and grab a gallon of water from a side compartment. "Your big brother is a pretty smart guy," I say. "I'd like to think I taught him that—the whole preparedness thing—but it was your mom who did that.

The older I get, the more I realize I'm the one that usually ends up winging it in this family. I just dress in collared shirts and have an MD after my legal name, so people seem to think otherwise."

I shoulder the bag and shuffle my grip on the water to shut the door. I lock it with a beep and set off toward the crows, but I only get a few steps before I pause, backtrack, and walk around the front of the truck. I dig under the wiper until I find it: a dirty penny.

I know the adage says these things are good luck, but I chuck it on reflex without really knowing why.

The baby surfs high and dry while I push through mesquite and creosote up to my waist, ignoring the ripping sounds my slacks make when one of the more persistent clumps snags at my right pocket. I check to make sure I still have my totem and push forward.

On the other side, I find the crows. Half of them are doing a strange back-and-forth hop that has undertones of *It's about damn time.* The flock smells a bit like wet dirt.

"I had to pack up the baby," I say before I realize I'm talking to a murder of crows. "It always takes more time than you think," I add anyway.

The crows do not deign to respond. The vanguard at the far end takes flight shortly after they see us, shooting forward over lumpy desert and through a ragged little valley into the wide sky beyond.

I look down at her, but she's watching the crows, so I set aside my screaming disbelief and start walking.

I CAN'T SAY how long we've been on foot—enough time to get completely lost, that's for sure. I'm sweating like a pig and covered in bits of foliage. The only thing keeping me moving is the fact that the crows are running ahead in little formations that make it very hard to believe I should be doing anything other than going where they lead. That, and every time I stop for any extended period of time, the girl starts crying.

I exit this latest canyon and can finally see where they're leading us, a huge stretch of flood-carved washout packed tight with overgrown creosote and mesquite bushes.

"Seriously?" I ask.

The crows slalom and wheel around and among the dense thickets like pros, but I see in an instant it's going to be a different story for the two of us.

I look down at my daughter. "They can go high, but you and me are going to have to go low. Okay?"

She looks up at me and waves the feather, yawning.

"Okay," I say rubbing my palms on my slacks. "I guess we're doing this."

I take a breath and press her to my chest as softly and firmly as I can, making sure my arm covers her face, and I duck low. I have no cogent plan except to follow the pockets of light. She doesn't complain, but my back does. I try to focus on the paper flutter of the crows and not the sound of the thicket absolutely destroying the sleeves of my last good oxford. It gets to the point where I think, *Fuck it. Just take the shirt.* And just when I think I'm about to slip a disc, we push through to flat desert. I stumble to my knees then turn and fall on my ass.

The girl sneezes, face to the sky.

"We're okay," I say, breathless. "I'm okay. You're okay." I pull her little pink unicorn water bottle from the side pouch of the fire drill bag and take a hefty slug from its chewed-up straw before putting it in front of her face. She drinks a good half of it while I look around to figure out what fresh hell we've found ourselves in this time.

We're in some sort of inset clearing a good fifty yards in diameter, maybe more. It's basically a flat ring in the middle of overgrown desert, with a haphazard boulder formation right at the center. Big rocks, each the size of a sedan, lean against one another like a badly built campfire to form a small cave entrance. The whole place has an abandoned-fort feel, complete with a Stay Out sign nailed right into the nearest rock with a railroad spike.

This is no kids scrawl, though, nothing like the No Girls Allowed signs we used to make when we would pull together the fallen logs in the fairy circles back in the woods of the Concorde estate when I was a kid.

This has an official air. I manage to get to my feet and take a closer look.

WARNING

FALLOUT AREA

NO TRESSPASSING

I go cold.

I look at the crows, hopping back and forth and flying across this dead spot like it's one big party. "What have you done?" I ask them.

I know about these places, mostly because I know what they've done to the people who come from out here. I've treated them on the oncology floor at ABQ General.

The quick and dirty is this: Nevada, right next door, is where nuclear weapons were born. The government blew up damn near a thousand nuclear weapons in Nye County, just testing. The fallout coated the south of

Arizona and a good swath of New Mexico like sticky pollen, especially around a few areas of the desert that happened to be in unfortunate weather patterns. I'd like to think the government didn't know that the Navajo that called this area home would be coated. But the longer I live here, the harder that is to believe.

Radiation is a generational poison. It doesn't go away. At the clinic, we put notes on their records that say "downwinder." These are the patients that come in with striated thyroids and lung cancer in their fifties and even forties. When we see anomalies like this, the first question we ask is if they're in downwinder territory.

The worst are the kids. Childhood leukemia isn't a common thing on the reservation except when it is. And when it is, it's because they're downwinders.

The sign is old, rusted. It looks like it was hung here to absolve someone somewhere of legal culpability decades ago. I'm fairly certain they don't test nuclear weapons here any longer, but when you're in the middle of the desert, on the run from things you don't understand, a certain anxiety takes hold. The radiation is probably in the dirt, in the stunted growth of the bushes. It's likely baked into the rocks.

I'm sweating profusely, and that sweat is stinging my striated face and hands. My daughter feels like she weighs about fifty pounds at the moment. Hot zone or not, I'm about to collapse.

The crows got us this far, and I don't think they did it to leave us for dead at a radioactive Stonehenge. Plus, there's shade under there, and I would bet at this point I'm tomato red.

"Okay, a quick break, in and out," I tell her, as if it's somehow safer beyond the bushes on the other side than it is where we're standing. I'm fairly sure fallout doesn't work like that.

I take a seat against one side of a wide, flat boulder. The sun is high in the sky now, but inside this place, the morning rays are sapped of their warmth. The rocks hold onto the night chill.

"Might as well get you changed, huh?" I tell her, and I rummage through the fire drill bag to gear up.

When I'm halfway through and she's still on her back, kicking indiscriminately at the air, I hear what sounds like a tree falling in the distance. She notices it too and stills. The crows turn toward the sound as one. Whatever it is, it's coming up via our approach.

The silence after the sound is a heavy thing. I finish dressing her and pack everything up like I'm doing field work on the front lines in the dead of night. Even the sound of snapping her onesie back up makes me wince.

Nearer now, I hear a tree limb stretching past the point of recovery. Then a series of small cracks, one after the other, followed by a big one, much closer. A smattering of crows alight from the other side of the overgrowth, flying in dead silence, until one flares out like it's been hit by birdshot and wheels to the ground. The others explode in a series of *caws* that rattles the dirt, and another handful take off after the first, swerving this way and that to avoid getting hit by whatever is peppering the sky.

More crows are struck down. A few of them land on our side of the brush wall, twitching. The shots that miss the birds hit the dirt one after the other, *piff piff piff*, kicking up sand in a line five feet from us. I cover the girl and squint through the dust, scooting to grab the nearest.

More dirty pennies.

All pennies smell a bit like blood to my mind, but

these smell particularly of blood, and they leave a tacky smudge on my fingers that very likely *is* blood.

I show my child like I might somehow be able to hash this out with her, but she's watching the crows chitter to each other. I strain to catch a different, darker sound on the other side of the brush. It reminds me of the half-strangled breathing of a big dog straining against its leash.

Bushes crack and snap. The wall we squeezed through is slowly trampled down by big boots. The rangy canopy above shudders.

I drop the penny and push back to the rock with my child. The crows sluice in to fill the space I left. Their message is clear: *Get behind us.*

I hold her tight and look for any way out of this place. I can't conceivably push through the brush on the far end in time. I'll get mired there and mowed down by this thing like a grunt soldier stuck in barbed wire. And even if I do push through with her, we'll be rewarded with miles and miles of open desert. Only a matter of time before we're run down again.

That leaves these rocks. The opening they make looks like it can accommodate us if I get creative. It's perhaps not the smartest of plans, I know, but I saw the size of the thing chasing us, and I doubt very seriously it will be able to follow. At the very least, I can buy us some time. Time for what, exactly, I don't know. But time is time.

"In we go," I whisper before I can logic my way out of it.

I duck through the cave opening easily enough, holding her to my chest. But once I'm inside and under these huge rocks, the space gets tight very quickly. Light cuts through in little patches here and there ahead of us like spotlights, and I think I see a stronger source of light up ahead, but to get there, I'm going to have to crawl. With a child.

Part of me has the madcap idea of sending her off ahead. Maybe now is when she becomes a crawler—I read that children often need forcing functions to hit milestones—but then sanity grabs hold of me again, and I am reminded that this is a cave. Things often live in caves. And even if they don't, there could be a pit or a rockslide of some sort that takes her. The thought makes me clutch her tightly enough that she whines, annoyed at the whole thing.

"I know," I say, trying to soothe her. "I get it. I'm not exactly a cave person either, but we're gonna have to go for it."

She's crying in earnest now, and I hold her tiny body close, legs and arms inside the ride at all times, as I flop over onto my back. My aim is to worm my way through with her on top, a bit like a human log ride. But I make the mistake of looking out the way I pushed in, and I see the giant break through the brush.

He's huge, easily seven feet tall, maybe more, and twice again as wide as me. He wears black canvas pants and black boots that divot the earth as he stomps the last few feet into the clearing with a roar that would scare off a heard of elephants.

The crows don't scatter this time, not even when he throws the limp body of one of their own into their congregation. They just flutter away and settle again, staring at it. When he spits the head of that same crow at his feet, I feel the bile rise in my empty stomach, but they don't make a sound.

"I hate crow meat," he says loudly, his mouth sticky

with blood. "I *hate* it. But I will eat my way through an army of crows if it means I can taste that child."

His eyes are black and piggish, and they track oddly with a type of ocular flutter that makes me think he can't see well, if at all. But his nose is another matter. He sniffs the air like a hound dog. He can smell her—I'm sure of it.

I lean back and start to kick my way deeper into the cave, holding her to my chest. "Don't listen to him," I whisper. "I won't let him get to you."

I say it because that's what you say to a child. I'm saying it to myself too. You can trick your brain that way. Your brain listens even when your heart knows otherwise. Brains are strange like that. What I don't say is *I'll die for you if that's what it takes, but once I do, odds are you won't be far behind.*

By almost every measure, I am a thin man, but this damn hole is going to take all the Houdini I've got. My shoes scrabble on the dirt, and my left shoulder presses hard against rough rock. I hear my shirt rip at the neck, and soon enough, it's stripped to the shoulder, and now the rock is ripping at my skin. I try to gut through it, tears in my eyes that I'd like to say are purely from pain but I've also got frustration like I've never felt, and it piles upon itself when I have to stop, bloodied and exhausted and perhaps a foot farther in than when I started.

I crane my neck back because I know a pocket of open space is back there. We're so close. And so far. My feet still are sticking out of the entrance like I'm the wretched desert equivalent of the Wicked Witch of the East.

My child wails. I angle my neck forward and look back the way we came, helpless to do anything else.

What I see is crows throwing themselves at this monster, one after the next, like a volley of black arrows.

And he's swatting them like a sloppy drunk. He misses most of them, at least at first. They gouge his blind eyes and rip at his already bloody face, but he gets each of them eventually, and when he does, he snaps them in half with his hands and mouth.

The crows are putting up a hell of a fight, but they are no match for this thing. He bleeds but doesn't care. He loses chunks of his face and then a whole ear, but he keeps his slow, growling press. And I can see why.

He holds a glittering black totem in his left hand. Black Bear gives him strength even the crows can't unseat alone.

I try to push deeper again, panicking and fully understanding that I am panicking. But I'm a square peg in a round hole.

I exhaust myself. She rides up and down on my heaving breaths. I put my shaking hand against the back of her head, still soft but damp now from the simple but powerful exertion of just being sad. I watch this thing approaching, and I talk to her.

"I love you, you know," I say. "I don't think I've ever said that. But I do."

Then everything really starts to come out.

"Check that. I *know* I've never said it, and I think it's because some part of me thought you're the reason Caroline is gone. But you're not. Caroline made that choice. And I did as well in my own way. And I'm sorry. I'm so sorry we couldn't see this through together."

I mean this stand under the damn rock of course, as well as this day, but also these past seven months, this journey to find Caroline. This life. All of it.

She cries and clutches her feather. The monster takes another step and another. He's perhaps twenty feet away now, and the crows are fighting but giving up ground, and eventually they stop their kamikaze runs. I don't blame them. Soon enough, the monster has a path.

When he senses the path, he stops. He drops one more poor, broken crow from his hand and takes a deep breath. "You're here," he says, in wonder. "I can... I can almost see you. Soon enough, I will. All it takes is blood."

He pulls a handful of bloody pennies from his pocket and drops them wetly to the sand. "For you."

He takes a crumpled packet of cigarettes from the remains of his shirt pocket and shakes them out, muttering. "For you. The dead crows are yours too. Not much. But soon, there will be more worthy blood—"

It dawns on me that perhaps this conversation is not directed at us, especially when the thing seems struck by a thought that shakes even him. He stares at his totem as if it's the receiving end of a bad phone call, turning it over and over again in his filthy hands. "No," he says quietly. "No, it cannot be."

He snaps his head around to look over his shoulder, back where he stomped his way through. "No!" he roars, hands pulled into fists so tight that they seem to squeeze blood from stone.

He shoots one more furious look our way, spattering blood on the rocks with the sound of rain, before he turns around and shoulders through the break without another word, taking huge steps that eat up the ground.

And then he's gone. And I'm left with is my wailing child and my panicked breaths and what remains of my valiant crow friends.

Something else is here, of course. *Someone* else. That monster stopped talking to me a while ago, and he wasn't talking to himself, either. The crows didn't give up that much ground on purpose. They made way because the game changed. And the game changed because we got a visit from a friend—a friend who landed right at the entrance of this cave and walked his way down the aisle to meet the monster for us.

I can't see him. But I know he's here, just as surely as the crows do. I smile through the sweat and the tears. "Hi, Ben," I say, my mouth dry and gritty. "Boy, am I glad you came by."

21

THE WALKER

I have trouble following soul threads on the move, but Owen and the girl are especially tough. She's a force, that one. I know from experience. I think she picks up on the fact that Owen is trying to hide them from these things prowling the Rez, and she's doing her part. She can make her soul quiet when she wants, and Owen's, too, to hide.

But me and crows, we see eye to eye. And when I see the souls of a hundred crows moving with the discipline of a marching army, I take notice. I drop out of the soul map with my back to a big rock formation, smack dab in the middle of a ring of desert dirt, socked in by the burliest thicket of mesquite bushes I've ever seen.

And here is Yé'iitsoh. The Big Giant. Eater of Men and the most powerful of the Anaye. He comes as a bloodied and inked man bigger even than Danny Ninepoint, but it's Yé'iitsoh, at least while he holds that black bear totem.

A fair number of my crow friends lie at his feet. He's somehow bigger than when we last met. Bloodier. Fat but sunken with hunger, as if consuming this place has revved the dark machine inside of him to want more and more.

He slows when I drop in on the scene, though. Blood drips in two lines from his nostrils over his lips.

These things seem obsessed with me, so I try a command. "Stop," I say.

He does. And I take the time to look around for the whole reason I'm here.

"Owen?" I call out.

Silence, of course. But you never know. A few of the crows at my feet shift to point their beaks directly behind me, and when I turn, I see Owen's fancy leather shoes sticking out from what looks a bit like a stone pizza oven.

"Owen?" I ask.

The big freak is blubbering on again, giving me pennies and shitty cigarettes and promising blood and saying he's *this* close to seeing me in all my glory and all that bullshit, and I want to cut his big black boots right out from under him, but I know I can't hurt him in this world. What I *might* be able to do, though, is get a thought across. *Let's see if you can scent this one, you big freak.*

"Your brother is dead," I say.

This stops the shitty offerings real quick, stops the blubbering, stops it all. Maybe he heard my words, maybe not. Either way, I got the point across. He looks at the black bear totem in his hand like it's burning.

"No," he says. "It can't be."

He turns around and pounds his way out, and I know where he's going—the Arroyo. I don't like it, but one thing at a time.

With Yé'iitsoh gone, the crows start leaving in twos and threes, chatting it up the whole way. I thought I might be able to talk with them for a bit, see what this place they found is all about, but no. Crows are like cats that way. They can save your life one minute and leave you for a ray of sunshine the next.

I'm dealing with a lot of shit at the Arroyo at the moment—it's pulling at me hard—so it's all I can do to just lie down and push myself back to where Owen and the girl are, stuck, breathing hard like foxes caught in a trap.

They can't hear me, but I talk anyway. "He's gone," I say. "It's just the two of you now."

I think she catches some sort of echo of me because her eyes target me hard for about three seconds before floating away. She presses her head back to Owen's chest because that's about all she can do. That's Owen's first problem. He's holding on to this poor girl for dear life.

"Owen, you gotta let her go. No way you're fitting through unless you pencil yourself, buddy. Arms high."

Owen does no such thing. He has no idea I'm even—

"Hi, Ben. Boy, am I glad you came by."

His eyes miss me, but he knows all the same. I easily pass through to the pocket he's working toward and sit back hard on the rock, ass in the mud, barely feeling either. And I smile. "What have you gotten yourself into, Owen Bennet?" I ask the air between us.

We sit for a while like that, and I feel his heart calming as the stillness of the desert comes back. I hear the call of the falcons return above and the low buzz of bugs coming back. A pair of white moths dance just outside the opening.

Owen relaxes enough to let her sit on him, and I'm amazed that she just sits. No squirming, no crying—just sitting.

After another five minutes, he tests the walls with one

arm straight up like a swimmer reaching. Never once does it occur to either of us that he could back out now that Yé'iitsoh is gone. Running from the monster was only half of the battle. The crows led them here because this is where their path lies.

"That's good," I say. "Let her go, just a bit. She'll stay where she is."

I don't know how I know she'll stay where she is except to say that I've been in some trenches with this little one already. Owen eases himself through where his shoulders got bloodied before. She holds on, awake after all. He pushes his other arm up.

His shoulders pass, then his hips. Then he's through, and she's through with him. I laugh because I can't tell who's more surprised to find themselves in here, Owen or her. Both look up at the dappled darkness with wide eyes. To them, this is just a pretty pocket of peace between rocks, but I'm getting a better sense of where we really are. On the living plain, this is downwinder territory, but on the spirit plane, it's something else, something different.

"You with me, Ben?" Owen asks, nervous. "No idea where we're going, but I think there's room for one more. Especially if they're already dead."

I smile again. Two real smiles in one day—no idea when that happened last. It's never exactly been in my skill set, especially recently, but I can't help it. Owen's always been good at gallows humor.

Of course I'm coming.

22

THE WALKER

The tug of the Arroyo becomes too much, so I split myself. Part of me leaves Owen and the girl in the stones, and part of me stays. I do this hundreds of times a minute—part of the job. People keep on dying no matter what happens to the ones you love.

Splitting too many times used to hurt like a bitch—a migraine on steroids. But that was in the early days. Now, it's barely a brain freeze, but that's not a good sign. If you spread yourself too thin in the flow of constant death, you sort of just... lose time. Maybe it's a day. Maybe it's a week. Or maybe more. In my case, it was five years. After I blacked out for five years and came to with all the people I love older and different, it locked a fear in me that no amount of grounding in the Arroyo can put to bed. I could easily lose ten years or a hundred. One day, I could come to and find everyone I know and love is dead.

The worst thing is the only real way to get rid of that fear—to kill that anxiety—is my work, jumping back into the flow. It's cruel that way.

The Arroyo helps too. I've spent a lot of time thinking

about this with a fractured mind, and I've come to see that the Arroyo is my last stand. If the Arroyo falls, I'll lose the last of whatever it is that ties me to this earth. My people are a people of the land. We aren't fucking around when we say that.

I swirl open the map and drop a good fifteen feet until I land like a rag doll on top of a rusted-out car, and not just any rusted out car. I recognize the big dent on the front right just above the gaping hole that was the windshield. This is the old flatbed Ford that's been anchoring the base of the Arroyo canyon since I was a kid.

I'm at the bottom of the Arroyo. I shade my eyes and find the lip above. Dust floats so thick in the sunbeams that I feel I could climb up the lines of light like a ladder. The veil hovers above me, waiting as I pick myself up, stand, and shake myself off.

"A warning about the drop would have been nice," I say.

It flutters in response.

A hand slams on the hood from below and scares the shit out of me. It's tattooed, scarred, missing nails on the thumb and pinkie. The rest of him follows. Blood Eyes. But he's not a monster anymore. He's just a man. He pulls himself up to the flatbed and flops down, rolling over, looking up at the veil, and at me.

"You who I think you are?" he asks in Spanish.

I nod.

He looks at his hands, shaking now. He looks down over the truck to where his body lies broken by the rocks of the desert. I have half a mind to try and break him again. But what's done is done. You can't break a man twice. And from the looks of that shattered chunk of obsidian now stuck halfway through his head, whatever hold Black Bear had over him is gone. All that he's left with is himself, which looks torture enough.

"It wasn't supposed to be like this," he says.

"It is what it is," I say.

He grabs me by the leg. "Santa Muerte, I've prayed to you—"

I try to shake him off. "Stop it. Let go."

"All the blood was for you!" he says.

I yank my leg free and kick his supplicating ass flat on the truck bed.

He looks up at me, eyes pleading. His hands reach for the tattered cuffs of my pants. The whole thing makes me sick.

"I'm not who you think I am," I manage to say, my voice thick when I'm trying to be all bravado.

He shakes his head. "But you are. You are *Death*! Bless me. Bless me!"

Enough of this. I look up at the veil. It knows what to do. On cue, it sweeps in, and not fast, either. This is the low, slow terror edition of the veil. *This man wants death? Well, now he's got it.*

"You know what *I* think? I think you backed the wrong horse, shithead."

He screams. Screams hard. It's the kind of scream that I know for a fact the body can hold in the lungs until the doomsday button is hit. The *last* scream. The veil slurps him up before he gets it all out.

One down.

I hear more shuffling, more movement in the shadows at the base of the canyon.

"Where is he?" Hosteen asks, pulling himself to standing by the rusty runner of the truck, fists still at the ready.

My day just got a whole hell of a lot harder.

Hosteen Bodrey was always so full of fury, but it's clean now, and it's amazing how different clean fury burns. "I dragged that fucker off a cliff," he says. "I'll drag him all the way to hell if that's what it takes."

I clear my throat. "He's gone, Hos."

I really don't want him to hear me, but he does. I can tell because he stops all his bluster, stops everything. He turns around and looks at me with clear eyes.

"Gone, huh?" he says. I nod and point at the body, speared through with the totem that brought him such power.

Hos takes one look and spits at it. Then he sighs. "And I can see you again. Which means..."

"It means you're gone too," I say.

I point behind him. I've been doing way too much pointing recently. Maybe there's something to all those old wives' tales of the grim reaper with the bony finger. But the truth is the newly dead seem to see everything but their own bodies. They need help that way.

Hos's is right behind him, beautifully painted in warrior ash, strong and young and fierce. And with his neck broken in at least three places.

A noise comes from up top, a scream I know all too well. It can come out of a million different mouths, but it somehow sounds the same. This one is Kai Bodrey, understanding what happened to her brother.

We both look up top as Grant tries and fails to keep her from turning herself ass-first over the lip and sliding down ugly and dirty, nicking her arms, her face, her chest. She bangs up her knees as she scrabbles in a half-fall down the face of the canyon, all thirty feet of it. She scrambles around the rusted flatbed Ford and falls to her knees at the body of her brother.

She screams that scream again.

"C'mon now, Kai," Hos says, and he gets his first lesson that Kai is beyond him now when he tries to put a hand on her shoulder and it passes right through.

To his credit, he looks at his hand for only a few seconds then stands back. He gets it a lot quicker than most.

"Shit," he says.

"I'm sorry, Hos," I say, remembering how this man helped his own ragtag clan from Dark Sky's prison back up to the land of the living. He's one of very few who have seen the shores of the dead and walked away. But that was then.

"Ain't no walking back from this one," I say softly.

He nods slowly, watching his sister, then rolls his shoulders and neck. "Weird. Don't feel all that different, you know? Bein' dead. It's like alive but... lighter."

"It can feel that way, if you do it right," I say, looking up at the veil. It's giving us a bit of time, which it doesn't have to do. I give it a nod of thanks. The thing can be a wet blanket sometimes, but other times, it's almost like a friend.

Hos is looking at his sister crying over his dead body, with a type of sad resignation I've never seen from him. His fingers twitch. I know he wants to be down on his knees crying with her, but he also knows his time on this dirt is done.

"How do you know if you did it right?" he asks, clearing his throat then wiping his eyes. He looks at his hands strangely when he finds no tears. Tears are for the living. "I ain't never done anything right," he adds, quietly.

I suck at my teeth. "I've brought more people through that veil than I will ever know or remember. Hard to say in death how well a life was lived. But I do know this. People don't cry like that over a bad man."

Kai is burying her face in her brother's chest, wrapping her arms around him, lifting up his limp body and holding him and shaking them both with her grief.

It's good for him to see, but the veil is moving in.

I clear my throat. "Hos, you might have come into this Arroyo a fuckup, but you're walking out a warrior. And you should be proud."

Hos shakes his head at that. "It's funny," he says. "Being a warrior used to mean everything to me. But in the end, all I wanted was to be a good brother."

He turns back to Kai one more time, and his face softens to something as close to happiness as I've ever seen on him. "Hágóónee', little sister," he says. "See you on the other side, in good time."

The veil comes down, but not like it did for Blood Eyes. This time, it comes in like a friend holding out a coat, waiting for you to shrug in. Hos looks at it without fear before he looks at me. "I'm done," he says, "But this ain't, and you know it."

"I know it."

"Good. Kick his ass, Walker."

Hosteen Bodrey steps forward and through and ends his time on this earth. Another Arroyo son gone. A warrior and brother both.

23

CAROLINE ADAMS

Black Bear is asleep on the couch he hate-gifted me. I didn't think dead men slept, even stubborn dead men who won't go away even though they've *way* overstayed the party. But he does.

Well, maybe *sleep* is the wrong word. He gets like this sometimes. After stumbling around like a drunk, his eyes pinpricks, he sort of... nods off. Sometimes, he conks out at the card table, head down like a child falling asleep in spaghetti. But recently, it's the couch. If I'm lucky, he even closes his eyes first. This time, I'm lucky.

He's been a busy boy. He was all the way down the hall in the third room for long enough that I started to get creeped out. Then he was in Sara's room right after, and I heard her quiet cries. I've got a pretty good idea of what happened. He dug out memories from these women. Special ones, and he main veined them, and now, he's absolutely stoned. Out of his mind high.

I've had what feels like ten lifetimes to think over what Sara told me, how memories are money here, for us. For him, they're drugs. He's time hopping, doped up on a joyride through the most meaningful parts of a life that isn't his.

And yes, I'm still in that awful midfall, facedown next to his feet on this disgusting frat couch. He froze me like this when he yanked the totem from my hand and threw me here.

That's how Sara finds me. This time, he left the totem with her before blacking out. I hear the patter of her feet and catch her out of the corner of my eye, but then she sees Black Bear, his eyes rolling behind closed lids, mouth open, tongue twitching like he's licking something in his dreams.

She freezes, mouths *sorry*, and backs away.

I scream inside, not because I'm angry but because I'm scared and cramped. My soul has been jammed in the middle seat of the longest flight of my life, way in the back, by the toilets, between two fat guys.

And I can't even blame her. If I was Sara and Black Bear was like this and I got left with the totem, I'd do two things: first, I'd really test this theory that we have nowhere to run. And if it's true and we're really trapped here, I'd spend the rest of my time doing yoga, just moving. And I don't even like yoga.

I expect Sara to go out the front door or maybe go into her own room, but I have enough of an angle down the hallway to see that she does neither. Instead, she walks down the hall to the third door and steels herself before she opens it. She has to force herself to look, and when she does, something terrible flashes across her face, and she runs inside, well out of view. I catch low murmuring, a voice I can't make out, speaking quick and quiet. A humming sound that takes me a moment to figure out is someone crying and doing their best to keep it behind closed lips.

Then Sara's back in the hallway, slowly closing the door.

She was the one crying. Tears don't seem to flow right out here, but the eyes don't lie. Neither does her smoke. She looks at me, lips pressed thin, threatening to break. Her hand tremors on the flat wood of her door, but she stays there in the hall, caught by her thoughts.

I know that look. That is the look of someone who's seen way too much of her room. She stares at it the way I used to stare at the hospital beds with the blinking blue lights above them. Back then, I was new to the constant low-grade panic of an oncology ward, and I hadn't learned to pause my brain when the code bell rang. I got caught a lot by my own thoughts.

Sara shakes herself free of whatever hangs on her and looks at me with a new clarity. She tiptoes into my room, past the sleeping bear, completely silent in a way that seems practiced, and when she kneels down to me, she puts her lips an inch from my ear and says, "Go into her room. There's no saving her now. He took her last memory, the one she held tight. Ask her about it. Find a way."

She looks at the totem and at Black Bear breathing too deep for any living thing. Her fear is written plainly in her smoke. Disbelief, too, about what she's about to do. "Then come back for me," she whispers, as she presses the totem into my hand.

My arched back eases, my corded neck sags, and I flop to the floor, breathing like I've run a marathon. Sara is on one knee, hand out like she's calling a woodland creature to her.

"Thank you," I say. I can't say I'll be back. I don't trust myself to do it, don't know if it'll sound like a lie coming out. I don't even trust myself not to pick up the stained card table from this fake set of what he thinks my life is and bash his head as many times as I can with it before he gets up.

Sure, I would be frozen for life in some horrible position. But at least I would have that memory to salt lick while I'm in my own head for the rest of my life. I'm pretty sure it would last me for a while.

But that's not why Sara gave me the totem. That's not why she's risking so much, frozen feet from where Black Bear sleeps.

I ease my way out of my middle seat from hell and soft step my way down the dirty plank flooring. Sara made this look easy. I feel like every step I take sounds like a tap-dancing cow.

I'm past the couch and out of the room. The front door still calls me, but the longer I'm trapped here, the more I believe that if there was a way to run, these women would have found it.

The third door is half open already. All I have to do is slip inside.

This room is from way back, so primitive it has no real clues to date it. The floor is dirt. Tattered buckskin nailed to the walls sheds little hairs that float everywhere. Fetishes hang from the ceiling on lines of sinew—balls of wrapped twigs, bones, and pieces of driftwood. Painted animal skulls spin from twine, their fallen teeth scattered about below them.

A young woman lies on a pile of straw topped with more dried buckskins. Her eyes are closed, but her left hand is out in that same *take it* gesture Sara has. They spoke before she gave the totem back.

I don't know what else to do but slip the totem into her hand, and when I do, she opens her eyes, but I know in an instant that she can't see me. The color has been leached from them, along with almost all her smoke.

She reaches for me blindly, finds my hand, then slowly moves to my face, marking my nose and cheeks and hair with the barest touch. "Another woman?" she asks, soft and sad. She isn't speaking English, but that doesn't seem to matter in this place. I can understand her anyway, the same as Sara, the same as Black Bear. I feel like I should introduce myself, but she's got the totem now. The power to move is hers alone although I doubt she's ever getting up off this bed again. She keeps the totem close to my hand like she doesn't even trust herself to hold it for long.

She lets out a small breath that somehow feels like a good half of what she's got left. "Sara sent you, didn't she? I already gave him the memory. I held it so long I can feel the place it lived inside, the shape it made. Echoes of it. But..." Her eyes shimmer, growing whiter by the moment. "But it's gone. I have nothing to tell."

She presses the totem back to me and freezes.

I sit on the floor with a huff, gripping the totem fast and hating the feel of it. Her eyes are locked on mine, and I hold their gaze. I could get up. I could go back to Sara, pass the baton, and assume the position on my shelf. But that's how I tread water here, not how I swim, and I can't tread water until Black Bear bleaches me too. I scoot forward. "How about this, then? How about you think of that place where he took it from, the shape of the hole it left behind, and you tell me anything that comes to your mind. Everyone has something to tell, even if it's just your name."

I press the totem back into her hands. They have almost no weight to them. I keep expecting the totem to drop right through, which would be bad news for all of us. But again, she hangs on.

"Stubborn," she says, with the barest echo of a smile. "Just like her. Just like me. I think that's how he likes his women. Because stubborn is strong."

She watches me, then her eyes relax, and I feel that she's trying, trying to feel the shape of what she's lost. She purses her lips and blinks her milky eyes. Above us, the strange fetishes spin in unseen air, and another tooth drops with a clatter that would make me twitch if I could move.

"I think of a brown bear," she says.

Okaaay. I'm not a huge fan of bears at the moment, but at least that's something I can work with.

"We have a story, our people. About Coyote's wife. Did you know Coyote had a wife?"

I know a few things about Coyote that I'm not thrilled about. He's a bit of an asshole, to say the least. But if living on the Rez has taught me anything over these past years, it's that there's always another side of the story.

"She came from a family with twelve boys. Just her and twelve boys."

That poor woman, I think.

"Twelve boys, and they never loved her because she was a powerful woman. More powerful than they. How could she not be, to love Coyote?"

"Her twelve brothers took Coyote hunting once, and they lost him in the valley where the spider people and the otter people lived. Coyote, being Coyote, threw one too many taunts, and the spider people trapped him while the otter people skinned him in strips. He howled in pain, but the brothers didn't hear. When they came home without him and his wife asked where he was, they didn't seem much concerned. 'Dead, for all we care,' they said."

"While they slept, she paced, for she truly loved Coyote. And her brothers infuriated her with their petty jealousy. So she left their lodge, only she was followed. The youngest brother snuck his way to where she went, and there he saw the truth. As she paced each of the four directions in her worry, she began to change. Her nose turned into a snout. Her shoulders popped, and her arms and legs filled and stamped. She grew coarse hair all over, and her teeth spiked and gnashed. She had become a brown bear, the very same that they used to run from."

"The youngest brother ran back to tell his worthless kin, and all watched as she huffed her way down the trail to the canyon where the spider people and the otter people lived."

Tell me she kicked their asses, I think. *Tell me she toilet wrenched all of them.*

"Coyote's wife got her revenge," she says. "She started way back, with the first people to hurt her husband. And she worked her way forward, destroying them one after the other. In the morning, she would stumble back to camp, bloody, and transform back into a woman, pulling arrowheads from her body and magicking the wounds closed. And every time, it drained her. But every time, she went back. She would not stop until all who dared strike her husband were dead. By the time she came after the otter people, they were so afraid of her they jumped into the water, where they would live forever."

"Last of all, she tracked down her own brothers, lured them to her, promising to live once again as sister with them, combing their hair and lulling them until she devoured them. Only the last brother was strong enough to withstand her, striking her down."

She settles, drops her chin to the hollow of her shoulder, but she holds the totem strong. I get the feeling she's been well trained. If there's such a thing as muscle memory even into death, a woman trapped here for hundreds of years would have it with this godforsaken totem.

"I always hated that part," she whispers, "the way that shifty spy of a brother struck me down. In my mind, the story stops before that."

Even though I'm frozen, some part of me must get the mouth drop across.

Her laugh sounds like it's coming from behind a door down a long hall. "Am I Coyote's wife? Maybe. Maybe not. I cannot remember any longer. But I feel that story is true. It feels right. I believe I fought for my husband like Brown Bear did, once. Coyote or no. I bled. I healed. And I revenged. The details of it are *his* now. But the shape of it is still mine."

She looks at me with all she's got left and holds my frozen cheeks in her hands. "You were right about the shape. Maybe you will survive this place. If you do, take Sara with you. I have nothing left."

She's drifting away, her hand weightless. I can see the words take the last of her smoke as she speaks. She places the totem in my hand, and the feeling passes back.

"Your name," I gasp. "Please. Please, tell me your name."

I shove the totem back, and her failing eyes open a sliver more. "Tábaahá," she says. "My name is Tábaahá."

Water's edge in Navajo. She's named after the shore. And that breaks my heart.

She pushes the totem away, and I grab it back. That push was a final push. Whatever may come, Tábaahá never wants to hold this thing ever again, never wants to move on someone else's account, and I get that.

"Thank you," I say although I doubt she hears it. I hope she doesn't. I hope wherever she is, it's a place where she can't see or hear any of this.

On the slow creep back, I run over every word she said. What matters isn't if she was *the* Brown Bear or if her husband was *the* Coyote. Her memory was powerful anyway, powerful enough that she held that story together even when all else was gone. Whatever memory Black Bear took, he got absolutely smashed off it. When I pass him, he's still drooling, eyes closed, licking air. It was that good.

The question is why.

And I have some ideas.

I pass the front door without a second thought this time. That way is not the way.

I return to Sara, where she kneels in my place. As stoned as Black Bear is, I doubt he'll remember how I looked, but I know now I have to be careful, very careful with what I say and also with what I think. Any and all of it could get snatched from me in a moment.

I put my lips to Sara's ear and whisper, "I have ideas. But I don't want to say them yet. I hope you understand."

I press the totem to her hand and feel my muscles seize up, feel the flash freeze hit me.

Sara stands, totem in hand. She nods. She understands. She's been in this prison a long time, but I see something in her eyes now that wasn't there the first time we spoke. I see a spark of new color, low and quiet at the riverbed of what remains of the smoke that flows from her.

I know that spark because I have it too.

It's the color of hope.

24

GRANT ROMER

Kai damn near broke her arm getting down to her brother's body. I think she'd have liked to shatter on the floor of the Arroyo, completely, just like the rocks that blow themselves to pieces once they get shook loose. I follow her, slidin' on dirt like mine cuttings, slowin' myself a lot more than she did, and I still hit the top of the rusted old Ford pretty hard.

She hops to the ground, groaning, but not because of the pain. Her arm got lucky, but her soul broke when she saw her brother like he is. She's kneeling and looking at him like there must be some sort of mistake. I remember doing that with Pap when he got killed. Something about losing such a huge part of you just don't compute right.

"Kai," I say, my hand fluttering in the in-between of touching her shoulder and lettin' her scream.

She hugs him and lies down next to him and buries her head in his arm and quakes with silent sobs as Chaco floats down. I hold out my arm for a spot for him to land.

My bird is haggard and angry. I can sense it in the way he's trying to shield his thoughts, and I can see it in the way he's still moving his neck feathers about after he got slammed to the ground by this thing. I'm haggard too. The only thing keeping me upright is how his soft weight on my shoulder somehow makes the sum total of all this shit bearable.

"You took a bad right hook," I say to him.

Chaco tests his wing again then looks down at the broken body of the fallen monster.

"So did he," Chaco says with a sharp snap of his beak.

The bell swells, and my throat stings with acid burn. I find I'm suddenly on one knee next to Kai although I ain't quite sure how I got there.

"Hos is leaving," Chaco says, by which he means Hos's soul. "It'll be over in a minute."

I know it will be, but it's another death, another poison coat glossed over the silver of this thing around my neck. I hold the clapper tight and breathe, trying not to look like a guy about to puke while his girlfriend is the one in real pain.

I can't even tell Ben to tell Hos thanks. I'm too busy holding the bell together. It stings all the way up my arm and settles in that pit behind my shoulder blade like a needle.

"He's gone," Chaco says. "He went out in strength. And in thanks."

The bell loses that intense burn and settles into the place on my chest where it sleeps. Or where it used to sleep. More and more these days, I wonder if it isn't sort of always on. A diesel engine on idle—suckin' just a little juice from my soul at all times, to stay ready.

Chaco flutters to the ground and bob-walks his way over to Kai, coming the long way around Hos's body so she can see him, and when she reaches out to him, he walks right over to her and nudges her, a gentle touch that maybe I coulda given if I could breathe right. And it resets her a bit.

Chaco knows my thoughts. "Go easy on yourself," he says.

My thoughts shoot back hotter than I'd like. "No goin' easy with this fuckin' thing on me, and you know it."

I expect him to chirp back. The bell is his charge too, after all. It has been for a hell of a lot longer than I've walked this earth. But all he does is nudge his smooth beak against Kai's splayed hand and say, "I know it."

She pulls her hands out from under her brother with such tender care that he barely moves against the dirt. She looks up at me, and her face catches every shadow, like the light can't reach it. Tears cut the Arroyo dirt on her cheeks.

"My brother's dead," she says.

And that's about all that needs sayin'.

THE SMOKER ROUNDS UP A WHEELBARROW, and Sani Yokana rolls out a line from the winch on his Bronco. We loop it twice at the head and foot of the wheelbarrow, and together we place Hos's body inside.

Ain't pretty. But Hos would understand.

Chaco perches on the handle by Hos's head. Kai guides it up from the base of the canyon. The two of us watch it all the way up, blinking away the falling dirt and grit.

"She's not doing so hot," Chaco says, talkin' about Kai.

"No shit. That makes two of us."

"She's the last of her blood on this earth now. That's a tough pill."

"I got no idea what to do to help her."

"Let her lead," Chaco says. "Just hold her hand, and let her lead. She's walking a dark valley."

So I do. I don't say anything, not that I'd have a thing to say that would matter now. When Pap died, I blacked out most everything. As I look back on it now, it's a big nothing. I know I knew more once, but brains are weird like that.

I see Joey up top, which heartens me. Him and Yokana came out of that death stare lookin' rattled, but they're at least pulled together enough to be gentle with Hos's body when they carry him over the lip.

Now, it's just me and Kai down here.

Kai looks down at the body of the thing Hos killed. She toes the shattered black totem with her boot. When it does nothin' and neither of us feel nothin', she steps back and boots it. Pieces patter off the walls and scatter to nothin'.

She rolls her bum shoulder and starts to climb.

"Kai, maybe we should wait until—"

"Let her lead," Chaco says from somewhere up top.

I drop my hands to my sides and watch her. She picks her line like a pro, of course. I bet this ain't even the first time she's climbed out of this thing. Ten feet up, her right foot slips, but her back tenses like a cat, her shoulders all corded, and she rights herself again.

I start up behind her.

"Don't," she says, placing one hand carefully in a split rock.

"Don't what?" I ask, testing the grips as I go, pulling off scree and chucking it down.

"Don't follow my line. If I fall, I'll hit you."

"You won't fall," I say. She's at twenty feet. I'm ten back now.

She snorts, or maybe it's a sob—hard to tell from down here. Looking up, I can see only her outline in sunlight.

"So sure," she mutters loud enough to hear, even as a clump of the Arroyo wall rolls past me on the right. "What if I do fall?"

"Why the hell you think I'm coming up behind you?"

"I told you not to—

"Kai, if you fall, you better damn well take me with you."

She tenses and holds hard to the wall. I do too. Chaco looks down, quiet.

She's stuck. In the between. I can sense it.

"That's the way this works, Kai," I call up. "It's both of us or none of us."

Another clump of the canyon crumbles over my hat, skittering off my back.

Kai gets unstuck and climbs again.

She's more decisive now, clear in her grips, and I'm not dumb enough to stray from her line. I do the same thing until I see hands grab her and pull her over, then those same hands grab me. Joey and Sani Yokana set us on solid ground.

Hos's body is lying on a cot. Already, the Arroyo folk gather around, prepping him, wrapping him in blankets. The Smoker burns sage and sings under his breath and streams tears, talking to the body like it's all one big mistake. Tellin' him he swore up and down it would be him first to the river. Lookin' back to the twins' hogan like he's lost.

Chaco answers my question before I can ask him. "Tsosi is almost in the Walker's hands," he says, weary. "It's all his brother can do to keep him here."

I look around at this broken place, this canyon that keeps swallowing the people that live here. We're already half as strong, now one more down, and before I can check myself, I say, "He oughta just let the man go. He's gotta be tired. Hell, I'm exhausted from livin' half a lifetime out here. He's been at this fight for at least a couple lifetimes."

I sit down on the dirt and dangle my legs over the edge and watch the sun throw shadows on a people in mourning—again.

The bell itches like something infected under the skin at my neck, but no matter how I shift it around, the thing still weighs the same. "You think you can love a place and hate it at the same time?" I ask Chaco.

He hops up on my shoulder and looks at me. "Sure you can. For me, it's most of this planet. The parts with people, anyway."

I smile, almost laugh, even.

"Buck up, Keeper. The fight is still on. Your dad had a run-in of his own," Chaco says. "With this guy's big brother."

This snaps me back into focus. "What happened? Are they okay?"

"He's with the Walker," Chaco says, then when I feel like pitchin' right back over the edge, he adds real quick, "As a friend! A friend!" Chaco fluffs and bobs. "Sorry. That just came out." He clears his little bird throat with a low roll like coins in a can. "But..."

I wait, wincing. "But what?"

"But I lost him," Chaco says, disappointed in himself. "And the child."

"The hell does that mean? Lost them?"

"I know they're still alive—"

"Shit, they better be!"

"They are! But they're... hidden. I think maybe they've found a thinning. On purpose."

I look at the crow hard. "But *you're* a thinning. Right? I mean, you're the thin places of this world made real."

"I am. But I can't see into them any more than you could take a look at your own brain. I'm too close."

A flash of memory comes back to me: the graveyard where my parents are buried, the main house, a garden where I saw a hand press through the air.

Another memory flashes: the deep desert, where a snake that wasn't a snake came for me. Chaco crushed it. Thinnings, both of them. And none too friendly.

"Why would Dad want to get lost in a thinning?"

Chaco looks at me side-eye. "Because sometimes that's the only way to get where you need to go. The good news is Big Boy didn't get 'em. Bad news is Big Boy knows his brother is dead, he's pissed off, and he's coming this way."

Great. Half my family is lost. The Arroyo is in burial prep for another one of their own. Kai is stone cold with shock. The twins—our last best hope—are too banged up to get out of the hogan. And another one of these things is on the way.

I sure as shit hope my bird knows what he's talking about, sayin' you gotta get lost to get found. Because we're about as lost as you can get.

25

OWEN BENNET

The sunset filters through gaps in the rocks and lies like sleep dust on me and my daughter. She lets the heavy light close her eyes, her little frame rising and falling with soft breaths at twice the rate of mine. Now that I'm through that pinch, there's much more room. And by *much*, I mean it's basically the size of an airplane bathroom. I even pulled the fire drill bag through and managed to change her, which was both a sweaty and smelly affair.

I suppose we could leave the shelter of the rocks. The eater has been gone for a while now, but even if we fought our way back out into the open desert, night would fall too fast for us to get back to the truck, and that's assuming I'm correct in remembering which sand-blown bramble I parked it next to. For tonight, at least, we stay here.

Caroline might call this *nesting*, albeit in a potentially radioactive fairy ring surrounded by strangely cognizant crows—and the corpses of crows. Which is another reason I think we should stay. Maybe the main reason. I'm not exactly what you'd call a sentimentalist. I don't know many in my profession who are. But the way those crows led us, and the way they died for us, it must mean something.

I'm here to find Caroline. That's my assignment. And over the years, I've come to see that crows understand the assignment.

The late afternoon sleep dust wants to take me too, but I have no such luxury. I rub at my face with my free hand and try to think of next steps. The crows are still here, which means the path is still here. This is the extent of the cave formation as far as I can see, and the crows aren't doing their leapfrogging anymore, so if you follow my crow-led logic, that means we are where we're supposed to be, for better or for worse. And yet there is no more path.

"Any ideas, Ben?" I ask. I still smirk even though I know he can't really help me. I bet it's driving him nuts. My daughter opens her eyes and looks to the left again. My eyes scan the same space. I can't see whatever she sees, but I trust she feels something, maybe even sees Ben. Especially in this half-asleep, half-awake state.

"I think she likes you," I say softly, struck by the strange sadness of sitting next to a friend—to another family member, basically—with no real way to carry on a conversation. I want to see him again but am terrified of the day I finally will. And this is but a taste, really, of what is his entire existence now. The want and the fear. It all makes me suddenly and inexplicably lonely.

The crows shuffle outside. They've started bringing berries and twigs to the entrance. One brought a dead mouse, like a cat might leave an offering on the doorstep.

They certainly think this is our new residence. For now, at least.

"Thank you, friends," I whisper, "But we're fine. Really. I think we'll stick to what's left in the fire drill bag for now."

They fly off, but I bet they'll be back with more. I feel like Snow White if she was a goth princess and the seven dwarfs were a hundred carrion-eating crows. As a matter of fact, for someone not from here, not steeped in the dust of this place, this might look a lot like a fairy tale. With a big monster trying to eat us, we run to safety in a metaphorical cave in the woods.

Except it's not. No fairy tales exist in my line of work.

"I know this place, Ben," I say. I can't hear him, but that doesn't mean we can't talk. "Or know of it, anyway. The blown-out sagebrush and creosote patches, overgrown to the point they become nearly impossible to pass through, then all of a sudden, barren ground and dried yellow rock. The sign we saw said as much, but I was busy trying to keep my daughter from being eaten at the time, so I filed it away. We're downwind of the Nevada Test Site, the nuke proving grounds."

The silence is too much, so I just keep talking. "I've treated more downwinders than I can count over my career. Thyroid cancer. Breast cancer. Childhood leukemia. Birth defects. All the uranium mining out here didn't help either, the radioactive tailings they left out like sandbox mud in the sun."

I turn to the side to look at the space where he might be. "I had a girl I helped with a thyroid goiter you wouldn't believe. But I helped her..."

I trail off, lost in thoughts of that bracelet that I once

had, that I gave to Caroline, that my child ended up with, that I lost again while running for our lives. I rub the spot where it was. "Who knows," I say. "Maybe you got caught up in it, too, with the glioblastoma. Hard to say what's circumstantial and what's genetic and what's just shit luck. After a while, it gets opaque."

She stirs on my chest and drops the feather. It floats to the ground like the air is syrup, floating way longer than it should. I can feel her breathing change.

I try to reach for it, but it's awkward. I can get it for her, but it'll take some nifty maneuvering. She's awake now and knows it's not in her hand anymore. I think she's about to let loose a cry like this rock hasn't heard in all its millennia of existence, but the cry never comes. She watches it settle and flutters her little hands and garble talks. Outside, I hear the crows settle too. The rocks get just that much heavier with their expectant weight.

Something strikes me in the settling. A possibility. An opportunity. Caroline talked a lot about thin spaces. We've run into them before, but I never really took note of the difference. I was always in triage mode.

I feel it now, though. Maybe it's just my daughter on my chest or the dead friend at my side. Could be the dappled light filtering through, dancing with desert dust or the crows resting like a blanket up top. But this is one of those thin places.

I'm tempted to think the nukes made it thin. But that gives too much credit to the nukes. If anything, the thinness of this place called the whole atom-splitting Armageddon down upon it. Egg before chicken. My guess is this pile of rocks was thin before humanity was a wink in the eye of the world.

The feather has landed in a strip of light that cuts

through from a crack somewhere way up top, a ray of sunset that fought to get here as hard as we did.

I feel like I should do something, like I should always be doing something, but my daughter just watches the feather. So I take a cue from my daughter, and we watch together.

26

THE WALKER

Owen looks at me and right through me. He needs help, but I don't really know how to help him. I felt the feather hit too. I felt the slow way it smoothed the air as it floated down. I know the girl loves that thing, and I know it comes from Chaco, and it has family magic too. It sat in the headband of Grant's daily beater hat for months.

Chaco's feather was a key before. Even Owen—always Mr. Science despite the fact that we literally wrestled Coyote together—even *he* knows it's a key.

We just don't know where the door is. So in the interim, we've been carrying on a sort of one-sided conversation from two sides, trying to figure out where, exactly, we find ourselves.

"I know about the downwinders," I say to him. "A lot of them ended up calling the Arroyo home. Joey and I used to call 'em cancer campers. We'd tiptoe around their sites because when we were little, we thought it was like a cold you could catch. Stupid kid stuff. But then I went and caught it anyway."

I realize I'm saying this quite clinically, like Owen would. His job was stopping death. Mine is taking over when the docs' races are run. Sorta like a baton pass. We're not so different.

I look around our little den and press my hands into the echoes of the earth here. It gives a little bit, like a sponge. "But I got some theories of my own about this place," I say. "We got a story, one you probably heard here or there, about the Slayer Twins."

The feather seems to test the dirt too, just a little, pushed around by a weird draft dropping in from the holes in the rocks.

"Their names were Monster Slayer and Born for Water, and they kicked ass everywhere they went. You could ask any Navajo kid on the Rez to name one of the old stories, and even the shithead kids who couldn't care less about the Navajo Way would know about the twins because they're everything us punks wanted to be. Powerful. Confident. Winners."

The feather flutters over itself once. I can't feel the breeze, but it wisps the girl's hair as she watches it move. The edges of the fletching dig into the flour-thin spread of dirt between us.

"They helped rid the world of monsters that look a hell of a lot like the ones we're seeing right now. The Slayer Twins stories are like an action movie. Hos knew 'em same as me—he's dead, by the way. You'll find that out if... *when* you get out of this place."

I press my hands to the sides of my head, willing my thoughts from straying even as I get pulled in a thousand directions. The brain freeze settles.

I clear my throat. Owen and the girl keep watching the feather.

"But the part of the Slayer Twins story that people sometimes forget is that between kicking ass, they were lost for a long time. On the run, trying to keep their family safe, they took the path of the gods and got stuck between mountains. No refuge. No life around them. Until just there, in the distance, they spotted a wisp of smoke.

"It was a smoke hole. Underground. A place I bet looked a little bit like this. And inside was Spider Woman, and when they looked down all scared, she looked back up, and her smile was kind."

I smile at the thought, lost in the memory of a story told to me years ago. "I remember the 'kind smile' part the most," I tell him. "I liked to picture it. Them all lost and scared and her smiling, meeting them like a friend, and she said, 'Welcome to my house in the ground.' And she asked them why the hell they thought they could take this path, this rainbow road of the gods. And they had no answer, no real answer until one of them said, 'We're here because we don't know where we *can* go.'"

Owen has a thousand-mile stare, hands rested lightly on his daughter's back. If I squint, I can believe he's hearing all of this.

"And Spider Woman, she says something I always thought was weird but now I think makes some strange sense. She says, 'You may rest here safely, my sons, but first you must tell me who you are and what you are running from.'"

I sit up. "You gettin' any of this, Owen? I think we found our way into Spider Woman's cave, brother. I think we pushed our way in—and I think we can find our way through, too—but first, we gotta come clean. With the world. With each other. About her. We gotta tell Spider Woman who we are and what we're running from."

The feather trembles and digs a little deeper, the quill tracing a fine lie detector-test line through the dust. Owen stares at it quietly, almost as if he's on the verge of sleep himself.

I rub my face. "Ah, forget it. You'd think I'd learn after ten years of talking to air—"

"I don't want to do this anymore," Owen says softly.

I drop my hands to my knees and look at him sideways. "Can you hear me?"

Owen doesn't look my way, doesn't even blink, but he keeps talking.

"I'm tired. Tired of walking worlds to find peace. Tired of waiting for the next mess to come my way. I'm *glad* the crow totems broke. I hope they stay that way. I never wanted the damn thing in the first place, all I wanted was another day next to Caroline, and that's all I want now, and I'm terrified I'm going to have to do all this alone. If that's what I have to do... I'll do it. But I'm not going to like it."

Owen brushes his daughter's hair back softly, barely touching her. "And my daughter is going to know, Ben. She's going to know I don't like it, and she's never going to forgive me."

He's crying without moving, without sound. A little slice of water, barely enough to notice, cuts from the outer edge of his eye down just under his ear and into the dirt next to the feather.

The wind blows, and the quill scratches then stills.

Owen's said his piece. He's quiet now. Outside, one of the crows lets loose with a three-caw blast, and the others shuffle feathers, but afterward, the desert is quiet. The offerings grow, berry by berry and twig by twig.

My turn.

"I think she's close, Owen. Caroline is. But she's on my side. And finding her—seeing her—it scares the shit out of me. I'm terrified I'll find her, and I'm terrified I won't. That I'm chasing another echo. Your life with her, your house on the Rez, that baby girl, I want those things bad. I'm jealous, Owen. It was something I thought I'd beaten, but it won't let me go. I love her. But I love you and Grant and that girl. I love that your life together happened. But at the same time, I wanted it to be me. Can you understand that and not hate me?"

Owen sighs, watching the crow-brought gifts grow. The girl stirs, and her eyes sweep my end of this little cave.

I rub my face. "Doesn't seem fair that I can hear you confess but you can't hear me. I'd be pissed about that if I was you. But you're not me. You just do what has to be done, man. I try to wrap my head around the job I got. I fight it and fight it. You just get your job done. I've always loved that about you. And I promise you, when we meet again, I'll tell you the same. And for the record, I hope that time is a long, long way off."

The wind blows, and the quill scratches and stills.

The girl climbs off Owen, and he props himself up on one shoulder to watch. He's so long that she follows his legs all the way back, basically to the opening, where she stops at the totem pile.

Because that's what it is. It's a totem pile, a goodbye. I would be too scared to touch it, but the girl still has that fearlessness, and she grabs all the things to herself. She pulls them in and does a sloppy pivot then pushes them back toward us. The sticks snag, and the leaves crunch, and the berries roll. None of that seems to bother her. She grabs handfuls of what she can, dirt and sand and all, and pushes them back to the spot between Owen and me.

Then she babbles something neither of us can catch, but the look that follows is clearly one that says, *Dad, get off your ass, and help me pull these things inside.*

Owen gets it, but he's wedged in here like a broom. He tries to catch a few straggling bits of twig and leaf with the toe of one loafer. He scatters the mesquite berries, and I smile at the *Are you serious?* look on the girl's face. She takes matters into her own hands and grabs a second batch, pushing them back on a wave of dirt, losing a few here or there but not caring. She sits and looks at the pile between us.

It's not right. She knows it. I know it.

"The feather," I say. "That's what this pile needs."

She looks at her own hand as if surprised to find it's not there. It's by Owen's shoulder, where it's been writing our stories in the sand. She starts to cry.

"It's right here, honey," Owen says, nodding at it.

The crying stops on a dime. She picks the feather up and puts it down again and shoves the crow gifts over it, burying it. Owen catches a few rolling berries and puts them on top, and the girl looks at it, and still she isn't pleased. She squints, cocks her little head, takes one hand and slams her fist down, scattering all of it.

She starts to cry again. I would too if I were her, halfway here and halfway there, touched by the river so that she can speak, then born into this crazy world mute again. She's expecting to magic a thing that the living world can't give her. The feather smushes, and the shaft of the quill breaks, which makes her sob.

Owen tries to calm her, and it seems like both he and she realize at the same moment that the crows have gone completely silent outside.

The feather sinks.

On my side, from what I see, it sinks. On their side, it's broken, but on my side, it's like whatever essence was in the shaft of the thing lets loose and starts cutting right through the desert floor. Sand follows sand down, down, and the pinpoint spreads until the cave becomes one part of an hourglass that I feel I've seen before.

The thin world trembles, and the dead world cracks, but the living world holds its façade, just like always. Owen is still listening for the crows. But the crows are listening for us now, waiting to see what *we* do.

The weight of the silence tips him off, though.

"Something happened, didn't it?" he asks.

Yeah, I'd say something happened, all right. Something's still happening. The desert is turning to quicksand all around me. Earth made liquid is sucking down through a point about two feet from his face. I push back to keep my footing, no time for smartass retorts.

"Ben, if there's a door, you have to go through it," he says. That stills me.

He reaches out and touches the very solid desert floor on his side of things, and I know in his own way he senses that on my side, it's falling apart. His own daughter did it. Blood talks to blood.

He grabs more sand and lets it sluice through his hands. "Me and her, we've gone as far as we can. The rest is up to you. Find her. And bring her home."

I realize I've been scrabbling back over liquefied sand until I could hear this, until I had this permission. I need this permission because if I find her, it's going to spring wide open a box I've held shut for years.

Not if I find her. *When* I find her.

I have more to say to Owen. I could sit and talk to him

for a lifetime. But once I let the quicksand take me, it takes me whole.

27

GRANT ROMER

Hos's body is covered now. A family blanket swaddles him head to toe. Kai stares at it while Sani Yokana does all the cop work. On paper, he died from a fall, but that's only because the chief ain't about to write "killed by a blood-eyed monster" on his notepad.

We left the shards of broken totem that powered the thing in the bottom of the Arroyo with the rest of the trash.

The twins ain't doing too good. Tsosi can't speak, and Tsasa won't. Tsosi lies still, eyes flicking behind lids like he's going through the pages of his life one last time. His brother sits watch over him, holding his hand at the same time he paints in the dirt by the hogan firelight. The sweat builds and dies and builds again, and he keeps painting the earth. The picture is coming together. It looks like a circular shield, with bolts of lightning and crowned figures in black, perfectly spaced. Intricate arrow designs mark the four corners.

I asked Sani if he thought maybe we should keep the cops here or call more cops in, given what Chaco says is walking our way. But Joey chimed in and said no. He said the cops would only be walking into a slaughter. Firepower won't win this fight, and there ain't enough Navajo cops as it is.

The chief took those words with him on a walk around the Arroyo. We'll see what he does with 'em. A few months ago, he would've had the FBI here by now. But a shitload has happened between now and then, and Sani's seen things. Blood Eyes made him see more things, same as me. He's got to wrestle with that on his own.

This waiting, watching, and mourning weighs on all of us. Joey sits for spells in the hogan, lending his voice to the sweat song, but he can't sit still for long, and neither can I. When we aren't with Maria trying to keep everyone fed, we're walking the tents and campers, stayin' busy with odd jobs and tellin' folks to keep an eye out.

They get it without really havin' to be told. They're Arroyo folk, after all.

Chaco circles high above, a black dart in a darkening sky, arriving as Joey and I carry flatbread stuffed with seasoned beef along the trenches to the hogan—food for the singers and the sitters and pretty much anyone that needs it. Maria's food is the best. But not even the best can get the twins to eat. By my count, Tsasa hasn't eaten in a day, Tsosi even longer.

Chaco wheels low and lands on my shoulder with a soft step, taking care not to unsettle the wrapped plates. "The Eater walks without tiring. His steps swallow the land between us. He'll be here in the witching hour. Dead of night."

"Of course he will," I grumble and relay the same to Joey. His nod is small, almost imperceptible, the nod of someone watching things align. Don't matter that the picture comin' together sucks. His totem pouch hangs dark from his neck, and I know he's had a tough time with it not working. Joey wants to go kick ass. But most of the time, when shit goes south, ass kickin' ain't the answer. What needs to be done is shit like this: feeding people, putting logs on the fire, shakin' hands and holding friends, standin' watch even when it hurts to stand. That's fighting too.

"Dad and my sister?" I ask Chaco.

Chaco twitches his head and settles. "No sign," he says.

I shake my head. Mom alive but with the dead. Dad and my sister dead to the world of the living. Quite the family.

When we come up on the hogan, the dyin' there gets so strong that I gotta take a minute. Joey sees it and takes my plates without saying anything. I make a show of standing tall, but it's all I can do not to claw at my neck and take to the flats. The second he ducks under the hogan, I turn right around and do my best not to run.

Chaco bobs along with me as I half walk, half stumble my way through the trenches back into the open desert of the Arroyo, where I focus on Kai, a hunched black blob in the distance, keeping watch over her brother—a smaller, much more colorful blob under the family rug.

"You okay, Ace?" Chaco asks, using the name he had for me when I was a kid. Somehow, it gets a smile outta me.

"No," I say, eyes on Kai. "I ain't okay, and I think you know it."

But whatever she's going through is worse, I think, as if Chaco wouldn't hear it anyway.

"Did I ever tell you about Manaba Morningrock?" he asks me.

I sit down on the lip of the mud trench and prop myself up by digging my palms into the dirt. "Yeah, the Keeper before me. Ben's grandmother. She died protecting the bell."

"She did," Chaco says, clicking his tongue. "But that's not what she'd want to be known for. She was a proud singer. A cornerstone to her family. You saw what happened when she died. The Dejoolis all unraveled. They went..."

"Up in the air," I say. That's what *Dejooli* means, Ben's last name. It always stuck with me. Makes me wonder every day if what we're given, things like names and bells, is what ends up defining us.

"It's not," Chaco says flatly, shuttin' that down and looking at me straight on. No side-eye, even.

Chaco sits down as hard as he can on my shoulder and puffs out to fill up the gap. I can't help but remember Pap, my grandpa—the way he would fill out his chair with his paper and his glass of whisky in his chapped hands after a long shift on the Lubbock rigs.

Chaco settles back and watches Kai with me. She hasn't moved in what seems like an hour, and I oughta try to take some water out to her again. Maybe a blanket. Night is coming.

Chaco speaks more quietly in my head. "Naba was Keeper for a long time. Only one person in the memory of man wore the bell longer than she did."

"Must have been a real shitkicker."

"He is. Because he's you."

I clear my throat. I don't like where this is going, but Chaco is on one, and when he gets going, he aims to prove his point.

"Grant, the bell found you as a child, and now you're a well-grown man. You've held it too long. And too closely. You were the first and only child Keeper in the entire memory of human time, it found you when you were *eight years old*—"

I stand, cutting him off. "I'm gonna go check on Kai. See if she's okay."

Chaco bobs right along with me with that supernatural bird-leg suspension he's got because he ain't lettin' go of my shoulder. I can tell he doesn't know what to say next, but he's hanging on, which is sayin' something. While I walk, he gives me a whole thirty seconds before he says, "The bell must *exist* here, but it does not *belong* here. It takes from those who keep it. It takes their life away from them. Every death a Keeper witnesses hangs on them like stones."

"I know this, bird."

"Point being this is not something that's gonna get better, buddy."

I stop halfway to Kai in the flat of nothing before the Arroyo lip, and I take a big breath. I take in as much baked mud smell as I can, sweet and sour at the same time, and I do it to keep from crying. And it works.

"I know it ain't gettin' better," I say, focusing on Kai's huddled shape, on losses greater than what I am dealing with.

She shivers like she's crying. I also know what Chaco really wants to talk about. I just ain't ready for it yet. "Can this wait for a day?" I ask softly. "Just one day."

Chaco does a bird sigh and tucks himself against me, upsetting my hat a bit. "It can wait a day," he says.

I gently settle my hat back, taking care not to upset him, and I go to Kai.

28

KAI BODREY

I know my brother isn't here anymore. Ben took him hours and hours ago. But I can know this and still not want to leave his side. Part of me thinks Hos would have liked a rock burial, the real traditional shit where your clan puts you out on the rocks for the birds. That would have been the most metal. But I think he would understand we're in the middle of a war here. War dead get buried as they can, where they lie, covered if they're lucky.

He would get that too.

Plus, there ain't no clan left except for me. I'm the last Bodrey. And the way things are looking—with what Chaco says is comin' our way—the Walker might be showing me the veil here before night falls again.

The clarity that comes when every other road—every other choice for survival—is taken from you is a strange thing. When the only real choice you have is how to face what comes, you get a real punch of perspective right in the face.

If I gotta face this thing—this eater of my people—I'm gonna do it right here next to my brother.

I can go out bigger, he says somewhere back in my brain.

"You dragged a monster to its death over the canyon," I tell the shell of him. "Nothing gets more metal than that."

Hos is gone from this world, but his voice isn't gone from my head, which means I doubt it ever will be.

I pull a dry strand of field grass from the ground. This area by the canyon lip is overgrown with it already. The wispy little things shoot out from the mud in clumps. Nature is taking over again. Back before the flood, the Arroyo folk lived all the way up to here. Now, those that did come back don't want to be anywhere near it. The camp has moved back, toward the brush line. I can't really blame them. For most of 'em, this canyon holds a lot of baggage: pain, fear, and probably a fair amount of regret right next to the rusted-out cars.

So you just gonna sit here and die next to me, then? Hos asks.

"I'm supposed to be in Arizona somewhere at college. Studying paleontology. You know that?"

You're supposed to be exactly where you are. Your people need you.

"My people are all dead," I say, louder than I'd intended, just as Grant comes around from behind and walks right into my crazy with Chaco on his shoulder.

He slows until he's in front of me then stops. He takes a measured breath and removes his cowboy hat, taking care not to clip Chaco, who leans out of the way of the brim in a sort of well-practiced dance I find insanely attractive on Grant at exactly the wrong time.

"I didn't mean you," I say lamely. "I meant... my *family* family."

"It's alright," he says. "Mine are too. Dead, I mean. All of 'em."

Chaco probably ain't meaning to, but he's staring a hole through me anyway. Grant looks at the brim of his hat and flicks at a speck that ain't there. "Funny thing, though, just when I ran outta family, I came up on some more."

I got nothing to say to that, but Grant doesn't seem to expect me to, and just like that, he's set the strange air between us down, and I want to tell him I don't deserve his kindness, his love. But I already know he would tell me to stop telling him how to love.

He ponders Hos's wrapped body and carefully puts his hat back on then looks out to the west, where the empty half-moon gives all it's got. Beyond that, the desert goes on forever.

"That's where Yé'iitsoh is comin' from," Grant says. "The deep desert. He'll be here in an hour at most. Chaco says he walks like he's eatin' up the land."

With a weak moon and no real campfires to speak of, the Arroyo is lit by a distant and cold starlight that makes the gathered brush at the flood line look like a low wall. I imagine this thing stepping right over it or walking right through it, chewing something.

Chaco jumps from Grant's shoulder and floats down to Hos with the sound of falling leaves. He settles on one of the cuts of pinyon pine I used to pin the blanket over his body.

Chaco ticks his head to take in the full rug, handspun wool Mom said we traded a month's worth of food for with the canyon shepherds when she was a child. Back then, the trading post had a loom, and enough people lived on the flats below us that knew how to use it. I know it's an heirloom piece, but when I look at it, all I think of is how far we've fallen. Those flats went from a full clan to a smaller clan, to one last family, to a brother and a sister, and now to me, losing more and more of the good along the way.

Sometimes, you gotta scorch the earth to get things to grow again, Hos says in the back of my brain.

I shiver in the dark. Grant is watching the line where that thing is gonna break through. He's thinking how we can stop him, probably, thinking what more we can throw at him. But when the Slayer Twins first put this bastard into the ground, they had the weapons of the gods, arrows made from lightning, sunbeam, and rainbow, firepower given to them by the Sun himself.

"We can't stop him comin' through," I tell Grant.

Grant tips his hat back and wipes his forehead. The weak, witchy moonlight reflects like dirty water off the bell around his neck. "We gotta try," he says. "Even if that's all we can do."

Chaco is looking at me again with that same unbroken bird stare. Not that long ago, I probably would've looked away. Even an idiot knows not to look a crow dead in the eye. But I'm tired, and I hurt lots of places, so I stare right back until he takes his arrowhead of a beak and snaps it on the wood he's standing on with a sound like a rifle crack.

Grant looks back at the bird over his shoulder. Then he turns away again. Chaco's talking, I know, but this time, I think maybe he's trying to talk to me.

"It ain't all we can do," I say. "That thing wants to walk in? Fine. Let it."

Grant settles his hat and turns toward me. "If it gets in, people are gonna die."

I pick another sprig of dead grass and rub my hand on the broken clay topsoil, dry as ash. I look at that brush line, spindly and jagged, full of the dried-out remnants of what once lived here. My hand settles on my dead brother's shoulder.

Yeah, people might die. People *have* died. But that is the story of our people, of *any* people, really. The point is to die well.

"I got an idea," I say.

29

CAROLINE ADAMS

Sara is in trouble. Black Bear has been in her room for way too long. I can't hear all of what's going on, but I hear tears. I hear him pressing, refusing to let go. He took that core memory from Tábaahá, and the hit was too good, and now he wants more, and he's got Sara up against a wall in there like the worst kind of drunk. I'd toilet wrench him in the back if I could. If I had one. And if I could move.

Hold on, Sara. Smother the memory. Eat it. Do whatever it takes—just don't give it up.

I have to sit here, frozen like a marionette while I listen to her slow struggle become silence. The tears I would cry jam up right behind my eyes, somewhere deep in my sinuses, stuck like the rest of me.

He comes stumbling in like a meth head, looking up and through the sagging roof, toward a sky only he can see. His fingers flutter, palms up, like he's trying to push more of the smoke of whatever hit he took into his face. The totem dangles from his right hand like a forgotten beer bottle. He stumbles back to that damn couch and sits like he's three hundred pounds.

"Come here," he tells me, fingers fluttering, face slack, too stoned to remember I can't move. Eventually, it comes back to him, and his mouth twitches in what might be a smile if he had more control of himself.

He shoves himself up and staggers my way, slamming his hip into the card table and shoving the chairs to the ground. He pushes the totem into my hands like a toddler, but I grab on the second I feel it. I blink my eyes a million miles an hour. That's the first thing I do now when I come back, the blinks. If you think the New Mexico desert gives you dry eyes, try not blinking for hours. Or days.

He stands all wobbly, like a baby colt. "Come to the..." He snaps his fingers a few times, processing at maybe ten percent. "The couch."

Poor Sara. Whatever he took from her was good.

I have to get to her, but first, I have to get through this thing.

"Tell me about your friend Ben Dejooli," he says, slurring the name.

"You mean the Walker?" I ask. Ben Dejooli isn't a name he should say or know. Ben is for me.

"No, I mean Ben Dejooli," he says, settling in and resting his long, thin hands over his stomach, watching me through lidded eyes.

I know that look. He's looking for one more bump to take him over the edge. If you didn't know better, you'd think I was the dealer. But the thing is, I'm the product.

Dose it out wisely, then.

Owen's voice is calm and collected in my head, a voice from the early days, when he was attending at ABQ General. I don't think the stress sweat of those days will ever wash off me, but Owen was at home there. Then we made a home together. And now, that home is far away from me. He's out there with her now. *How long has he had her? Is she crawling? Walking? Driving?*

Dose it out, Owen says again.

"Ben and I know each other pretty well," I tell Black Bear, which makes his eyes glitter.

He's looking for a nightcap, and I'm looking for Sara. I think we can meet somewhere in the middle.

"You know I touched him once, through the veil. He and I touched."

I have his attention now. His breathing slows. "Touched what?"

"Just our fingers. Through a spot between the worlds that was so thin it hardly felt like anything at all."

I'm lost in that memory now, remembering the way it felt when we moved the waters of the river of death, the sucking and the pushing, the way the shattered blade blew open a place between worlds that was so huge and so tight that it held everything and nothing but one touch.

And even as I speak the memory, I feel it fading, flitting away from me like a dream upon waking.

Black Bear leans his head back with the force of it and closes his eyes. His breathing is deep and slow. I read somewhere in some trash magazine about how someone survived a bear attack, and all she could remember was the breath of the thing. It smelled like death. You'd think Black Bear, of all creatures, would smell like that times a thousand, and I'm pretty sure he does on the living plane. But here, he smells like an old newspaper left out on the stoop in the rain then baked in the sun. He smells forgotten.

He's down and out. But I know he could wake up at any time.

I wrap my fingers tight around the totem and tiptoe out of my room, past the front door, to Sara's room. I move to push it open, but I'm hit by such a strong sense of déjà vu that it nearly staggers me. In this place, where memories are money, the flashback is blinding, and it's of me walking through Ben's old duplex in the way-before time. The front door was just like this, half open, but his was snapped at the lock, kicked in by Danny Ninepoint. I remember walking through the living room and finding the place turned upside down. Things were broken, glass glittering, and that terrible sound of final breaths was coming from the back room, where his grandmother was.

And here is Sara, frozen and faded, a bleached husk of herself, rolled on her side in her dreadful iron cot. No blood, no mess, but an ending just as sure as the one I stumbled upon in that back room then. I fall to my knees next to her, and everything feels slow—flipbook fashion, one page at a time. This paper-thin husk of a woman risked everything to come over to me, to open my door, to help me understand how this place works.

I can't tell you which death was worse to come upon. But I can tell you Sara had one thing left to tell me, just like Ben's grandmother did.

All Sara has is a finger. Her arm is flopped out of the bed, lying flat against the same dirt-crusted wooden floor I have, the softness of her forearm up, wrist exposed, fingers curled except for one pointing at the hollowed-out television, another of Black Bear's ridiculous props.

This piece of junk is her equivalent of my frat couch. I can imagine Black Bear coming in with his dumb head through the hole where the screen should be. Maybe she accidentally dropped that she had a fun night watching whatever rowdy revue was on in the community center's only television, black-and-white 1950s style, and he obsessed over it like a stalker.

One time at ABQ General, I mentioned to a creeper patient that I like chocolate ice cream, and he dropped off a pint of it on a random Tuesday a month after he was discharged. I hid in the break room until the orderlies eventually escorted him out, and all I could hear was him saying, "I thought she liked it! I thought she wanted it!" When he was gone, I opened it and found the imprint of what I *really* hope was his thumb pressed deep into it. My nurse manager came up later that day and said, "You gotta be more careful what you tell people," like it was my fault.

That's how I imagine Black Bear did it. *You said you like television, right? Now... tell me more.*

The same unfelt wind that spins the painted skulls in Tábaahá's room stirs the sand dusting the top of the TV here. I walk over to it then crouch and look through. More sand is here, too, but it's deeper, and something sticks out, a corner of a piece of paper, just a point. I pull a note free, folded in that end-over-end way I remember doing as a kid with the notes that were really special, the real deal stuff that mattered about boys and other girls and teachers. I guess some things cross generations.

I look back over my shoulder at what's left of Sara and ask, "For me?"

I can barely get it out because I know I'm talking to a shell, but it feels so good to talk to someone who wants to talk to me for me instead of what I can give them.

I open it carefully. Unfolding it one bit at a time, not even daring to smooth it in case it rips or smudges the thin scrawl of ink, and I start to read.

I see what is happening to Tábaahá, and I know it will happen to me. Together, we've tried to test the boundaries of this place. Every time, we have failed. We ration memories like food, hardly daring to touch them ourselves any longer, for fear they will somehow show brighter for him *to take. Between us both, we know four things:*

1 – We probably will never leave here.

2 – Unless we pass on what we know to the next woman, our loss will mean nothing.

3 – You cannot defeat him. Only he can defeat himself.

4 – The key is in the memories he wants most.

A list—I like this Sara more and more. It's a shame we didn't have more time together under better skies. I think she would've been a good girl to watch trashy television with on a non-frat couch with low-sodium popcorn that we eat enough bags of to make up for the low-sodium part.

Here is the memory he will take from me that will end me.

My hands shake so that it's hard to read. I clear my throat and wipe my eyes with the back of the hand that holds the greasy totem. I'm squeezing it so hard that it hurts, but I would rather have the pain as a constant reminder than do something dumb like set it aside to wipe my nose and get stuck here for him to find.

The memory is of my husband crying. It's not much more than a moving picture of perhaps five seconds. His back is trembling from the tears.

It's hard to say in a piece of paper how much it means and why. Just enough room to say I was rich and he was poor. My clan proud and sprawling, his clan withering. He couldn't understand why I would love him. Never mind that I fell in love with him when we were children, when a beam of moonlight and the soft rain of one night gave us strength to survive the schools. We were together from then, but the more we grew, the less he believed. My family has always mistaken a soft-spoken man for a weak man, which is why they protested our marriage on the day it was to happen.

But that is not the picture I have in my mind that matters. That is not the day he cried.

That day, when my mother stood and said in front of our clan that she would not support us, I stood too. And I slapped her.

My father stood and rebuked me. I slapped him too.

No one else stood.

I turn it over, holding the edges.

We were wed. And on the night of the wedding, well after we lay together, I awoke in the middle of the night and looked to my side, and that is my memory: him, with moonlight across his back once again, crying silent tears. I pulled him to face me and found his tears weren't hard rain. They were soft rain. And when I cupped his chin with my hand, he took it in his and looked at it with pride and said "The hand that strikes for me. You fight like Coyote's wife. You are my warrior."

I asked him if he believed I loved him now.

He said he did and would forever.

That is my memory. That is what he will take from me, but if you have it too, he can't take everything. I am gone, and now, it is up to you to figure out how to break him or, if you cannot, to pass on what you know to the one who will.

When the days feel like they become nights never-ending, remember this. We may not be with you, but we are not gone. Nothing is lost forever.

I look over my shoulder at her husk and blink my bleary eyes clear. I hold the note for a good ten seconds, letting the memory she shared wash over me, letting it stick. Then I carefully rip the note to pieces with my free hand and my teeth, then I eat it. It doesn't even scratch going down.

I stand.

Sara's list rolls over and over again in my mind. *One, two, three, four.*

Three and four loom largest. They're in a bold font in my brain.

Number three: *Only he can defeat himself.* That makes sense. This isn't a place where trickery works. He sets the rules. What Sara means is clear. Nobody leaves unless Black Bear is gone.

That takes us to four.

I turn from what's left of Sara and close her door softly behind myself. No use blubbering. Sara wouldn't want it, and it makes me vulnerable to *him* showing up. Emotional control is key here, which isn't exactly awesome for me.

Back in my room, on the couch he "gave" me, Black Bear twitches in his stupor. His hand lolls over the edge a little bit like Sara's did, but his fingers point nowhere. He has no intention of going anywhere except from room to room, getting wasted on what his girls give him. And I'm all that's left of his stash at the moment.

I clench the totem in my hand so hard it hurts. Pictures of me smashing him again and again right on the bridge of his nose waltz unasked through the forefront of my mind. But this isn't that kind of fight. This isn't the kind of fight we had back at the Arroyo with him, either, where brains and faith and sleight of hand won the day.

This is a battle of the heart. It's about who has the heart to win and who is willing to risk everything not to lose. I got him on the former. I have so much heart that I wear it on both sleeves. I have so much heart that I feel like I would go to war for either of the two women I literally just met.

It's the second bit that worries me, if I'm willing to risk everything.

Black Bear strikes me as crazy enough to destroy himself to keep his little shack and all his precious boons hidden forever. But I have way too much to live for, including the daughter I've only met in passing.

Right now, the thought of going back to that little stained spot on the couch and bending back into the same awful position I was in when this monster passed out makes me sick. My room gets more and more disgusting the longer I look at it: the oily trail that tracks the floor, like a leaky trash bag at a dive bar; the bloated and dented can collection that screams botulism; the way the curtains move in clumps like greasy hair; the way I can't *feel* the stupid breeze that moves them. All I get is still basement air that smells like open sewer drains.

I've made up my mind. I may not be able to run, but that doesn't mean I can't leave.

"Come find me, asshole," I mutter, and I turn toward the door.

I wish I could say the desert outside this crappy cabin is a welcome break from my day to day as part of a doll collection, but it's not, not really. The desolate sky, the same color as the sand, makes it hard to see where ground ends and sky begins. The only hint I get that something might be out there beyond what I can see is the faintest sound of moving water scraping slowly along its banks. A lot of moving water that wasn't there before.

I follow the sound without thinking until I start to meet the invisible barrier Black Bear showed me about ten lifetimes ago. The air gets thicker and thicker the harder I push. I know if I go much farther, it will suck over me and trap me where I am like a bug in sap.

I step back. Like I said, this isn't about running away. There is no running away. This is about turning the tables.

Tábaahá's core memory—the roundabout way she shaped it through the story of brown bear cleaving her way through the forest and smashing her husband's enemies—has been running circles in my head since she told it to me. Same with Sara's final note, the way she stood up to her own clan—struck her own parents—for the love of her husband. Both women were devoted in their own way. Powerful enough to stand on their own, they chose to stand for the men they loved. The key is there somewhere.

I close my eyes and run down Sara's note again in my mind. Back in the day, nursing student Caroline would've gone over that thing with a highlighter, plucking out parts of it that struck me as something particularly important, like I did in the textbooks that still gather dust somewhere under our bed on the other side of reality. And one bit in particular would've glowed.

Coyote's Wife.

Sara wrote that her husband said she fought for him like Coyote's wife. Tábaahá said her memory was shaped like Coyote's wife—how she took arrows for her husband, loved him until she bled, and made others bleed because of what they did to him.

That's the thread I need to follow to the heart of Black Bear. That's the string I have to tug to unravel this monster.

The river sounds louder now even though I'm standing still. Chaco says that on the other side of the veil, the path the river cuts is always changing. I wonder if the river is searching for this place just like the veil searches for Black Bear.

Just like Black Bear is going to search for me. I turn away from the sound of the river and look back toward the cabin. He'll be awake soon. When he finds me, I want it to be head-on. I want him to know I'm not afraid.

I sit down cross-legged in the sand, holding the totem in both hands in the space between my knees, and I start tugging at the strings of memories I've found. If I can just let my mind wander over the stories of the women I've met here—over the story of this cabin itself—maybe I can find the key that unlocks Black Bear's dark heart.

30

GRANT ROMER

With every step Yé'iitsoh takes toward this place, the bell gets a little heavier and stings a little more.

Joey calls him the Eater. He's about ready to bash his way through the flood wall, then he's gonna find himself here at the Arroyo, with plenty of people to eat up. The first of them is Kai, still sitting there by her brother's body, waiting. She's got the dried washout of the flood all around her now: driftwood, branches, leaves. All part of her plan. She wears her beat-up leather jacket against the cold blue morning, one hand resting lightly on the blanket covering Hos, her back to us here at the hogans. I can't believe I'm leaving her alone out there, but that's what she asked, and I'm followin' her lead.

The Arroyo is dead quiet. We siphoned all the gas from the generators and spread it on the flood brush. That's also part of her plan. Kai has a path out of the gas-soaked mess around her, a path that'll take her back here to us. But I'm fifty-fifty on if she takes it.

I think this plan she's got might be her way of saying

she's goin' the way of her brother. I could keep fightin' her on it, but I'm fifty-fifty on all of us goin' the way of her brother anyway.

"She's gonna run, right?" Joey whispers. "Light it and run?"

I look at him long enough that my answer, "Sure she is," says everything I feel but can't quite say.

Joey lets out a slow breath and leans back, elbows first, on what's left of the pinewood fence. He looks from Kai to the hogan where the fire burns low. The twins are still in there with Maria, the Smoker, and Sani Yokana, who's havin' a tough time coming back from whatever Blood Eyes showed him and is guzzling Maria's tea as fast as she can brew it.

Everybody else rings the Arroyo, waiting.

"Feels like an end," Joey says.

Chaco chirrups on my shoulder, and I translate. "We ain't dead yet, Joey."

Joey's the one should be buckin' others up, and he usually is, but this fight has all of us second-guessing ourselves. I'm about to tell him as much when the bell rakes a little harder down my sternum, and Joey pricks up his ears.

"You hear that?" he asks.

The sound of steps floats over the still air. You really shouldn't hear steps. They should just be a part of the background of life. But these are *look at me* steps. They sound like they're goin' out of the way to crush the loudest shit they can find.

Then, there he is, big and blue in the dead light as he shoves his way through the flood wall and half stumbles into the flat of the Arroyo.

Chaco said this thing was more than just big, and I

catch his meaning now. When I hid in the small space between my bed and my dresser as a kid, I pictured monsters just like him. It's like the air withers around him. He carries a headless crow in his hand and chews slowly as he takes in the Arroyo with eyes that light up like a desert cat's at night.

The crowd that rings the Arroyo does their best to keep their horror to themselves, but it comes out anyway. The collective sound reminds me of the *whoosh* Pap made when he got knifed in the gut.

Yé'iitsoh drops the crow from his right hand. In his left, he holds tight to something of a deeper black, the totem. Chaco tenses like he wants to go out there single-handed, but I rein him in. "If he eats your head, can you come back?" I ask Chaco.

He pauses to think. "I'm not sure," he says honestly. Then he tenses again to jump anyway because he's a bit of a dumbass like that despite being older than the mountains. I grab him by the back, which is somethin' I almost never do.

"You ain't goin' nowhere, you hear me?"

"Kai's gonna die out there."

"She has a plan. She don't need no savin' any more than the rest of us."

Chaco scoffs and swipes his beak at my hand. "Her *plan* is to burn next to her brother."

Before Kai lost Hos, I would've said such a thing was out of the question, but losin' every ounce of blood family walking the earth changes a person. Still, I know Kai Bodrey. She'll give more than she gets.

Chaco tries to jump again, and I grab him midair, which is really pushing things with him.

I bring him down and sandwich him between my hands. "What the hell do you think you're doin'?"

"I'm timeless and ageless, Grant Romer, I cut the sky and walk the great rope. I will fly where I will—"

"Shut up."

Chaco looks at me with about the heaviest sidelong gaze he's ever shot my way. "I am a thinning. *The* thinning. I am the weight you feel when you know there is more to this world than you see. This monster is nothing to me."

"Yeah? Well, he looks like he ate about twenty of your best friends on his walk over."

"Let me go, Grant. I am the—"

"Would you shut up? You think I'm the indispensable one just 'cause I wear this thing around my neck? You always think I'm the one needs protecting? Let me tell you somethin'. I die, the bell goes to someone else—"

He bucks in my hand, but I hold on. "Don't you say that," he says.

"There are a million of me, Chaco. Only one of you."

I've been keeping my thoughts close so that even Chaco ain't got a hold of all of it, but I think he and I have been comin' around to the same conclusion, just in different ways. The bottom line is my time as Keeper is running out, and we both know it.

There's more to be said, but Yé'iitsoh, Big Giant, the Eater of Men, finds where Kai is sitting vigil, and all of us go still. Chaco covers my hand with his wings like a glove, so I can feel the heat of his body and the flutter of his heart.

The monster stops his shattering steps about ten feet back from Kai and Hos. He spits out a mangled crow head and a dollop of blood black as oil then picks his teeth with his finger.

"Where is my brother?" he asks, his voice a thunder rumble.

For the longest ten seconds of my life, Kai says nothing. She's talking with Hos. I can tell because of how softly she presses her hand on the rise of his forehead under the blanket.

Then Kai stands.

31

KAI BODREY

This thing standing before me is a monster—ain't no two ways about that—but it was a man once. Tattoos cover his hands and arms. They snake up under his torn shirt and wrap his neck and face and head: gang signs, symbols, pictures. Some of them I recognize, but I doubt this thing would recognize them himself now. It wears the skin of a man the way my people wear masks during the big dances. He holds that black totem so tightly that his forearm bulges.

The Eater.

I know all this in a glance. The smell is enough, spoiled milk and roadkill. He breathes like a bear, which makes sense because a bear sent him here. A bear I beat and banished has still found a way to terrorize us with nightmares from our past. And here one stands, right in front of me. And everything in my body screams *run*, screams *wake up*. But I know there's no waking up from this.

"Where is my brother?" he asks with a voice like bubbling grease.

And despite all of it—the oily coating of blood, the smell of him like a cloud around us—the only thing I can think is *How dare you speak of brothers?*

I stand.

"Your brother is dead. My brother killed him."

He watches me with black eyes that roll in their liquid like marbles. He smells the air deeply, and for a second, I think he's caught on to the gasoline we've drenched everything with. But no. If he cared about it, he wouldn't have stepped over the wall. There's enough gas on the ground here that they can probably smell it on the highway. It didn't stop him. Something tells me his nose tunes into other things, like pain. And children.

He looks over at where the Arroyo edge drops, and he smells his dead brother and knows I'm telling the truth.

"He died well," the monster says, looking at Hos under the blanket. "Took one of your warriors with him."

I had some things to say, some shit to talk. I had a lot I wanted to unload on this thing, but he ain't even here, really. He exists outside flesh and blood. I'd just be wasting my breath. It's a soft realization but heavy, like stones piling up slow on my chest.

"Nobody really dies well," I manage to say. "We just die best we can."

I pull out the lighter, a battered old Bic I found in Hos's truck. Once one twig catches, I'll run. But damn if those stones don't sit heavier and heavier.

One flick. No catch.

Two flicks, three. No catch.

I turn toward Hos. "Really?"

You ain't goin' out that easy, I hear him say.

Yé'iitsoh grumbles. He sounds as disgusted with me as I am with myself. He lunges forward and grabs my hair and in one swipe puts a fistful of it in his mouth. I feel it snap under his teeth like tense twine. I think I'm screaming. I'm probably screaming. Or maybe that's Grant screaming behind me, rushing in.

Take your time, my love. His stomach is big enough for all of us.

He throats my hair like a snake, and with each bite, I'm drawn closer to his mouth. In a flash, I'm inches from the black teeth. My hands slip on his face, pushing away, but he doesn't seem to care. Then he stops.

He scents something. I see that through tears and sweat. Some smell gummed him up. He takes one big breath and one more ripping bite that flays a whole flap of my scalp before he drops me. And just like that, I am forgotten.

I hold my head together, try to ignore the pulsing warmth of the blood that seeps between my fingers, and kick away as fast as I can.

He's looking at the hogan, where the glow of the fire is growing, and the eastward door is darkened by someone coming out.

Tsasa's head is bowed, his shoulders so stooped that he doesn't even have to duck. He walks slowly, humming to himself, hands clasped in front, draped in the blanket that has covered his knees for a thousand stories around the fire. The lightning weave runs jagged over both shoulders. Steam rises from his body as he cranes his neck to take in the Big Giant.

Yé'iitsoh stares back, picking my hair from the roof of his mouth. I heel my way back to my brother's body.

Tsasa's voice is old, and he wheezes, but it rings as clear as ever. "Three times, you have shown yourself on our land, Yé'iitsoh, Eater of Men. This fourth will be your undoing."

Yé'iitsoh pulls a crumpled feather from his teeth, flings it to the ground, and speaks in ugly, broken Navajo. "Who are you?"

"We are old men."

Big Giant narrows his eyes. He wanted cowering, fear, food. He does not want this.

"We?" he asks. "All I see is you. And all I smell here is death. Old and new. Like layers of buried bones."

Another body darkens the eastern door, this one even more hunched. The Arroyo drops into a heavy silence, like we're back in the flood days, submerged, all holding our breath.

Tsosi makes his way to his brother's side.

He takes his time, and everything waits. He barely makes it to Tsasa, where he almost collapses, but his brother hooks him arm to arm, and together, they shuffle toward me.

The wind shifts, and the hogan smoke blows our way, carrying a strong scent of burning sage and something more I can't quite pinpoint.

"I want the young," says Yé'iitsoh. "The old have no taste." He works his jaw all around. "I would have saved you both for last. So you could watch me eat the rest."

Tsosi and Tsasa keep walking, Tsosi has his head down, back curved like a horseshoe, his focus on his feet.

But Tsasa speaks. "There is no *last*, Yé'iitsoh. There is only next." And here, he looks at me.

His eyes are all for me, and they shine. And in this second, I know I'm seeing the last walk of the elder twins. It all hits me before I even notice Maria and Joey and Grant holding each other back and holding each other up at the same time. A string of devastating crow calls from Chaco seals it.

But those eyes, and those words—*no last, only next*—were for me.

The smoke shifts again, and the twins are obscured, but the voice that rings out carries the power of both of them.

"We will not be here for the next, Yé'iitsoh, eater of our people. But neither will you. The difference is, we go in beauty. You will go in flames."

I know the smell now. It's burning wool, like a rug thrown on a smoldering fire.

Or a Navajo blanket that holds a fire within.

The air clears for a moment. Tsosi lays his head against his brother like a child listening to a story. Only this time, the twins aren't telling it. They're living it.

The blanket they share bursts into flame all at once, and the sound is soft, like a sheet catching the wind on the line. Then the ground around them becomes flame, and the flame races out like fault lines in every direction. Yé'iitsoh crashes backward in a haggard retreat, but it's like the fire has a bead on him. All lines point to him. He stomps at the first while the others circle him, eating the wood with a furious hiss. He swats as they climb his legs, but they split and jump, and soon his flesh is burning.

Time to go, little sister, Hos says.

I turn and find my hand still on my brother's shoulder. The smoke is thick and white now, and for a second, I think I see him sitting there on the other side of his body, a swirling cloud of himself.

This fire is not for you. But fire is hard to reason with once it gets going.

Big Giant is screaming and sizzling, and the flames are already looking elsewhere, closing in around us.

I'll hold the fire. You hold the Arroyo.

"I love you, brother," I say.

I lean on him and press myself to my feet. My line out of this inferno is in front of me, but the smoke is doing its best to blind me. I catch a glimpse of the hogans and set my feet that way, then all is white. No time to wait. I run, blind, through a world of fire. Only the hard feel of the Arroyo earth underneath my boots keeps the panic from eating me whole.

I don't say goodbye to Hos this time and don't say goodbye to the twins, either. 'Cause it's like they said.

No last. Only next.

32

THE WALKER

I'm walking through a forgotten pocket of desert just to the left of the land of the dead. I can hear the river of souls nearby. Sometimes, it rushes like rapids, and other times, it rolls heavy and wide, and you feel the weight of the water more than you can hear it. The only things moving are the sky above and the sand below, both of them so subtle that you'd miss it if you didn't know what to look for.

The feather knows the way to Black Bear's den. I hold it in my open palm, and it flutters on a strange breeze I can't feel, just strong enough to spin it like a compass.

My mom got really into dowsing right about the time my sister was about to check out of the living world. She thought she could use these spinning rods to find pockets of energy to help heal her. I'd seen so many different things fail Ana: Navajo medicine, Western medicine, thoughts and prayers. All of it was worthless, so I wasn't in the mood to believe in anything ever again, and I got into a fight with her about it. I remember slapping one of those bent coat-hanger lookin' things out of her hand and saying something like *stop looking for what ain't there and face what is*, and Gam scolded me with a quick snap of "Grandson!" which to me was as good as yanking on the leash of a barking dog. I shut up real quick.

The feather points over low rolling hills of rock that drip with sand like they're slowly dissolving. I walk that way, and I soon find my feet leaving footsteps. I look back at them more than I'd like to admit.

After Gam snapped at me, I remember dinner was quiet that night. Dad was off drinking, and Mom was in the middle of packing up for ABQ. Ana was too sick to eat. It was just me and Gam at that yellowed countertop, eating her chicken posole and fry bread that had no right to be as good as it was, coming off that wreck of a stove with one-and-a-half burners working. I asked Gam why she got mad at me. She and my Mom never got along. Seeing them both in the same corner was strange, especially over some weird spirit stuff that felt more like gold-miner shit than Navajo medicine.

She said, "Everywhere you walk, you walk with everyone who was ever there and everyone who will ever be there. Your mother is just trying to hear them as best she knows how."

Then she went back to her posole.

I think of those words a lot. I think of them now when the feather—a feather that was part of Chaco and then part of the little girl who sits up top with Owen, waiting for her mom—flutters into a little course correction that takes me under more falling gardens of sand, up and over shifty crops of limestone, and to a large flat stretch of desert dotted with little boulders.

One of them, way out by the horizon line, looks like it's

smoking. The feather corrects again, catching that phantom breeze, and it points right toward it.

I walk. The horizon stays the same, all the rocks that dot it showing themselves one by one as rocks, except for the smoking one. That one is a house—more of a shack, really, with a drunken lean and crooked windows. The smoke comes from a stovepipe bent like a crazy straw.

So this is what Black Bear wanted to upgrade from with his Arroyo sweatshop, Dark Sky at the whip. I don't blame him. I've seen better on the wrong side of the tracks back at the Rez. I walk around it, giving it space, and it seems to lean my way no matter where I am, a bit like a haunted portrait.

I see her well before she sees me.

She's sitting cross-legged and facing the house with her eyes closed, waiting like she's expecting someone, although I don't think it's me. I know it's her because my phantom lungs stop breathing, and my phantom heart starts racing at the same time.

Caroline.

Even the distant sound of the river seems to drop off. I feel like I'm seeing something behind the scenes, a view I shouldn't have. And it's as if I've been given a pocket of time to prepare myself. Although for what, I can't say.

She looks different. Older, yes. She wears the years beautifully on her cheeks and chin and at the corners of her eyes, but mostly, she looks stronger. Nothing on her is wasted. Where she was soft, now she's defined. The Rez has been at her like a sculptor.

Out of nowhere, I'm hit with a bolt of nerves like a high school kid at his first dance. I'm embarrassed about everything, about how I look, how I lived, and how I died. She's gone on to live her life. She's different because of it, better. And here I am, preserved in a jar, cut off, soaked in universe juice like formaldehyde and slowly losing my mind.

Years I've wanted this moment, but now it's here, and a voice I thought I'd left behind is telling me I'm not up to it.

Sometimes, at my day job, I'll arrive on a fresh soul, and for a while, they'll be stuck on the last thing they said, the last thing they felt. I remember when I was dying in that hospital bed at ABQ General, some of those strong drugs would do the same thing. When they hit, your body takes a sort of snapshot of your position and your thoughts, and your brain holds on. You feel frozen in time, on a loop.

I know Caroline loves Owen. Hell, *I* love Owen. I love Grant and the new kid too. I love them all, and I know Caroline is where she needs to be when she's with them. But when I died, some part of my heart got stuck in that muscle-memory loop of loving her, and I can't kick it.

I'm embarrassed about that too.

It's enough to make a living man turn around and try again another day, but I've been dead a long time now. I don't have any more days.

She's lifting her head now and turning around, and she sees me.

She actually sees me.

33

CAROLINE ADAMS

I'm sitting on the sand and thinking about my daughter, thinking about the word *daughter*. Somewhere, I have a daughter. I feel—*know*, really—that she's with Owen. And I bet she feels like his daughter. I bet he looks at her and goes, *That's my girl*. Or maybe Grant's been taking care of her, and say she's sick or whatever, and he calls Owen at work, and Owen pauses his three o'clock and says, *So sorry, my daughter seems to have come down with something. I'll have to reschedule.*

What a strange word, *daughter*. I wonder if it'll ever feel right to me, ever feel less sandy on my tongue. And then I think, *Well, the only reason it feels sandy on your tongue is because you don't feel like a mom*, which makes me wonder when moms *do* feel like moms. Whenever it is, I'm pretty much definitely sure every other mom is feeling it before me. I then conclude that makes me a terrible mom. And here we go: spiral, commence.

Then somewhere behind me, I hear the soft shift of sand in a way that's totally different.

I've listened to these sands for what feels like lifetimes.

I know when sand moves that isn't supposed to move, and it makes me open my eyes and turn. And I see Ben Dejooli.

There's nothing but blasted sky behind him, and he's so sharp, so clear, that he seems cut from the air. I stare at him until some little postage stamp bit of my brain yells, *How about we don't drop the totem right now, Caroline?*

I hold tight and stand.

He smiles at me, and in one second, I get a sense of him like I'm picking up an earmarked book. The decade behind us feels like nothing but a night. He has the flair of his position. His skin is pale, feathered with black. He wears a faded, threadbare NNPD uniform. But other than that, he's the same—lean and strong but soft too. The weight of what he does now blunts him a bit, just like the cop work did when he was alive. You can see it on his shoulders. He's tired—tired but keeps showing up. He was like that then, and he's like that now. But he *feels* different. He has a weight, even standing barefoot on the sand, barely sinking. He has such heavy weight.

We walk to each other in silence. For me, it's because I don't quite believe this, and if I don't, he probably doesn't either, and if this is a spell or some sort of strange twist of this forgotten land, I don't want to pop it.

I come over to him and touch his face. If this is the dream of a woman finally driven insane, his face won't feel like anything but memory. Instead, it feels like smooth soap, and the soft weight of his hands holding mine is real enough—real enough for me.

"I see you, Ben Dejooli," I say.

He hugs me. I think he wanted to say something, but he couldn't, which I get, because those five words took about everything I had, so I hug him back and hope that what passes heart to heart is all those other words we can't say.

I've had this waking nightmare in the endless frozen moments in which a younger version of me makes one left turn and misses Owen entirely, misses our life together because of a decision made here or there in a heartbeat. History rewritten. Part of me thinks Ben could have been that turn, and if I ever saw him again, I might throw everything away.

But I don't. There's nothing of that. Nothing about Ben right here and now means anything less of Owen.

He presses his cheek against mine, and I know it's his way of saying what he can't. When he bows his forehead into my shoulder, I know it's his way of saying a little more. And when he says softly, "Let's get you home," I feel like what's passed between us is *way* more than four words could say.

I take a long moment, maybe a bunch of moments. Who knows how long a moment is, really, especially here.

Then he says, "Owen is waiting with her."

That's when I realize that there is another way out of here, one I never considered, one that doesn't take a fight, one where I just disappear. Ben walks these lands. He knows the path that got him here. He can take us back.

I could just leave with him.

I do leave, for a second. Ben holds my hand still, and I take a good four steps with him, and the barrier I felt before is nothing. He cuts it like butter. But I still hold the totem, and I find myself looking back.

And I stop. And I gently let go of his hand.

"I can't leave them," I say. "Their souls are still there. They had smoke. They can't be trapped like this forever.

"Who's they?" he asks.

I'm walking toward the shack again before my mind even makes the decision. So that's that, then. I wonder how many times I looked out that door. It's *nuts* that I would walk back in. *Nuts.*

Somebody has to do it, Owen says in the back of my brain.

"Come on," I say. "If we can be quick and quiet, then..."

But I don't even believe myself. *Then what? We get to smuggle out souls like kids sneaking beer then wait until Black Bear brings more fresh hell our way?*

Ben places a hand softly on my shoulder, and part of me will never get enough of it. The feel of his hand. Real and true.

"He's in there?" Ben asks.

I nod.

"With others?"

"Sort of."

He doesn't ask, just nods. He glances at his shoulder like he wishes Chaco was there. And he knows I know that, and he smiles sadly before taking a deep breath of whatever air he breathes.

"Alright then," he says. "Lead the way."

34

KAI BODREY

The fire has burned itself out on the Arroyo, but the smoke refuses to leave. It muddies the low air just above our heads, swirling this way and that, blocking the rising sun and turning the whole place the color of rust.

I walk the flats off the canyon edge with Grant, Joey, and Sani. All of us are in a line, looking for any signs of Yé'iitsoh or the elder twins. Joey ripped his tattered flag of New Mexico into pieces, and all of us wear a strip of it around our face and mouth, bandito style, to save our lungs, but the smoke and ash still stings my eyes.

Grant doesn't look good at all. I keep eyeing him, and he keeps catching me and half-smiling, but I don't buy it. Neither does Chaco. He's flapping about on Grant's shoulder one second and stiff the next. They're having some conversation, and Chaco doesn't like what he's hearing.

When we're close to the center, where Yé'iitsoh and the elder twins met across the body of my brother, Grant stumbles. Joey catches him, but not before Grant cracks the baked ground with his knees. Chaco flaps, agitated, like he's trying to help pull him up. His *caws* are loud and concerned.

"You go on," Grant says. "I'm just gonna sit here a spell." He flips around and sits right here in the dirt and ash and takes off his hat with his free hand. The other hasn't let go of the bell.

"How bad is it?" I ask.

He takes the water Joey offers and swallows it all in big gulps. "It burns like hell, a heavy sting I ain't felt before. Those were big deaths."

"Can you take it off?" Yokana asks, brow furrowed. He's still comin' around to all of this, which is good 'cause he can ask the questions we all want to know.

"Don't matter none," Grant says through breaths that sound too wheezy for my liking. "The burn waits for you. The bell needs a Keeper to do more'n just carry it. We shoulder our share of the death it takes on unless we want to let it ring."

Seeing him like this makes me sick, him taking a knee while trying and failing to hide the pain. I know Grant, and he'd gut out just about anything rather than show how much it hurts.

"I'll be alright," he says, squinting up at me in the weird, bloody light. "It gets better after a bit. The pain evens itself out."

Joey crosses his arms and looks flatly at Grant. "How much better?"

Grant pauses, which is all I need to know. Then he says, "Mostly better."

"Mostly better," I say, drily.

"Yeah. Mostly. Now, go find that totem. I'll just sit a spell."

He puts his hat back on and digs his heels into the dirt and avoids looking at all of us.

I flutter tap my fingers on my hips, something I do when I'm nervous. "Fine. But we ain't done talking about this."

"No, we ain't," he says, looking at Chaco.

I know he's trying to keep the defeat out of his voice, but it ain't working, and now Chaco's looking away, refusing to meet his eye, and I know in a way I can't describe that all of this is going somewhere I don't like at all. But one thing at a time.

Sani, Joey, and I form up the line again and keep walking, eyes on the ground. Sani does it like a pro. Something tells me he's walked way too many of these lines across the desert before. Falling ash dusts his black hat. "So we're looking for a black totem, obsidian or something like it," he says.

"You could go back to the station, Sani," I say, and I mean it. This is no cop out. This is me trying to give an old man a chance to retire on the high desert in peace. "You could just let the Arroyo deal with this."

He gets my meaning, but the look he gives me is enough to put that to rest. "You'd be surprised at what I've seen," he says. "I know what you're thinking. You're thinking an old man saw a monster from the time of the gods and his brain might not be able to take it."

He takes another step, kicking aside flash-burned shells of driftwood that flutter to ash. "Fifty years I've been on this force. Twenty as Chief," he says, then he looks at me rock steady under that ashen brow. "I think we could swap story for story well enough, Kai Bodrey."

He takes off his hat and rubs his forehead. His fingers leave perfect smudges in the faded felt of the brim. "Monsters don't scare me. What scares me is that before these two became what you saw, they were men—men who caught the attention of something worse than themselves.

Sani walks on, but Joey stays back, looking at me.

"What?" I ask.

"The Chief is with us."

"That ain't true. He can walk out still. He's got a police department to run—

"He can't walk out any more than you or I could," Joey says. "And thank the creator for it. We need all the help we can get."

Sani stops out on the plain, about ten yards ahead. He takes a careful step back and looks my way. "Here's Hosteen," he says, quietly.

I don't want to find a charred corpse. I keep thinking about that shack near the border and how that family died. But I also don't run from bad shit. So I walk back to my brother and rip off the Band-Aid.

No trace of our blanket remains, but it's not nearly the mess I was afraid of. His skin is a black char on his bones, but the fire turned everything inside him to ash. He's an open book now, facing the sky, drenched in red morning light. Our people believe fire is sacred but two-faced. It gives life but also brings death. Here with Hos, it does both. For the first time, I feel like his death is real and also right. The flames took all that weight he had and turned it to smoke. He's light now.

I look around for the bodies of the twins. They dropped their fire close to here, only a few steps back. I trace the paces from memory, and when I get there, I see nothing.

Joey's here too, looking for their bodies, but it's very clear very quick that we ain't finding bodies. I see where they stood clear as day. It's a divot about the size of a car tire scooped right out of the desert. The dirt here glitters black. Logs and char smolder at the edges, but this spot is flattened for ten or so feet in every direction. It looks like a bomb went off.

It looks like one of their sand paintings.

The blast marks stretch past my brother's body, but he lies in peace. Yé'iitsoh does not.

The body of the Big Giant is blown to pieces. His boots remain, but the rest of him is nothing but a long line of bones. Leg bones are blistered and black. His pelvis is shattered. The links of his spine thrown like chicken feed. Arms, hands, completely mangled. His skull is fifty feet back and so charred that it looks like someone dipped it in black paint.

"Over here," Joeys says.

All three of us meet up at the splintered bones of a hand, where we find the totem. The bear is broken in half, and the stone looks muddy and flat. Floating ash lands and leaves. None of us is in a hurry to pick it up.

Sani clears his throat. "So this was the source of..." He trails off, thinking.

We wait, partly because our people don't jump in like that, but mostly because Sani's looking for answers we can't give. 'Cause we don't know.

"The source of this man's power?" Sani finishes.

"Somethin' like that," I say. "But it wasn't his. It's Black Bear's. And it's a boon, a favor he won from someone. Or something."

"Something pretty fucking bad," Joey adds flatly. "Maybe the king of the Anaye himself."

"I see," Sani says even though I know he doesn't see.

None of us sees, not totally. But we fight anyway because that's what the Arroyo does.

"And how many of these *boons* does this Black Bear have?" he asks.

"No idea," I say. "But the first took my brother. This one took the twins."

Joey clears the smoke from his throat with a low growl. "That is a hell of a price to pay to break a rock," he says.

"From what we know, Black Bear has a lot," I say. And 'cause I know what the Chief is gettin' at, I add, "More boons than we got people."

Joey turns to look at the ring of tents and scattered cars. The buds of the new Arroyo have been blasted to ash again. "Our people haven't had numbers on our side for generations. If this is a war of attrition, we will lose."

"We held the line this time," I say. "Maybe we will next time too."

"How?" Sani asks, all cop clinical. "If another one of these things comes our way…"

He trails off. No need to dirty the air with what we all know is true. If another one comes, and us without the twins, it ain't gonna be good.

But I'm thinking of Ben Dejooli. I'm thinking of Owen and his little girl. All are walking the rainbow road to the land beyond. That busted-up crew is also somehow our ace in the hole. I'm not sure I would've sent anyone else even if we could have, except maybe Grant. But that would've killed me.

"We got people working for us on the other side," I say, eyeing the broken totem. "It's a long shot. But it's a shot."

35

THE WALKER

Caroline is trying to explain something about how she found a pattern to Black Bear's stories, something about a woman named Sara and something about a woman named after the water's edge, but I'm having a hard time keeping it all straight because she's holding my hand. She's actually holding my hand.

Touch is such a gift for the living. Real touch—to be able to touch someone you love. You have no idea what a gift it is. You can't. It's something you do every day, so your brain is wired to think it's nothing. But it's everything. Once you hit this side of the river, you'll get it. Then, hopefully, you slip into the water and forget it.

Not me. This is all I get. So yeah, I'm feeling a little bit like a teenage kid, right up until we hit this shack.

She stops in front of the busted-up plank door. I can tell she doesn't want to go back in there. I don't either. But hers is the kind of no that's working itself up to a yes, so I case the place as best I can with the moments I have.

I remember a place we used to bust for bootlegging back on the Rez, called Sancho's Broken Arrow. The door looked just like this, greasy and chipped. It was off the main drag but near enough to the casino that it caught people in a gambling mind like flies to shit. We just couldn't quite kill it. Funny how things come back around. Maybe when Ninepoint and I were clearing that place out for the hundredth time back in the day, I should have looked a little closer at the bar back. Maybe I'd have found a Black Bear totem tucked in the corner by the jars of Bodrey moonshine.

"Do you feel them?" she asks.

"Who?" I reply, touching the old wood of the door. Witchcraft, all of this. We're really pushing our luck here.

"Sara and Tábaahá. Their souls, you feel them, right?"

I reach out into the map, and I don't find them, but I see where they *should* be. That means yeah, I feel how they're missing and have been for decades, their tracks covered up by the shifting sands. But that's a lot to explain, so I nod.

"He fed off their memories. Mine too. We all gave bits of our past to him. The pieces that hit him hardest—the really good drugs—was the stuff that fit his own narrative. He's trying to piece together what he lost with *our* memories, Ben. The key is in his past."

I guess that's a lot to explain too, so I nod.

She pushes the door open, and it creaks like a dried-out coffin. I'm tense, all wound up to fight the king of monsters, the architect of all this pain.

What I get is a drunk, but not the kind sleeping it off wherever he happened to land.

This drunk is wide awake, leaning against the table, waiting for us, eyes mottled red with fury. He looks like a cross between a dad about to beat the hell out of his kid for coming in late, and a bear someone fucked with before it could sleep off the hibernation hangover.

"You walked into the wrong cave, Ben Dejooli," he says, pushing the words out in a low growl. Then he turns to Caroline. "And you. Since you love those dry shells of women in the back rooms so much, you will join them."

He slams his fists into the table and stands in one motion then tosses the whole thing at us. I step in front of her and shoulder it hard, and it cracks down the rusted-out middle, bits of cheap plastic and jagged metal raking along my shoulder. Both of us stagger back, nearly going down on a weird little shelf that runs along the wall.

I brace for him to run at us, but Black Bear takes to one knee instead and starts slamming his fist into the planks of the floor—swing after swing, like a sledgehammer. I expect his hand to splinter with each blow, but when the cracking sound comes, it's the wood that gives, first bending then buckling. All the time, he's seething, staring at the same spot, spit dripping from his lips.

"I have more boons than you have bodies. I will send waves and waves. I will crush your people. Grind them to dust, and turn them into totems."

He pounds his way through with a snap like a tree limb giving out. He looks up at us, and his face is wet. His eyes are swimming and narrow as he roots around in the guts of this place and pulls up another black totem. His smile is a grimace of pain and mad pleasure.

Caroline squeezes my hand in a way that screams, *We're all done for,* but I'm thinking of what she said outside.

"The past," I say. "I can do the past."

She holds me tight, bracing to take the charge. "Well, we have to do *something!*"

"Do you trust me?" I ask.

She squeezes my hand again. "Of course!"

I pull her close. Black Bear roars and runs at us, and I roar back. Caroline too. Or maybe she's just screaming.

I slam my hand onto Black Bear's forehead right as this newest totem swings our way in his fist, and I spin my roulette wheel of time.

Everything goes end over end: my thoughts, my breath, my body. All of it is plucked backward into darkness.

36

THE WALKER

I sail us over a cliff into Black Bear's memories. The drop doesn't stop. All I can do is grip his face with one hand and squeeze Caroline tight with the other and ride it out.

Chaco could've done something impressive like climb inside the guy's brain and give us front-row seats to just the right moment in his past, but I ain't Chaco, and Black Bear ain't exactly the kind of brain I'm lookin' to climb into, so your basic mega rewind is gonna have to do. We'll see it how it plays out. I'm just hoping I don't rewind us all into oblivion.

Black Bear twitches—nothing huge, but enough to show me he recognizes something or someone in all this backwards blur. That's enough for me to pull the emergency brake.

We land with a jerk that drops even my long-dead stomach. I reach for Caroline, but she staggers away and falls. I try to keep one eye on Black Bear, but my eyesight clicks at the edges like I stepped off a spinning top.

When the world comes back together, on the horizon I

see Mount Taylor—the holy mountain we call Blue Bead —so I know we're still on Dinetah, the homeland of my people, but it's different, thicker, less scraggly, and lusher. The rocks and low brush are here, but the trees are bigger and spread way back, almost to the horizon. There's more water, too, and more... things. Living things—animals and birds and insects all around us are making a low hum in the light of the setting sun.

And above it all is a sound hard to ignore, coming from a crude lean-to inside a grove of piñon trees.

At first, I think two people are crying inside, holding each other close, but soon it's clear that the sadness is as least part pleasure. Two people are having desperately quiet sex in there, keeping the sound as low as they can.

I help Caroline to stand, and she looks around, dizzy, and dry heaves a few times. "You do this for a living?" she asks.

"Not always. Sometimes. Not usually as far back as this."

She takes a few more deep breaths, holding onto my shoulder, and I try not to lean into the weight of her just because it's there, then she stops and tilts her head, finding the sound, finding the shelter. "Is that—"

"Yep."

She looks from me to Black Bear, who seems to have forgotten we're here. He watches the shelter and listens carefully, like he knows every note of the music they make together.

"If this is his past, that means his young self is in there—"

"Pretty much."

"Okay," she says, rubbing at her face. "Wow. We're in deep."

Black Bear shrugs off our words with an animal flinch. He still holds the totem, but he's walking toward the tent with tunnel vision. He holds his head up and closes his eyes as the sounds grow tighter, faster, and when they peak together, he opens his own mouth just a little bit, his arms raised like he's conducting.

My guess is he's been here more than a time or two. I can't tell you how many times I've walked back moments like this—not necessarily sex stuff, either, just any sensation stuff. Pure feelings. Moments when you eat life. Hard not to when you get lonely.

The quiet that follows is something I know too. Or knew. That moment when lovers just hold each other. Spent. That quiet holding is the part I miss most.

A minute later, Black Bear of this living memory emerges from the lean-to, still slick with sweat and so full of life I can almost hear the blood screaming through his veins.

Our version of Black Bear watches closely as the man of memory walks to the edge of the trees and looks out. The land relaxes into the flats that way, and there in the near distance is a small cloud of dust.

"Someone's coming up on them," I say.

"Yes," Black Bear says, with a deadness that chills me more than the anger that dripped from him before. "Death is coming."

Then she emerges, a beautiful woman adjusting a well-worn elk skin around her shoulders with innate elegance, as if she's settling a diamond necklace. She has a smooth, broad brow. High cheekbones drop to a razor-sharp nose, smooth jaw sloping to a small chin set in stone. By any standard, she's beautiful. But by my guess, we've gone back four hundred years or more. And four hundred years ago, our people bore the scars of life heavy and forever and had no real shelter from the world we lived in. In her own time, she would've been a goddess.

I catch a cold glint of silver resting softly between her breasts as she dresses. I know that glint. She wears the bell on a sinew thong around her neck. It clinks softly with a small obsidian knife threaded next to it. She was a Keeper.

Our Black Bear walks up to her and reaches out to brush her cheek. His hand falls through the replay, but he expects this. He would've done this before too, a million times, maybe. Again, I hate that I get it.

"She's beautiful, isn't she?" he says. "She walks like a warrior, more grace upon her brow than all the chiefs of the clans combined. But fearless. The kind of woman who fucks in the face of death. Her name was Tala, first daughter of the Blood Moon clan. And she was mine."

"And the cloud on the horizon... That's death?" Caroline asks.

Black Bear tears himself away from Tala and looks out with narrowed eyes. His lips peel back from his teeth. "Her brothers," he growls.

He's finding his footing and filling with mad fury again. He looks at me and Caroline like trespassers. Best to keep him unbalanced. A wobbly bear can't charge.

"Alright," I say, grabbing Caroline's hand. "We ain't got all day."

I swipe us forward. The cloud grows and grows, then we're in it. And figures emerge one after the other from within. The brothers ride bareback on horses slick with froth, controlling the mounts with their knees and wielding weapons in their hands. Knives. Long sharp spears. Bows and arrows.

The riders churn a circle around Tala Blood Moon

and Black Bear, kicking desert dust into a vortex that blots out the morning sky. They whoop warrior cries like the piercing calls of hawks. Caroline and I step back even at the memory of this, but Tala and Black Bear stand tall inside it, back-to-back. They seem to be expecting this.

Their tornado flashes with sharpened obsidian, and the thunder of hooves mixes with the sound of spinning ropes slicing the air. Blood flies inside, spinning out in arcs that spatter the ground beyond.

The churn slows, and the dust settles, and Black Bear is beat up bad, his face weeping red, one ear in tatters. He took almost all the hits by design. Tala is dusty and bloody, but it's not her blood.

"Step back, sister," says one of the brothers. "We do not want to cut you down."

"But you will?" she asks, her voice steady and loud and somehow still unafraid.

"If it means we keep the bell in our clan," says another, "then yes."

The horses canter around now, their hooves a low, threatening rumble.

"I will not leave his side," she says.

This gets sneers and spits.

One brother on a spotted white roan flecked with blood uncoils a net looped around his shoulder, weighted at the corners with something resembling bolas. He starts to twirl it. "Then we will take you from him," he snarls.

His toss is expert, hard and clean. He clips her at the knees, wraps her, and pulls her away, shredding what's left of the tattered buckskin she wears. Black Bear's memory screams for her as the deadly stampede fires up around him again.

A drag like that would put me down for the count, but

not this woman. She slits a clean line down the net with one whick of her knife and tumbles out with enough sense to grab a good length of slack while her brother circles around for another pass.

She stands naked and bloodied and whips the line back on him, looping his neck, and she twists with all she has at just the right moment. One second, he's on the horse—the next, the horse is riding off into the sunrise without him, and he's crooked and dead on the dirt.

She doesn't stop to take any of this in. She prowls back to the pack, and even though I know it's a memory, I step back to let her pass. Caroline does too.

The other brothers notice too late. She lashes out with that black knife and slits an unlucky horse along the length of its side then dips and catches the one that follows at the tendon above the hoof. The first bucks, the second staggers, and both brothers fall. One gets his head caved in by his own horse. The other, she plugs with her knife two, three, four times in the back, finding the spaces between ribs like an expert butcher. He staggers off to drown in his own blood.

The others notice her now. The bell drips, and she pulls at the strap and takes in a deep breath. I know that look. Grant has that look. The bell is soaking up death. It's saturated with blood and crying to be rung.

One brother, with murder in his eyes, leans at an impossible angle off the side of his horse and draws back a bow black with use. His arrow hisses and catches her right in the neck. She's brought to her knees and touches it, fletching end first then the bloody tip sprouting from the other side. The brother leaps from his horse and rolls to his feet, closing fast.

She pulls the arrow through. The fletching takes a

chunk of skin and something gristly and white on the way out, and she wheezes once. As the brother leaps for her, she turns and buries the arrow in his gut. The look of surprise on his face, the way a man can go from murderer to murdered, is almost funny. Then she shanks him three times where his shoulder meets his neck, and everything is wiped from his face.

This leaves one, but he has already reached Black Bear, who looks unconscious. His right arm and leg are at bad angles. Arrows protrude from his side, and flaps of skin are missing from his chest.

The brother that holds him is small and cruel looking, and he wipes his own buck knife on the leather of his breeches as he yanks Black Bear's hair high and shaves up along his forehead before digging in at the hairline for the scalp. He gets about an inch deep before Tala sweeps in from behind and slits his throat. Blood bubbles from the razor line then weeps, and she shoves him aside.

Tala falls to her knees and wheezes for Black Bear. She tries and fails to speak, and I realize she hasn't been able to breathe since the arrow pierced her.

"The sun will never set on our love," our Black Bear says, his voice thick and low as he walks up on the memory. "That's what she said to me. I've spent many days of men here, listening to that wheeze, unearthing her words."

Caroline has her own hands to her throat, covering her mouth, her eyes wide with shock. All of this happened in the span of time it took the sun to pierce the horizon.

Tala is turning an ashen shade of blue. She holds the bell, looks at it hard, then shakes her head. She falls to the ground, and as she closes her eyes, Black Bear of memory moans himself awake. He sees her, pale in death, and tries to scream, but his injuries won't let him, and the sound sticks in his throat. He crawls through the churned dirt to her and brushes her face, puts his hands to her throat, and tries to shore up what's already bled out.

Death is crawling over him too. His breathing is labored, rattling. His head drops by slow degrees.

She holds the bell in a death claw, but he pries it open. The real Black Bear takes a knee and watches as if he's having a hard time recognizing himself.

"I thought if I couldn't keep her from dying, I could at least keep her from leaving me," he says.

He closes his eyes in pain as his old self rings the bell.

The force of all the death around him comes out at once, and the man of memory is blown from his body full and whole, rolling shoulder over shoulder until he settles, splayed out.

He spends a moment feeling his face and his side, feeling that first hit of *nothing*. The first shot is wonderful. When you ring the bell and all the pain goes away. You think it's a miracle.

At first.

Next, he sees what all this hell wrought. Five dead brothers are in a line, walking away into the desert, their deed done and their eternity awaiting them. The veil sweeps in through the piercing light of the morning and the still-settling dust, taking them one by one. I'm sure they think glory awaits.

But the same river is waiting for them that waits for all of us. The only difference is how you float it.

Tala is the last soul standing, but Black Bear is beginning to understand now. This isn't the reunion he was expecting. There is no stopping what comes, no stopping the veil.

He reaches for her soul and finds she's too horrified to touch him—not by the veil making its silent way toward her, but by him.

She knows what he did, what he's become.

That's the look she has when she's taken. The veil doesn't care who died or how. The veil just keeps coming. The blood-red curtain envelops her then sweeps around Black Bear before it falls into the sand itself.

Somewhere, a crow cries three times, sharp enough to make us all flinch. Chaco, maybe, witnessing another handoff. Black Bear falls over her body and tries to cradle her head, but his hands pass through.

His loneliness has only begun. Our version knows that. He has centuries ahead of him to slowly lose his mind, thinking about that last look she gave.

"She swore our love would never die," he growls, "but when *she* did, it fled from her."

Caroline isn't having that. "Maybe she saw your true face," she says. "The face I see. The face all those women saw."

"She saw death!" Black Bear snaps. "And I knew if I ever wanted her to look at me like she did when we were alive, I'd have to shed death from me. In my time of living, I was a good gambler, and good gamblers never lose. They just bide their time between wins. I knew then that I would win my way back to life and meet her face-to-face on the other side, one boon at a time."

He's recovering himself again. He lurches toward us, off kilter and drunk with the emotions from his past, but I don't stick around this bloody battleground to see what kind of punch he's trying to land with that totem. I rush right up to meet him and spin us all the way forward until we hit the wall of the present, and it staggers all of us back to the lost desert outside his forgotten home.

We roll on the sand, landing a lot like Black Bear did after the bell rang. The vertigo rushes in like a wave and pulls out like a riptide, and it takes me a minute to realize that the ringing in my ears is actually the river. It's close now, a short walk away. The water rushes in the center but eddies at the sides, which means we're to the chaos side of center but not far down.

Caroline helps me up this time. Of the two of us, she's got the sea legs here. I settle my head and try to find Black Bear, but he's still on hands and knees, looking at the river.

"It's never been this close," he says.

"It's been looking for you for four hundred years," I say.

"It will look for four hundred more," he says, pushing himself to full height, like the man who stood in the center of that storm of death.

"You drink the love of others because you're too chickenshit to face the end of your own," I say. The thought of that is so disgusting to me, so selfish—and he did it to *Caroline.* I'll bring the river to *him* if that's what it takes. Drop by drop, right through his fucking forehead. Not sure how, but I'll figure it out. I got time. My anger threatens to boil over, but then Caroline cuts between us.

She walks over to Black Bear and stares him down from a foot away. He's taller than her, but right now, it doesn't feel that way.

"You took me away from my daughter," she says, her voice thick. "You know that, right? And the whole time I've been here, all I wanted was to watch you suffer. But hate doesn't get you through these dark, never-ending days.

You know what does? Thinking that maybe others aren't so miserable. Owen, he gets to see her. He gets to watch her grow. And even if I can't picture her, I can picture him. And he's happy. And that's enough."

Caroline grabs Black Bear's face with both hands, and he's too stunned to react. Both of us are. "Tala saw an ugly face when she looked at you. You know it, and I know it. She wanted to die with you, and you ruined it. You fled from her. Your fear made you ugly. And every second you stay here, every second you hide, it gets worse."

He tries to tear himself away, but Caroline holds him and stares into him, looking at him the way she looks at things when she sees colors of smoke. When she finally does let him go, she gives him a little shove toward the river, and he staggers back, staring at her like she's a stranger, a thief who replaced the woman he stole. But that's only because he doesn't really know her or what she can do.

I'm not talking about her seeing smoke, either. I'm talking about the way she can understand a person, how she can turn over rocks lodged in the hard dirt of sad souls. She can see the truth in you, yeah, but her real power is making you see the truth in yourself.

Caroline points at the river. "She said the sun will never set on your love. That's why you hide in an endless afternoon. But you can't hide from the fact you've been breaking that vow for four straight centuries."

That's the dagger.

The river is three steps away then two. I think it's got a bit of the veil in it like that. Once it senses a thing it has lost, it makes its slow way there, hell or high water. These are the great tools of the balance. You can run from them, but they'll find you eventually.

And today, the river of souls has found Black Bear.

Or maybe I should say Caroline found the real Black Bear, and the river followed her.

I find myself grinding my teeth, praying that he'll just fucking walk out into the water. *Just go. Scream if you want. Gnash your teeth. Spit venom. But go. Please.*

His toes are inches from the water, and it ripples toward him, eager. He looks at the dead sky and says, "The sun will never set."

He turns around, and I mutter a string of curses, roll up my sleeves, and get ready for a fistfight I ain't gonna win, but he just stares at me.

"When everyone you love is gone, it'll happen to you too," he says—clinical, matter of fact. And it lands a gut punch worse than anything he could've thrown by force. "The days will blend until you forget your own face."

He looks back to Caroline. "Maybe the river will help me remember."

He opens his arms just like he did that day, walking on water out in the Arroyo, and falls back in a silent, sucking splash, watching me the whole time.

I look for his soul light, but it's lost in the depths of the river in an instant. Chaos took it so quickly that it never got the chance to shine.

37

OWEN BENNET

You may be wondering if, in fact, I'm still with my infant child inside a very possibly radioactive rock pile. The answer to that is yes. But in my defense, I'd like to mention two things. One is that she seems to be having the time of her life. She's been watching the floating dust and the shifting shadows like it's must-see TV. Sure, she's on her second-to-last diaper, and since we're out of baby food, I've been feeding her bits of a protein shake which I'm quite sure will destroy the diaper she's currently wearing, but right now, she's doing fine.

The second thing is I've set a timer, not on my watch but on the rocks. When this shifting sunbeam hits a certain spot on the rock wall that looks a bit like the red eye of Mars, it's time for me to go. At that point, I will ask her to sit in this hollow above my right shoulder and tell her not to worry at how Daddy might look, wiggling like a stoat in a sack. Then, when I get to the place where I had trouble before, I will tell her not to worry about the bad words Daddy will say as he attempts to fold himself out of here.

Then we will regroup, and we will look for Caroline again some other way. Because if this whole claustrophobic disaster has taught me anything, it's that I am willing to play the long game. And I'm not willing to accept a world in which I don't get to at least say goodbye to her.

The thought makes my wildly acidic stomach lurch. That protein shake was for me, of course, but this is what happens when you have a kid and you get yourself wedged in a tough spot without a real plan. You give the kid the food and instead eat at yourself mentally. I am aware that providing for her first makes very little evolutionary sense at the moment. If I don't make it out of this rock, she won't. But I would hazard a guess that not a whole lot of evolutionary biologists have been stuck under radioactive rocks with their infant children.

A funny sound comes from her as she lounges across my diaphragm once more, grabbing at motes. At first, I think maybe she's burping up protein shake, and I wouldn't blame her in the least, but then she turns toward me, and she's smiling.

She hiccups again then giggles. She swipes at a mote and just so happens to swat across my face at the same time.

"Are you laughing?" I ask, helpless not to smile myself. "Are you laughing, baby girl?"

I think of how wonderful it is to be able to laugh in this place. It's easy enough to assume she doesn't know where she is or what got her here, but I think she does. And she's laughing, which scratches something deep in my brain. First of all, I don't really think I've heard her laugh before. Maybe she bubbled a few things up here and there, indistinguishable from gas, but never a real laugh.

No, I would remember this sound. It's pure and clear and somehow defiant, almost like a war cry. That scratches a little deeper, and I remember something Joey Flatwood told me once. He said the Navajo believe no child is truly safe until they laugh.

I strain my head to look at her as she giggles once more then sighs, watching the sun, her butt pressed happily against my cheek.

38

CAROLINE ADAMS

He's gone. Black Bear is gone, and now, it's just me and Ben on this endless shore.

"Why can't I shake the feeling he's just gonna jump out again or something?" I say.

Ben squeezes my hand. "Because for many lifetimes, he did. He did jump out at you. And that feeling ain't gonna go away. That's what they call trauma. It's tough to shake."

I cock an eye at him, impressed. He may be frozen in the body of the young man I knew, but he's grown so much in other ways. I suppose it's hard not to when you've seen what he's seen.

"Trust me," he says. "That river scattered him. It was like taking a lighter to a piece of four-hundred-year-old paper. He's gone."

Behind us, the ground groans. I turn to find the shack leaning heavily to one side.

"It's coming down," Ben says, "just like Dark Sky's house did."

My mind flashes to the rooms where Sara and

Tábaahá lie as frozen husks. The thought just doesn't sit right with me. "The whole thing is going to collapse?" I ask.

Ben nods. "My guess is these things, these hideouts, were built on boons. You saw how he bashed his way through the foundation to find the next one he wanted. But when he went, the boons went too. It's all going back to the sand."

"It'll be a tomb," I say, and I'm already speed walking toward it then running. "I can't let them be buried like that."

Ben runs after me. "Caroline, we really can't mess around with this stuff. This place is quicksand for the living."

I look over my shoulder. "Do you trust me?"

I don't even need his nod. I already feel it.

So yeah, we're running back toward what's essentially a burning building. Maybe it's something like Stockholm syndrome or whatever, but I'd like to think it's just me doing right by my friends, leaving here on my own terms.

I shoulder open the door and find everything groaning and shifting. The guts of the place are sloshing around, crap crashing off the walls, bottles shattering, cans rolling left and right. That stupid folding table and the godforsaken couch slide my way. I dodge them and cut down the hall, Ben right behind me. *Tackle the farthest from the door first and work your way back*—good ol' listing logic. Tábaahá first.

The floor of Tábaahá's room is breaking in half. The boards bow and crack, and the fetishes and skulls spin wildly and fall from the rafters one by one, popping like lightbulbs. But she is still where she was, under ratty old skins in the corner.

"Her," I say. "Can you... I don't know, help her? I mean, I know she's dead, but—"

I'm trying for words and failing and tearing up, but Ben just puts a hand on my shoulder and steps over to her. It's so hard to find people you don't have to explain yourself to. By my count, I've only got three, and one of them is dead.

Ben kneels down, steadying himself as the ground shifts, but he's all focus. He looks her over, head to toe.

"Tábaahá," he says after an endless half minute. "There you are."

He smiles and reaches carefully with one hand right through her forehead. He closes his eyes and makes a bunch of tiny movements, like he's spinning the combination on a safe.

A big rumble gives him pause, but not for long. He pulls a tiny spark from deep within, a firefly gently caged in his hand.

He turns back to me and holds up his closed hand. I could kiss him. But we have another stop to make.

Sara's room is harder. The floor is already pitted with gaping holes that yawn wider and wider. Ben takes one look at it before telling me to wait in the hall, then he jumps across to her iron cot. Her husk has rolled off onto the ground and cracked nearly in half. The busted television that hid her last note rolls toward a break in the floor and pitches in.

Ben braces himself with his left forearm, gets low, and does the same careful lockpicking. Something deep within the house snaps with the sound of a cosmic whip, and I brace myself in the doorway just like a good little elementary school kid. Never mind that the doorway is crumbling off in my hands.

Ben is oblivious to the world around him falling in chunks to his left and right. Some part of the ceiling collides with his shoulder, but he only freezes a moment before going back to his work.

Part surgeon, part sorcerer, he pulls Sara's spark free. And only now am I really considering who we have on our side here. The old Navajo stories have characters that do stuff like this. They call them holy people. They call them gods.

I'm not gonna say that out loud though. I have a hard time squaring it with my memories of sitting with him in the front room of his tiny duplex a lifetime ago, talking about everything and nothing to keep his mind off the chemo.

He hopscotches his way back, and the floor falls to sand seconds after his steps. We run down the hallway as it crumbles behind us. I lower my shoulder to blow through the front door, but Ben yells from behind.

"Your crow!"

Of course. My crow totem. Black Bear pinned it to the wall with two railroad spikes under each wing when he found he couldn't shatter it himself. I should've taken that as a sign it might come back to life one day.

If I think about it, I'll freeze. So I don't think. I scamper like a spooked rabbit until I reach the far wall of my room. Every step I take pops the slatted boards like gunshots. I grab the crow and turn back to Ben, but between us is black quicksand.

"Jump!" he yells.

If I think, I'll freeze. So I don't think. I jump.

Ben catches me by the hand then the waist, and together, we spin with momentum to hit the door. I lower my shoulder, bracing for the crunching pain, but instead, it folds over me like a bead curtain. Both of us tumble out and over the porch. Ben half helps and half throws me forward, and only once we're twenty or so feet out do we both steady each other and turn around.

By now, the shack is a lumpy wax candle of a thing, all burned out. It sounds like the tail end of a massive rainstick as it oozes itself out, and I spit at what's left, which surprises me. I despise spitting.

The absence of the place makes me incredibly tired. It's like looking at an excised wound. The gap that remains is painful, yeah, but it's also tiring. So much lost. So much that needs to heal. In a lot of ways, the cutting out is the easy part.

After long minutes, Ben holds up his gently cupped hand, and I see the two sparks moving slowly in and around each other inside.

"Are they hugging?" I ask, and the tears are back, and the words come out kind of slobbery.

"I think they want the river," Ben says.

So we go to the river.

Ben can touch the river, can go all the way in and out and between, so he takes them in, wading carefully until he's up to his waist. Then he sets the sparks down like flower petals. At first, they freeze, but then they grow and grow until the sparks aren't sparks anymore—they're more like candles then flashlights then lanterns. And once they're lanterns, they move around each other again, weaving and passing through one another with something that can't be anything but joy. They do this for a bit, then they spin around Ben before moving side by side to the shore. They glow softly a few feet from where I stand, and I feel like they're waving at me.

"Goodbye, my friends," I manage to whisper.

They linger for a moment more, then they float off to the right. Ben watches them with a small smile. My guess is that way is the side of order, the side of peace. And peace has been a long time coming for these two.

Ben wades out of the river, then the two of us walk along the shore together.

I had a whole laundry list of things I wanted to talk with him about if I ever got the chance. So many things have happened to me or with me—or to Grant and Owen —that made me wonder, *What would Ben think?* If only he knew how much he helped me figure out being alive without saying a single word.

Now that I'm here with him, I forget all of them, natu-rally. But one thing I know is still true.

"I miss you all the time," I say. "You know that, right?"

He glances at me, and there's that small smile again. "I know it. I feel it too. Sometimes..." He works his mouth, struggling for the words. "Sometimes, I feel like missing you is all that keeps me from..."

He flutters his fingers away from his temple. He means *spinning out*, losing himself, becoming something like Black Bear, obsessed with a life he couldn't have. Afraid of what the river holds.

"Sounds a lot like my day-to-day," I say. "And everyone else on the planet. It doesn't matter what you *think*, Ben. All that matters is what you do. And you do wonderful things. You help people. You help *me*. And I need you here, helping. We all do."

As he mulls that over, something catches my eye. It looks like a little black ribbon, rolling our way over the sand on a breeze I can't feel at all. Both of us stop and watch it approach. As it gets closer, I see it's a feather. A crow feather is tumbling end over end to rest right at my feet.

"What's this all about?" I ask.

Ben looks at me, and not even that little half smile can mask how sad his eyes are.

"I think you should pick it up," he says.

I reach down and touch it with my finger, brushing it along the fletching, and I get a powerful vision of the exact color of my daughter's smoke. It's so real and so rich that it's almost like I can smell her—that strong, just born, fresh-from-the-ether smell of new skin and new beauty and new life.

"Oh," I say, quietly. "It's her."

"She's waiting for you with Owen," Ben says. "Just on the other side."

In the time it takes me to grab the feather and move my focus to Ben, everything gets darker and quieter, like a movie is about to start.

I take Ben's hand, and he squeezes back, his eyes glittering, then there's nothing but the touch of our hands. All around us is soft darkness. I get the sensation that we're moving through the black, going back home.

"Is this goodbye?" I ask, and I move in closer and put my head on his chest.

"It is."

"Will I ever see you again?" I ask, trying to capture feelings and memories like snapshots I can tuck away forever. But I'm failing.

"One more time, maybe," he says. "But I don't think either of us in a hurry for that one."

He trails off because I'm feeling for him, feeling for his face and all its parts and brushing his lips like a blind woman trying to read the life I might have had if I'd turned left instead of right.

It's as if our lips find each other's of their own accord. We press everything we have into that kiss, as well as everything we don't. Then we pull quietly away from one another.

He doesn't know what to say. I know that, even in the total dark. But I do know what to say because I've had this conversation with him before in my mind. Many times.

"I deserve that as much as you do. Let's call it a nod to another timeline. You know I love you, Ben. You know Owen loves you and Grant and my daughter too. You may be out here by yourself, but you're *never* alone. And you are not Black Bear. You are everything he isn't. You're kind, and you're strong. And you have to stay strong. For us."

The movement in the darkness around us slows, like a train coming into the station. I see a faint hint of color in the mist, a small patch where the dark breaks a bit like ripples of light in the deep water.

I feel him nod and hear him swallow hard. He still struggles for the words, always has. But that's okay. Everything he could possibly say, I feel anyway, more deeply than he could express. And I think he knows that.

Ben and me, we've got muscle memory.

So I make it easy on him. I gently let go of his hand, turn, and walk away through the mist. And the whole time I walk, I keep him right behind, because if he's right behind, he can't even get a hint at how hard it is for me to keep it together.

Although he probably knows that too.

39

GRANT ROMER

I'm sitting in the sunwarmed mud, leanin' hard against the twins' hogan—too hard, probably. This thing is a hundred years old, maybe more, and it ain't good to be leanin' this hard on anything that old, especially now that the twins are gone and ain't proppin' it up anymore. But the truth is I'm more tired than I ever been, and I ain't got nowhere else to go.

Black Bear's broken totems puffed to ash a few minutes ago. We're all pretty sure that means it's over. Our two-front war is over, and I guess we won even though it don't feel that way.

Joey sits here too, both of us kinda like spent horses tethered to a post in a ghost town. The thought of standing is too much. I picture myself trying and staggering, all gut shot, probably crawling to Kai then dragging her down, both of us under the weight of the blood-soaked silver that hangs around my neck.

If I was Kai and I was with me, I would get the hell outta Dodge. I know that's easier said than done, but she don't have to leave Navajo country. She can do anything.

The way things are goin', she ain't gonna be able to do it with me, but that's okay. She'll get by.

I look back at the ballsy kid I was, trying to get her name and number back in high school, and I wonder how that kid had the strength. I'm afraid that kid is gone. I don't want her to see how weak I've become.

Then she's here, lookin' down at me. She's wearing her old jeans and tank top, but they're so covered in ash that they're all one color now. She smells like this mix of smoke and clean sweat and soft skin that I can't quite describe right because it's a bit like describing the color of her soul.

She looks down at me, and I ain't felt like so much a broken boy since I sat crying at those graves back in Midland.

"We need to talk," she says.

I know this means terrible shit. What a terrible set of four words. Ain't no need for those words unless it's an ending, but she ain't even privy to the half of it.

"Alright," I say. And I ask Chaco if he'll sit on my shoulder again. And I know he might not. But it's now or never, and I need him.

And he comes.

The way he settles is so soft. I think he does it on purpose, brushing me with his wing tips, because this ain't gonna be easy, not by a long shot.

Kai starts.

"Grant," she says, and she starts crying. She tries to stop it. Looks up. Looks away. Wipes her face. None of it works. Kai ain't ever really been able to cry her whole life, so she ain't got practice in stopping it. "I think you're drowning," she says through the tears. "And I know why. It's that goddamn bell. But I don't know how to help you, and it's fuckin' killing me because I love you. I love you, but I don't know how to help someone drowning in a thing I can't understand."

I hold the bell up from my chest, and it's like ripping grass at the roots. I drop it to my chest, and it thumps like a gong inside.

I look at Chaco, he looks back, but he's quiet in my head. Which is how I know he's listening.

I don't know who came around to who, but I'm gonna say this was his idea.

I look up at Kai, drenched in loss and love and more beautiful than I've ever known her. "There is a way you could understand," I say. And this part hurts a lot, but I've gotten to a point where holding pain in don't work anymore. "And you could help me too."

Kai looks at the bell and at me and then away. "What are you talkin' about?" she asks, but she asks it like she knows.

It can get real awkward, trying to ask your girlfriend to save your life. But it's ride or die now.

I hold my arm out, and Chaco hops down to rest on the ground between us.

"You could take the bell," I say to her, trying to keep it casual, like I'm handing off keys to my truck, but when the words are out, the sound of them is so stupid—that anyone who's seen what I've become might want this thing—

"Okay," she says.

Then it gets really quiet. And I know Joey is trying not to let me know he's listening, but the fact that he's as tense as a jackrabbit gives it away.

"Okay?" I ask.

Kai grabs a handful of old ash and pollen from the

east-facing door above us and brushes it through her hair. Then she sits next to me.

I try to shuffle to make room, but I don't got it in me. I used to be able to shift the weight of the thing around, to hold it in my back one day, shoulders the next, neck the next. But it's too heavy for that now.

She looks down and picks at the mud that won't come out of her knuckles since the flood. "Except... what about Chaco?"

There it is. I didn't want to hear this from Chaco. It's why I shoved the thoughts away, but he's been planting this seed in my brain for a little while now, ever since it got so I couldn't keep my head up right.

He won't talk to me mind to mind, no matter how much I try to stink eye him. My guess is he thinks if I hear his voice in my head like I always have, I might back out. And he's probably right.

He does press his head under my hand, though, and I trail my finger down the crown of his head.

"Well," I say, turning to Kai. "You'll be able to talk to Chaco. He'll become like a brother to you. Hell, he *will* become a brother to you."

You who have no family left. You who need a brother more than I do now. I don't say these things, but they pass between all three of us anyway. Me gettin' dragged down by the bell is only part of this decision. It's the best for everyone, but that don't mean it don't hurt.

Kai looks off at the big sky. "And you?" she asks, so soft I can barely hear.

"I... won't be able to talk to him. Not anymore. His charge is the Keeper."

"I can't do that to you," she says. "I can't take him away from you. I won't."

I lean back on the Hogan and take my hat off and put it on my knee. "If you don't, pretty soon, there won't be much of me left for Chaco to talk to anyway."

She blinks big tears down her cheek and holds out her hand for Chaco, who hops over to her and runs his crown along her palm too. He knows the stakes of this, maybe better than anyone.

"Okay then," she says barely.

I nod and run my hand through my sweaty hair and put my hat back on. I feel like I'm watching myself, like I'm walking through a dream. "Can I have a second with him?" I ask. "To say goodbye?"

Kai is full-on silent crying now, and she gets up without a word and walks away, hugging herself. I get it. It's hard to need something and not want it at the same time. Joey stands too and looks at me with a pride I ain't seen in him for a while. Then he walks away.

It's just me and my bird and the desert.

"I can feel Caroline again," Chaco says, looking out toward the horizon.

"I can too," I say. And I mean it. She's coming back. I don't know what she did or how she did it, but it just feels like the scales are settling again. It's in the even spread of the sunrise. The world has the right weight.

We're quiet for a bit. Then Chaco hops up my arm and settles in his spot on my shoulder again. "It's the right thing, Grant. You know it, and I know it."

"Of course it is," I say, but tears fall anyway. "That don't make it easy."

"I know," Chaco says and he presses softly against my neck.

"So how do I do this?" I ask, hoarse.

"You give her the bell. A willing giver, a willing recipient. That's all it takes."

"No, not that. How do I say goodbye to you?"

Chaco's voice is small, quiet. "I'll still be here... You just..."

"Won't be able to hear you. Won't have you here with me, sharing this space in my head. My oldest friend."

I dig at the tears with the heel of my palm, but ain't nothin' stoppin' 'em this time. All my life, it's been Chaco that's stopped the crying. Now, I'm doing it on account of Chaco. And I know it's the right thing. I know it. But it still—

"Still sucks," Chaco says softly, bobbing his head. "I know."

Maybe he knows I ain't ready yet, not just yet. So he says, "How about I tell you a story?"

Yes. A story. I'll be losing his voice soon, and I want all of it I can get.

"Alright," I say.

"I am an infinite thing, so to speak, and I've had many different forms over the eras in which I've walked, but there are certain stories that have found a way deep inside me, to a special place even I cannot understand, which I think you might call a soul."

He stands on my shoulder and looks at me, but I can't look back because I think I'll dissolve.

"No matter where I go or what I become in my task as a thinning, these stories never leave me. And this is one of them," he says, then he looks out at the way the sun is breaking over the Arroyo like a cracked egg of pure light. He's looking back in time too, visiting that space inside, maybe.

"Years ago, my kind sensed destruction coming. First, the imbalance of the river and the escape of the creature of chaos. Next, the imbalance of Black Bear cheating the death he deserved. Any one of these things alone would have been catastrophic, but to have one after the other, all so closely tied to the bell... Well, let's just say my crow brothers and sisters had basically given this world up for lost."

Chaco shivers at the thought, fluffing up his small feathers and settling them again. "Only a few of us held out hope, the ones that were there when Ben Dejooli freed his sister, Ana, and took upon himself the mantle of the Walker. That was a selflessness we hadn't seen in generations. So we had our ally on the side of the dead, but that was only half the battle. Agents of chaos were close to Ben at the time of his death, and in order to protect the bell, he had to throw it through time and space. A terrible risk but the only choice. And so it was lost, and my kind mourned again, and as the world tipped, I began my search."

"I searched and searched, and I felt my spirit sagging. Sometimes, the enormity of all this existence is enough to even crush the soul of timeless creatures. But just when I was about to give up, I sensed something: the bell but... different. From the beginning of time, whenever the bell found a new Keeper, it rang out in a voice only I can hear —a loud voice—but not this time. This time, the bell called out softly. I redoubled my efforts, but I strained to keep the sound in my ear. At times, it was so quiet that even my wingbeats would overpower its call. I overshot the spot several times. But when I eventually located it true, I dreaded to think what I would find. What could quiet the bell like this? Was the bell frightened by what it saw?"

Chaco turns back to me and walks the length of my shoulder until he forces my eye his way. Deep and dark, he's a velvet universe of his own. "And when I dropped out of the soul map into a dark desert night in the heart of Texas, I found you. And I realized two things. First, the bell wasn't quiet because it was afraid. It was quiet because it didn't want to scare you. That snake tried its best—surely it was an agent of chaos itself, seconds from claiming the bell as its own but seconds too slow. I speared it without thinking. I would have speared all the snakes in the world if I had to."

Chaco flashes his beak to prove the point and in the new light it takes a razors edge. But when I run my finger along it, the softness returns.

"The second thing I knew in an instant was that, with you, we had hope—a child equal parts strength and sadness, but with a heart that shone like a diamond in that dark night. If only you could have seen it yourself, Grant, you'd have believed in yourself so much sooner. But that is the way of humans. So much of your beauty is only visible to others."

Chaco leans against me. "For the first time in many lifetimes of men, I felt hope because there, in front of me, was that selflessness again. Ripped jeans, dirt on his face, mixed with tears. A young boy looking for a friend. A boy with too much worry and too much wisdom for eight. Who asked, "Is this a dream?" when I first spoke to him then simply nodded when I told him it was not. A boy who started giving of himself to a greater cause—the great balance—the second he put that bell on, and who hasn't stopped giving since."

Chaco looks over at Kai, who sits with Joey, and I can't tell who is comforting who. They both look pretty miserable, and they're trying their hardest not to look my way.

"But you don't have it in you to get burned up by the bell, Grant. You know why?"

I shake my head and hang it low and sob, but Chaco speaks through it into that soft place in the back of my mind. "Because that would be selfish. And you are not selfish. So you're doing the only thing more painful than getting crushed by the bell. You're giving it up—the bell and me—to a woman you love who needs me more. Self-lessness. You're still doing what that eight-year-old boy would do. You, Ben, and your mom and dad are selfless. All of you. That's what saved us, and if another terrible storm comes our way, it is selflessness that will save us again.

I nod, but I think it's hard to tell, on account of my shaking shoulders. And I hold up the bell. It's time.

Chaco grabs it very gently in his beak and pulls it tight against the strap. He means to break it, which makes sense. Already, I feel the lanyard stretching. The second I nod my consent, it began to fray. The bell knows.

He looks up at me with that knowing bond, and his voice settles itself in my mind one last time.

"You don't have to hear my voice to know I will always love you, Grant Romer," he says. Then he breaks me free.

There's a pop like a joint set right again—extremely painful but then quickly quiet, muted and warm.

I use that voice in my brain and reach out. "Chaco?" I ask. But I already know it's different. I'm just talking to myself now.

Chaco stands on my knee and watches me. I reach out to him through my tears, and I think for some reason, he won't recognize me anymore. Maybe he'll fly away. That would truly bury me.

But he doesn't. He bows and runs the crown of his head along my finger, in silence. His voice is lost to me now.

But that pop took away a weight too. And for the first time in years—maybe in my whole life—I feel like I can stand tall.

So I guide Chaco to my shoulder in silence.

And in silence, I stand up.

40

CAROLINE ADAMS

I'm following the light, but I walk through the darkness alone. And yes, it does occur to me that maybe "following the light" is not the super smartest thing to be doing when walking across the land of the dead, but the alternative is a beach that eats everything and a life without my family, so yeah, anyone would keep walking.

I think the light is changing color. I'm not sure, but with each step, it turns into something more and more familiar, then the most familiar, smoke I would know anywhere. It fits around me like a glove. It's her. It's not that new-chick fuzzy yellow anymore, and I'll table how much that kills me a little inside, knowing I wasn't there when that fell away, but a bright yellow that sparkles like a diamond and rushes toward me. First, my tummy, where it was at home, then it explores the rest of me, going in and on and around me, drawing me in closer.

The darkness takes the forms of rocks, heavy things that crisscross above. And I take one step that crackles on dusty ground before I'm grabbed by the ankle.

"Who is it?" Owen asks, harsh and tired. It's the voice of a haggard man still ready to throw himself back in front of the bus again if that's what it takes, the voice of a father with his back against a wall, a man who is stuck.

Not hard to see why. This cave is the size of a broom closet, and he's wedged in with our daughter.

The weightlessness is leaving me, but I'm in that in-between, neither here nor there yet. And I grab him under the arms, and press his arms to her, and as one, I push us through the last of this thin place while it's still thin.

He tenses and scrapes, holding her tight, but the rocks still sense me too, and they seem to breathe a little bit. It's not much, but it's enough.

We three sprawl out on the hot sand outside the rocks with the morning full-on now, and I almost scream when about fifty crows take flight at once, cawing back and forth like they just got the gossip of the century.

Owen's smoke practically oozes out on the dirt, spreading out like it hasn't stretched in ages. He sees me and tries to come to me, but he's weak, and he's been all folded up, so he struggles like a baby giraffe until I can scoot over to him and put a hand on his chest. Him first. I love her, and I will see her and greet her like she greeted me, but him first.

"It's me," I say. "It's just me."

He shudders and tries to steady his breathing until he can say, "You came back."

I'm already working at his smoke, settling it with touch.

"You came back," he says again, and this time, he seems to believe it. He has so much to say. I can see it written on him, but there's time for that later. Right now, I calm him with a kiss. First his forehead then his cheeks then his lips.

"You came *back*," he says a third time, bewildered and streaming with the same bright blue smoke I know and love, like a well running over.

"Of course I came back," I say. "There was a memory, a memory that kept me alive. The one I would never share with Black Bear—"

He tries to speak, but I put my finger to his lips. "I'll explain everything. But I have to tell you now."

"A memory kept you alive?"

"Yes. The one I couldn't let him steal. The one at my heart. It was you, Owen. The day you asked if you could come with me. Remember that? Out in the parking lot? With the crows above?"

And he laughs. "Of course I remember that. As far as I'm concerned, that's the day you said yes to me."

"Best decision of my life."

"So far," he adds, holding up a finger, which makes me laugh. What an Owen thing to say.

And then she laughs, too, and that's the moment I know we've finally come through. That's when I know we're safe.

41

KAI BODREY

Joey taps me on the shoulder and points that Grant is coming my way, with Chaco holding the bell.

I shake my head. "He's really doing this. Why is he doing this? He can't do this."

Joey folds his hands and rests his elbows on his knees. "It's happening. The question is are you ready?"

I look at Joey like my slackjaw cousins used to look at me back before one and then another thing plucked them all from the face of this earth. "Are you kidding me? Ready? I'm gonna go ahead and say no. I don't even have a *home*, Joey—"

"You have a home," Joey interjects with infuriating calm.

"You know what I mean. Everything I own is in my brother's truck."

"I think you can call it your truck now," Joey says.

I elbow him, and he allows it. "Fine. But I can't take Chaco from him."

"Nobody can *take* Chaco. You don't think he's had a say in this?"

They're closing in now, the two of them. The bell glints. Chaco's eyes have a literal weight to them. "I'm gonna puke," I say.

"Wouldn't be the first," Joey says.

"You're a real piece of work, Flatwood."

"I think you need to ask yourself a question, Kai Bodrey," Joey says, dusting his dark jeans off and standing, holding out his hand to me. "And that question is this. Can you accept a gift that you need?"

I look up at him. "What the hell is that supposed to mean?"

"You Bodreys were mostly shits," he says, with such strange deference it somehow comes out not terrible. "And yet somehow proud. Too proud for help. That is a bad combination. I thought your brother was the worst of you. But he proved me wrong."

"Uh. Thanks?"

"You were always different—night and day, the best your whole clan ever offered to this world. That is also a bad combination, but in a different way. You've been surrounded by such darkness that you've had to shine twice as strong. A hard thing. And one that will burn you as sure as the bell would burn Grant if you hold to it. So maybe you'll be the first Bodrey to understand you cannot do this alone. And maybe you will take the damn help that is offered you."

That hits me so hard that I do have to take his hand to stand. And he has to set me right on my feet. Joey ain't usually one for compliments. If that was a compliment. Anyway, he ain't really for talking all that much, so when he does, it's best to listen to him.

"Will you stay with me?" I ask suddenly. I don't know why, but I have this feeling he might dip out on account of privacy between Grant and me or whatever, but he's been here though all this, and it wouldn't be right.

"I can," he says, nodding.

Grant walks over to me with that Texas gait that says he ain't in no hurry but he's gettin' where he's goin'. His eyes are red, and his face is puffy over his desert tan. I fix his hat right on his head, then I look at Chaco, who has the bell on a string of leather and walks from Grant's shoulder down his arm. Before I know what's happening, Grant extends a finger, and Chaco jumps from him to my shoulder.

He feels weird, a little prickly but the perfect weight. And the prickly I think I could get used to. He turns back to Grant and holds out the lanyard. Grant takes it in both hands.

"Listen..." I say to him, and he pauses. I can tell he's made his decision and cemented it. I have too. I just feel like this turning of the page needs noticing. I lay both hands on either side of his chest and lean into him.

"Thank you," I whisper.

He loops the bell over my head then steps back and takes a huge breath.

I feel a slow, soft pressure, like I'm sinking just a little bit—but not in a bad way. Just like I have a bit more to swing around.

Joey appraises me and nods. "Ya'at'eeh, Keeper."

Both men step back and watch with that patented Navajo nonsmile. Grant's pretty much got it by now.

The bell finds its place within me, and the silence is like that moment just before the break of dawn. I get it in an instant, what Grant means when he says it's dangerous. I don't feel the killing weight yet, but I sure as shit feel the potential, like a loaded gun.

Then a voice comes from a place in my head I thought I'd boarded up forever, a place of quiet waiting, not all that different from the way the trading post used to be on a dark night, with low clouds and everyone accounted for. A family place.

He talks to me like a father. Like a mother and a brother. But most of all, he talks to me like a friend.

"Hello Kai," he says. "My name is Chaco."

42

OWEN BENNET

We're outside the rocks, and Caroline is holding our girl, taking that perfectly slow Mom way of getting reacquainted, and she watches Caroline like she's come upon the biggest birthday present on the planet. She hasn't stopped touching her mom's face. I couldn't either, but I guess the both of us pawing at her was too much, so I stepped back to give them time. I've had more than my fair share.

The sun has risen on a new day. I guess you could call it the next day although I feel like I've been underground for a decade. The rock formation doesn't make sense to me, looking from the outside in. I can't quite figure where I found a way inside. There are cracks and crevices, but no real door. Not anymore.

"Do you know where we are?" Caroline asks.

"Kind of."

"No cell coverage, I suppose."

"That would be correct," I say, turning back to her, struck dumb for a second by the sight of her holding our daughter, of them both looking at me in the same way, just several decades apart.

"So how are we gonna get out of here?" she asks. "I've been down below for a while. I'm a little rusty. Do the crows work?"

I take mine from my back pocket and unwrap it from the black kerchief I've been burying it in. I touch it like I'm testing a hot pan. Then I grab it.

Nothing.

Caroline pulls hers out and rattles it about. Nothing. Our girl reaches for it, and Caroline makes a tsk-tsk. *Not for you.*

"Strange," I say. "I thought they'd fire back up once Black Bear was gone."

Caroline tucks hers back into the saggy pocket of her hospital gown, and I carefully fold mine away. "Maybe they need, like, a reboot or something," she says.

"Maybe," I say. Although if I can be perfectly honest, I would be fine never touching a crow totem ever again. I said as much to Ben, but I suddenly feel ashamed saying that to Caroline. *I can shoulder the burden. I can fight for the Circle. The crows are a gift.* These are the things I tell myself, but when I look back up at her and see the quiet way she watches me, I remember that she sees beyond the little lies that people tell themselves.

"Well, if we can't phase out and get help, I guess we improvise," she says. "How did you get here?"

I look around at the ground then trace up the piñon trees. All around me are specks of black in the washed green, quiet as graves.

"Them," I say.

"The crows?"

I nod. "I followed the crows here."

"Well, maybe we can follow the crows out?"

I stand with my hands on my hips, looking up at the canopies. "Sounds reasonable," I say.

I walk up to my scattered murder of crows, black dots within the green, floating with the breeze like bits of pirate flag.

"Alright, my crow friends," I say. "We all need to get out of here so we can get some water and food and continue to live. Can you help us?"

They stare down. A few shuffle about in the branches. That's about it. The girl coughs. It's been a good five hours since she ran out of diapers, which means she's not peeing, which means she's probably quite dehydrated. My own lips feel like sandpaper.

I flap my hands. "Fly? Hello?"

Nothing.

I walk up to the nearest tree, but all the crows do is jump up to higher branches.

"Great," I say. "These guys were giving me a king's ransom worth of field mice and berries an hour ago, but now they pretend they don't know me. Pretty rude, if you ask me."

"They're waiting," Caroline says.

I turn. "For what? Black Bear is gone. It's over."

The girl half cries, half mumbles, and reaches out to the trees. The crows titter. Caroline and I freeze.

"Okay," I say. "That was certainly something."

Caroline looks down at her. "She needs a name, Owen."

The crows titter again.

Bingo.

I run my hand through what's left of my hair. It feels gritty, more sand than follicles. "Well, I've tried, but nothing feels right. I mean, I like a lot of names. Then I hate them. What about Caroline Junior?"

Caroline is looking down at her, running her fingers over the tops of her little ears. "What about Ana?" she asks.

The breeze drops in an instant that stills all of us. Three caws shatter the stillness with such force that I cover my head for a second.

The crows start to titter again, stretching their wings and moving to the edges of the branches for takeoff.

"I think we have our answer," I say.

Caroline walks up to me. "But what do *you* think?"

I look down at our little girl. "Ana," I say, testing it out. "After Ben's little sister?"

"A young warrior," she says. "One who walked both worlds."

I nod. "In a way, she was the start of it all. A little girl who changed everything."

"I think this one will do the same. In her own way."

"Ana," I say again. "Yeah. I think that fits."

And no sooner do the words come out of my mouth than a hundred crows explode from the trees. They flock close and circle us so tightly I can feel the wind from their wings. One calls out, then another, then others on and on in a circle that doesn't end until the line peels off, and they point our way home.

"This way," I say, smiling at Caroline and down at Ana.

Up above, the crows lead the way slowly and deliberately, alighting and landing, and on the ground, we walk, joining the flock.

43

THE WALKER

I f you drive due west from the city of Albuquerque, New Mexico, for two hours then cut north before you hit the city of Gallup, you'll see a big stretch of glass—flat nothing dusted with sand, slightly lighter in color than the rest of the Red Rock Country to the north.

Our land has this strange power of making you want to dive in and drive by at the same time. You could call it a trick of the light, where things seem wavy one second then crystal clear the next. I've walked this entire planet. I've seen sides of this world no living man or woman will ever see. And still, when I look at Navajo country on a clear evening with the sunset slicing sideways, it's enough to make me stop still.

The Arroyo is rebuilding, constantly rebuilding. I walk the half-moon lip of the canyon and watch this clan make it happen. They *are* a clan, even if they come from different clans. And the patience with which they remake things—reset tents, clean out campers, dig out firepits, and level campgrounds—is a kind of beautiful stubbornness that I hope lingers here forever.

My mind juggles a lot of places and a lot of times. I have a memory of this place that is deep and strong, one I've played in my head time and time again, where Joey and I count coup against yellowed campers and rusted cars, ducking and weaving under a bright moon, moving from campfire to campfire. I can see us here, doing that.

That Arroyo is gone. The one here now is different, changed. And you might think that's bad, but let me tell you, coming from a man who is dead, the best thing about life is that it changes.

Joey is scrubbing down his bricked car, plopping mud off in shards the size of dinner plates. The faintest hint of that bitchin' mural he drew on the side peeks through now, a crow painted the colors of the sunset. I can see the hint of red under Chaco's wing.

Joey's in that focused mode of his, humming to himself, and I think he would go about cleaning this thing for a day and night if it weren't for a flutter from the totem pouch hanging around his neck. I know it because I feel it too, like the buzz of a hummingbird right by your ear.

He grasps his pouch and looks over toward the old gates, not buried anymore but not swinging anytime soon either, and that's where I leave him. I know who is coming, and I want to take in the quiet of this place before the joy. The quiet before joy is the best kind of quiet.

I walk the half moon to the twins' campground, where I find Grant and Kai at the fire and Chaco on the top of the twins' camper. Maria sweeps the stairs of the ash that won't quite quit. The twins' home is hers now, and she's as ripped up about it as she is proud.

The twins are here too although only me and the bird can see them. The veil, vengeful old shroud that she can be, does have a keen eye for the great ones, and in my time, I've seen the way she lets them stay for a little while. It's hard work to be great, but it pays, even in death. Maybe especially in death.

"Nice of you to join us, Walker," Chaco says, same old snark. You know what they say: the more things change, blah blah.

"I hear you got a new charge," I say carefully. I felt it, actually, the passing of the torch.

Chaco fluffs up then settles down. "You heard right."

"Are you okay?" I ask.

"It's never easy leaving a Keeper. It crushed me to leave your grandmother. It crushes me to leave Grant. And I know it'll crush me to leave Kai. That's how I know it's the right thing to do."

Used to be I couldn't understand a damn thing that bird said. I just flew with him, so to speak. The fact that he makes more and more sense to me must mean I'm getting old, even for a dead guy.

"And Grant?" I ask.

"A badass. As usual."

I nod. Sounds about right. He's digging out more trench, probably doing anything to keep his mind off what he's lost. Looking at him now, I can sense the sorrow. But there's something new there too, a fresh green stitch to his soul thread, like a little sprout pushing through to the light for the first time. He's still heavy, but he won't be for long.

And as for Kai, well, she shoulders the bell well. True, the weight hasn't hit her yet. That takes years. But then again, her scars have made her strong. It's a shitty thing to say, but the bell sitting on top of all that is something she is more than capable of handling. For now. It helps that they've got each other. The way they share looks, it's hard to tell who props up who, which is a good sign.

The twins are quiet souls. I sense that they're here only to bear witness and won't be for long. So when they turn their attention toward the front gate of the Arroyo, I follow them, and the three of us stand side by side to witness the return of Caroline, Owen, and the child they named Ana. A good name. Strong. Right. My sister would have been honored.

Caroline is in front. She carries Ana, and Owen is a step behind. Joey met them at the gate and is leading them along the upper ridge, looking back over his shoulder constantly like he's afraid they might disappear again. Pretty much all of the Arroyo files in behind, bodies in a line throwing long shadows in the late light.

Grant greets his little sister with such warmth that it brings a glow to this whole corner of the soul map. He picks her up and holds her and talks to her and says her name with a light and easy smile that I haven't seen on him in years. He hands her to Maria, and soon enough, the Arroyo circles up around the fire, and Ana is getting passed around. The twins sit in their chairs, left as they were by the Arroyo. They nod at Ana as she passes through them, and I swear she follows their spirits with her eyes. I'm pretty sure she looks my way too. That shock of white hair will always mark her as a child who spent more than her fair share of time on the other side. But already, her soul is being woven into the fabric of this place. She's forgetting about the before time, which is good. There are things you need to know to survive down here, and there are things you need to unknow until it's your time for a visit from the veil.

Grant hugs Caroline like he's about to drag her to the

dirt, like the tentpoles holding him up finally give out, and now he's really and truly crying and trying to explain that Chaco isn't with him anymore even though he is still kind of with him, and all of it just rushes out of him until Joey suggests everybody take a seat where they can around the fire. That's what they do.

Kai stays back, unsure. Chaco is up on top of the double-wide, already helping her through it.

Then Joey, Caroline, and Owen take their totems out, skin to stone. No phasing. Nothing. *And yet…*

"I felt it too," Caroline says. "They want to wake up again."

"Are you sure?" Owen asks. "Because it's good if they sleep too. Sleep is good."

"They need each other," Joey says. "They need the Circle."

He holds his out, and Caroline places hers against his, and I feel that thrum again, louder. Owen hesitates, biting his lower lip, but he eventually puts his hand in too, all three stones touch, and the thrum kicks into a higher gear that dims all the light like a passing cloud.

In an instant, all three are gone from the living world, phased to the windblasted sepia of the thin place.

For just a moment, though. Then they're back.

Joey is elated, Caroline relieved.

"See?" Joey says, settling holding up his totem pouch. "Just a little reboot, that's all. They needed to remember what they are."

Owen holds his in that old black kerchief, and he ponders it for a long stretch of moments. He catches Caroline's eye, and something passes between them, because both of them look toward Grant.

Grant, for his part, is doing his level best not to look up

at Chaco, but I know he wants to. My guess is he's calling out to him in the way he used to, over and over again, and trying to come to terms with the silence.

Owen walks over to him and touches him on the shoulder. Grant starts, embarrassed, which makes it even more heartbreaking.

"You okay?" Owen asks.

Grant pauses long enough for that to be an answer in itself before he says, "Kinda. Up and down. But mostly up."

He steals another glance at Chaco, who watches them.

Owen leans his elbows against the mud-spattered fencing that marks the edge of the twins' backyard, and the two men are shoulder to shoulder. He starts to speak, but whatever words he had fail him, and he's quiet again. Maria's bringing tea around, and the yard is settling into quiet sips. I'm getting tugged in all directions, but I fight to keep myself here.

After a few moments, Owen tries again.

"Son... I know that life has asked a lot of you. More than anyone should give, really. You were put to work at eight on the front lines of a fight you couldn't really understand. Getting the bell was a burden, one I'm fairly sure I'd have tried my hardest to talk you out of taking if I'd been there, knowing what we know now."

Owen shields his eyes from the sun and finds Chaco atop the double-wide. The bird chirrups. "And giving it up is a burden too. I see it in your eyes."

He looks at the kerchief in his hand with a sigh. "What I'm trying to say is once you show yourself as strong, the world keeps testing that. And you are strong. Like your Mom."

"Like you," Grant says, watching him now.

Those two words are enough to halt Owen and bring tears to his eyes. The Owen I knew when I was alive would've denied it. The Owen of a year or two ago might have shrugged it off.

But this Owen nods. "I guess so, yeah. Like me. But your strength and my strength are different. Which is why I want to ask something of you. Yet again."

Without quite realizing it, our whole little family has gathered around the two of them. Kai settles on the fence to his other side, while Joey and Caroline move in beside Owen. Even Chaco sails down, flapping to a gentle landing atop a gatepost worn blunt by the years. Ana clings to Caroline, resting her head on her Mom, but her eyes are open and sharp.

Owen unfolds the black kerchief in his hand and looks at his totem with a small smile. He tilts it so it glints cloudy red in the sunset.

"This totem has shown me things I never could have imagined even in my wildest dreams as a lonely little kid on the east coast, pretending to be a doctor to the neighborhood teddy bears. It's brought me across the world, to the land of the dead, and everywhere in between."

He looks up at Caroline. "It showed me your Mom. And it showed me you too. It showed me this place, my home. And now, it's shown me to Ana, your sister. And I think I'm about done."

Grant pushes himself slowly from his lean to stand tall. He looks at his dad and takes off his hat, brow furrowed. "What? Done?"

"It's funny. Holding this in my palm, I can go anywhere in a blink. But these days, I don't want to *go* anywhere at all. I want to *stay*. Right here." He folds it up in black like a little present and holds it out. "So, I was wondering if you might take it."

"Really?" Grant asks, his voice small and edged with wonder.

He looks from it to Owen, who nods. For a long span of seconds, the Arroyo sits in stunned silence. Until Joey speaks.

"Grant Romer, a member of the Circle of Crows has offered his place to you. Do you understand what that means?"

Grant stares at the black present. He looks back at Kai, who nods at him, eyes shimmering.

"Grant Romer," Joey says again. "I asked if you understand what that means."

"I do," Grant says softly.

"Yes," Joey says. "I believe you do. And do you accept?"

Grant finds his Mom last. Caroline picks up on his pleading look instantly. "Honey, you don't need my permission to do things anymore. You're practically thirty. But if you're asking, heck yes. We've already fought side by side. Might as well make it official."

Grant reaches out a shaking hand, and Owen hands him the kerchief. "Thanks, Dad," Grant manages to say.

"No," Owen says. "Thank *you*, Son."

"Owen Bennet, your totem has been passed, and your watch is at an end. Rest easy, my brother."

He turns to Grant and grabs him by both shoulders. "Grant Romer, your watch has begun." He thumps him hard enough to make his hat go crooked. "Ya'at'eeh, brother! Welcome!"

Joey sets Grant's hat right. "The Circle is unbroken!" he calls aloud.

"The Circle is unbroken," Caroline repeats, walking in and giving him a big mom hug.

"The Circle is unbroken," Owen says, smiling. He leans against the fence again and lets out a big breath.

Chaco takes to the sky with big wingbeats, and once he's up high, he caws and caws and caws. Soon, he's joined by other crows until the sky above is a spinning ring of black and the calls of the crows are so loud that they echo against the canyons before they shoot off in every direction at once, off to share the news and keep their own watch. Chaco soars high on thermals, watching them go.

That's when the twins rise up and look at me, which to my mind means two things. One, the balance has been found. And two, it's time to for them to leave.

I walk through the crowd, letting the sounds wash over me. Joey is telling Grant he has so much to show him. Caroline is telling Owen she's never been prouder of him. Ana is laughing at everyone who holds her. Kai is speaking to Chaco, making sure he isn't about to shoot off anywhere just yet. And Chaco is telling her he ain't going anywhere.

I join up with the twins, and they nod to me, speaking for the first time since they died. "Ben Dejooli," Tsasa says, smiling. "It is good to see you again."

Tsosi grabs me by the shoulders and brings me in to a hug that is way stronger than I expect. "You do your people proud, Walker," he says. "Keep doing it."

"Grandfather, I don't know how long I can. The longer I stay, the more chance I have of becoming like *him*."

Tsasa laughs. "Like Black Bear? No. I do not see that in you."

"I do," I say, blunt. True.

The twins allow it. There is a rare truth in death. It can be very refreshing under the right circumstances.

Tsosi scratches at his chin, once mottled and sagging, now growing younger by the minute. "In that case, I would suggest you stick to what grounds you. Keep it close."

"It's this place, these people. Keeping them alive keeps me sane."

The twins nod. "You deal in death," Tsasa says. "But it's life that keeps you together. The great balance."

The veil, which has been very polite about this whole thing, is finally making her presence known. The twins see her as clearly as I do, and they face the curtain like she's the sunshine after the storm. I'm old hat at this, but still, seeing them about to cross makes me panic—all that knowledge, gone.

"Wait, Grandfathers, please. When will I know to go? Will someone have to come after me too?"

Tsosi turns back to me. "You will know when to go. Even Black Bear knew when to go. He just ignored it. All who walk the rope get the choice, in the end. What you choose is up to you."

Tsasa holds his hands wide. "Look to your people. They let go and rebuild every day. They will show you the way."

They hook elbows and escort one another toward the veil. Tsosi looks over his shoulder at me, all vestiges of sickness wiped from his face. "*Hágoónee'*, Ben Dejooli. We will meet you in the river, in good time."

"Hágoónee' Grandfathers. Until then."

The twins walk through the veil with smiles on their faces.

The veil stays for a few moments once they disappear,

and I nod my thanks to it. "That was good of you, letting them watch things settle like that," I say.

She still lingers, her cloak billowing crimson red in the silent breeze of the land of the dead.

"What?" I ask.

More billowy silence.

"I'm fine," I say, knocking my head to show it's solid. "Totally not crazy. Trust me."

This seems to be what she wanted to hear. She pops out of sight in an instant.

And looking back over the way the sun sets across Chaco Rez, I realize that's true.

I *am* fine.

I am *not* going anywhere.

As long as this place and these people stand, I will too. We're tied together at the soul. I lived here. I was alive here, once. I'm more dead than I ever was, but every time I see this place and these people, I'm alive again.

Black Bear forgot who he was. But I know who I am. It's reflected in the family I see growing all around me.

That's the difference. And that's more than enough to keep me walking.

AUTHOR'S NOTE

The tales of Monster Slayer and Born for Water are among the most action packed in the Navajo creation story. The two are understandably popular characters—twin brothers who use their strength, brains, and the weapons of the gods to destroy the monsters that plague the early Navajo.

Binaye Ahani and *Yé'iitsoh*—known in lore as *Monster That Kills With His Eyes* and *Big Giant*—are only two of many monsters that the Slayer Twins kill. These two monsters fascinate me because of how they consume: through eyes, nose and mouth.

Big Giant is considered the strongest monster in the stories. But equally as frightening, to my mind, is the thought of a creature that kills with a stare.

As I wrote in the narrative, what sometimes gets over-looked in the tales of the Slayer Twins' many victories is the fact that in their quests, they despaired as well. It's written that they were tired, hungry and cold, and at one point "could not decide which way to turn."

This is when they meet Spider Woman, who offers them shelter and asks them two things: *Who are you?* and *Where do you come from?*

Deceptively easy questions with surprisingly revealing answers. I hope to have conveyed as much when Ben and Owen are forced to ask the same of themselves under similar circumstances.

As for the Slayer Twins, they reply: "We are here because we do not know indeed where we can go."

A wonderfully honest answer.

One final note about the battles of Monster Slayer and Born for Water: In the stories, at the end of each fight, the brothers salvage something to take back to their clan. After they beat Yé'iitsoh, they salvage flint destroyed by lightning so that their people can use it as knives. In their words: "That way we can turn Yé'iitsoh's evil into something good."

One of the most humbling aspects of researching this series is how often I see examples of the Diné people looking to create good from devastation. That, to my mind, is true strength.

Thank you so much for reading. What a joy it is to know that you have been right alongside me for six of these novels now. There is more to come.

Sincerely,

-BBG

ABOUT THE AUTHOR

B. B. Griffith writes best-selling suspense and fantasy. He lives in Denver, CO, where he is often seen sitting on his porch staring off into the distance or wandering to and from local watering holes with his family.

See more at his digital HQ: https://bbgriffith.com

If you like his books, you can sign up for his mailing list here: http://eepurl.com/SObZj. It is an entirely spam-free experience.

ALSO BY B. B. GRIFFITH

The Vanished Series

Follow the Crow (Vanished, #1)

Beyond the Veil (Vanished, #2)

The Coyote Way (Vanished, #3)

The Wind Thief (Vanished, #4)

Child of the Sky (Vanished, #5)

Den of the Bear (Vanished, #6)

Gordon Pope Thrillers

The Sleepwalkers (Gordon Pope, #1)

Mind Games (Gordon Pope, #2)

Shadow Land (Gordon Pope, #3)

The Tournament Series

Blue Fall (The Tournament, #1)

Grey Winter (The Tournament, #2)

Black Spring (The Tournament, #3)

Summer Crush (The Tournament, #4)

Luck Magic Series

Las Vegas Luck Magic (Luck Magic, #1)

Standalone

Witch of the Water: A Novella